DON'T TELL

ALEXANDRIA CLARKE

❀ Created with Vellum

hey told me it would be an easy first day. They never put rookies in overwhelming situations unless something unexpected came up. The first day was a trial run. You were assigned to a senior officer, rode in the passenger seat of the squad car, practiced radio calls, and got used to wearing several extra pounds of gear on your chest and around your waist. The belt was heavier than I expected. Each item —handcuffs, radio, baton, taser, and firearm—was one more brick of dead weight. There were two other women—Jess and Angela—in my rookie class. Both of them were stockier than me. They effortlessly buckled their belts as I struggled with mine. Their sturdy chests and arms filled out their vests like the guys did. I had to request a size down. The only thing I had going for me was my height. I was five feet and ten inches of skinny rookie cop, and about as intimidating as a chihuahua wearing a bite warning vest.

"I heard at least one rookie quits on the first day every year," Angela said, her voice echoing off the metal lockers and vinyl floors. "Who do you think it's going to be?"

"My bet's on Ryder," Jess answered, jerking her head toward me without any attempt at secrecy. "She's shaking in her boots already."

I did my best to ignore them. They were right. My hands trembled as I laced up my boots. I'd forgotten to eat breakfast that morning, and my blood sugar was in the toilet. I tied a double knot in each lace then got to my feet, towering over Jess and Angela as I approached them.

"Anyone got a protein bar?" I asked, pretending I hadn't heard them talking about me. "I'm starving."

Jess tossed me one from her locker. I caught it with deft fingers, unwrapped it, and took a bite.

"Thanks," I said, spraying crumbs across their crisp new uniforms. "Oh, and shut up."

As far as I knew, the Tampa Police Department didn't see the same kind of action that a place like New York or Chicago experienced. I wanted a simple job in a simple town. Part of me hoped I'd never see any action on the street. I'd be comfortable desking all day. As long as I was serving my community, I was okay with whatever my role at the department entailed.

Carter, one of the few women on the force,

knocked a clipboard against the locker room door. "Yo, listen up, rookies! We're assigning your training officers in two minutes, so get your asses in gear. Don't make me look bad."

I liked Carter. She was scary as hell, a no-nonsense woman with dark skin and perfect, tight braids. Her biceps were bigger than most of the guys and she never let anyone call her by her first name.

"Never let anyone on the force call you by your first name," she'd instructed me, Jess, and Angela. "Especially the guys. A last name means respect. A first name means they think you're soft."

Ever since that talk, I corrected anyone and everyone who called me Alex. Two other guys on the force were also named Alex, so it was easier if everyone called me Ryder anyway. It avoided confusion.

Jess hastened to reach Carter first, her shoulders so squared off that I thought they might turn into cement blocks. "I'm excited about my first day, ma'am. Any chance I can get you as my training officer? I feel like we've bonded over the past few weeks, and I really admire your work."

Carter looked Jess up and down. "You know what I hate more than the rookies' first day? Suck-ups. Get moving, Jones, and loosen your belt. It's not a damn corset, and you ain't looking for a husband. If you wanted to show off your waist, you should have picked a different career."

Jess's ears turned bright red as she shuffled past Carter as quickly as possible. Angela followed suit.

"Hi, ma'am," she said as she sidled by Carter. She saluted the older cop, an old habit leftover from Marine Corps training. Angela had dropped out during her second week on Parris Island. "I mean, good morning, Carter. I'll—*ahem*—see you out there. Right."

Carter didn't spare Angela's odd greeting a second thought. She waited until we were alone in the locker room then banged her clipboard again. "What are you waiting for, Ryder? A written invitation? I don't do calligraphy. Move your ass. And wipe that smile off your face. Schadenfreude isn't a good look on you."

After I got my belt on, I joined the rest of the rookies in the big conference room. The senior officers were there too, laughing, nursing coffee, and munching on that morning's batch of fresh donuts. Lieutenant Marín stared longingly at a glazed cruller in the box. When I'd first met him at the Academy, he was twenty pounds heavier, but he wanted to set a better example for his younger officers. Since then, he'd lost his enormous belly and double chin at the expense of no more donuts in the morning.

The room buzzed with conversation. The recruits eyed the older officers and muttered about which one they preferred to ride with. The senior officers inspected the recruits and whispered behind their hands about us. I'd heard the senior officers had a pool going on. They bet on which of the recruits would bow out, make a mistake, or misfire their gun first. I stayed quiet and leaned against the back wall as the rest of the cops gossiped and chattered.

"I pray to God I don't get Carter," said Miller, a muscled rookie with a buzz cut and blue eyes. "That woman scares me. Plus I heard she drives like a maniac. Wouldn't want to ride in her squad car for a minute, let alone a whole day."

Miller's buddy, Ryan, had a swimmer's body. The shoulders of his uniform were too tight and the waist was too loose. He crossed his arms and snickered. "Don't worry, Miller. I heard Carter picks one of the girls to ride with her every year. We've got nothing to worry about."

My stomach flipped. As much as I liked Carter, it was no secret that riding with her meant one of two things. Most of her rookies quit during their first week, but those that had made it through the training period with her turned out to be some of the best cops in the nation.

Lieutenant Marín coughed, and the room quieted. Some of the senior cops still spoke in lowered voices, less worried than the rookies about being called out for disrespect. Meanwhile, the rookies and I gave the lieutenant our full attention. Carter passed off her clipboard to him.

"Listen up!" Marín said. He flipped through the pages on the clipboard. Carter knew the rookies best, so she was the one who paired us to the training officers. Marín nodded approvingly at her choices. "Let's make this quick. We've got to work to do. Adams! You're with Officer Grady. Bedford! You've been assigned to Officer McMahon."

It went on in alphabetical order. We were the largest rookie class the department had seen in several years. What inspired a bunch of twenty-somethings to become cops? For me, it was a lack of direction. It wasn't a stretch to get into the police academy. My uncle—a retired cop in New York—had referred me and written a letter of recommendation. For the first time in a while, I committed to something. Law enforcement wasn't the career I'd dreamt of, but at least I had a career.

"Miller!" Marín called. "You're with Officer Perrone."

Ryan stifled a laugh. "Sucks for you, man," he said to Miller under his breath. "Perrone's a dinosaur. You'll be lucky to see anything but paperwork."

"Ryan!" Marín barked, making the rookie jump. "You're with Brant."

This time, I had to abstain from snickering too as Miller cracked up. Brant was eternally red-faced, and he released his stress through flatulence. His squad car and the immediate area around his desk smelled of whatever his wife had made him for dinner the night before, and there was no way to escape it.

"Ryder!" Marín said.

"Yes, sir?"

He checked the clipboard. "You're with Carter."

Repressed groans made their way through the room. Some were rooted in sympathy, others in jealousy, and still others in humor. Everyone had an opinion on Carter's rookie. Carter, on the other hand, wasn't having it.

"Shut up," she ordered the room. "Lieutenant Marín isn't done."

The officers fell quiet once again. As Marín read off the rest of the names on his list, I worked on not swallowing my tongue. It felt huge in my mouth, like a bee had flown in and injected me full of histamines. My throat closed up, and no amount of relaxation techniques helped my breath move in and out of my lungs as anatomy intended. Before I had processed my fate, Marín tossed the clipboard aside.

"You have your assignments," he said. "Here's a few tips. Get to know your partner. Ask them about their job and their life. Learn how to trust each other. Don't do anything stupid. Welcome to your first official day on the job, rookies."

The room dissolved into chatter again as the rookies paired up with their training officers, shaking hands and introducing each other if they weren't already familiar. Carter didn't approach me, holding a conversation with the lieutenant instead. Jess bumped my shoulder as she followed her senior officer out.

"You know what everyone calls her?" she whispered in my ear. "Carver. Because she likes to carve up her rookies like raw meat. Good luck with that, Ryder."

She clapped me on the back. Angela stopped by next. She'd been paired with Officer Moretti, a stern but friendly woman who worked drug busts. Angela was lucky. She'd get a decent education, see some action, and make plenty of arrests.

"Don't listen to Jess," she said to me. "She's arrogant. Thinks she's going to make detective first. You and Carter are a good match. You can handle her. Don't think you can't."

Like Jess, she clapped me on the back, but it was a friendly pat versus Jess's vindictive slap. As the room emptied out, I waited for Carter to end her conversation with Lieutenant Marín. Minutes passed. They chatted and chuckled without a glance in my direction. I went over to them and cleared my throat.

"Excuse me, Lieutenant—"

Marín checked his watch, resetting a timer. "Four minutes and seven seconds. Smack in the middle of the sweet spot, Carter. You've got a good one here. Observant. Proactive. Don't scare her off."

"What was that about?" I asked Carter as he left.

She chuckled to herself. "Every year, I strike up a conversation with the lieutenant at the end of this meeting to see how long it will take for my recruit to cut in. Some of y'all jump in right away. I don't like that. It's pushy and disrespectful. Others will wait until they think I'm done with my conversation. Once, it took my recruit twenty minutes to introduce himself. I don't like that either. It means you lack initiative and don't have the confidence to step in. Between three and five minutes is the sweet spot. Nice job, Ryder."

Pleasantly surprised, I hurried after her as she headed outside to the parking lot. The rest of the officers and their recruits were gone, save for the ones who started on desk duty. Carter parked her cruiser in the same spot every day, closest to the door, and no one dared take it from her.

"You been in Florida long?" she asked.

"About a year. I moved from Santa Fe."

She clicked her tongue. "It's dry there. Wet here. It rains a lot, especially in the summer afternoons. I don't like to get my hair wet, and everyone knows it, so I get to park closest to the building. What's in Santa Fe?"

"Sorry?"

She unlocked the cruiser door and gestured for me to get in. "Did you have family there? Friends? Is that where you went to college?"

"Oh, uh, yeah. I went to community college though, not a university."

"No shame in that."

Carter's cruiser was impeccable. I'd seen the inside of a few cop cars. They were littered with paperwork, empty Starbucks cups, crumpled napkins, crumbs from eating on the go, and various other items. Not Carter's. She wiped a speck of dust off the dashboard and flicked it out the window.

"I've got three rules," she announced as she turned the key in the ignition. "Number one, don't eat in my car. Number two, do as I say. Number three, refer to numbers one and two. We clear?"

"Yes, ma'am."

The engine growled under the hood, and my seat rumbled. Carter had a fiery sports car under that official police department paint job, and she liked it. She revved the engine, either for fun or to show off the amount of horsepower she had to play with.

"I'm not playing," she said. "Do as I say. Every time one of my rookies failed, it's because they forgot to follow rule number two. I don't care what situation we're in. I don't care if you think you know best. I don't care if you believe you're going to die if you follow my instructions."

"I don't think—"

"I'm not done."

"Sorry."

She adjusted her rear view mirror and backed out of her reserved space. "My number one job is to keep you safe. My number two job is to make sure you don't mess anything up for this police department. Oftentimes, they go hand in hand. If you listen, we'll be fine."

I waited a beat to make sure she was finished. "Yes, ma'am."

"Great." She pulled out of the parking lot. "Let's see what we got."

Tampa Bay wasn't the hotbed of criminal activity or

seedy deeds that New York or Chicago was, but there was enough illegality to go around. Two patrol divisions covered everything from Tampa's peninsula, the football stadium, the university, and all surrounding suburbia. Carter also happened to be a member of the ROC—Rapid Offender Control—squad. She was familiar with crime patterns and repeat offenders, and she patrolled high-crime areas to stop offenders before they had a chance to do intense damage.

"We'll take it easy today," she said, turning toward the neighborhoods rather than the seedier part of town. "I don't want to throw you into something you can't handle on your first day. How about some coffee?"

"What about rule number one?"

"Coffee doesn't apply," Carter informed me. "*Unless* you spill it on my seats. That's a different story."

We stopped at a boba tea place rather than a Starbucks. Carter ordered a Vietnamese coffee. I got a taro milk tea. The drinks came in bright blue cups with a cartoon monkey printed on the side. Seeing Carter suck tapioca balls up through her reusable rainbow straw was one hell of an image. No wonder she never brought her drinks into the station.

We cruised through the streets and listened to the radio as the sun beat on the windshield. The tint on my sunglasses wasn't dark enough to keep my eyes from watering. I was sweating too. The AC was on full blast, but the polyester uniform didn't allow for much airflow. Worst of all, I was damp. Santa Fe was hot, but the air was dry. Summer in Tampa was like sticking your whole body in a dryer halfway through a cycle. My thighs chafed, and I'd sweated off the organic deodorant that claimed to be one hundred percent effective. I cupped my hands around my drink then patted my face with the cool condensation. The milk tea was my only source of relief from the heat.

"What made you want to be a cop?" Carter asked as she drove. "I heard your uncle retired from NYPD. Does it run in the family?"

"Not really," I said. "But I ran out of options job-wise, so here I am."

Carter sipped on her coffee-boba combo. "You're going to have to change your tune, Ryder. That's a poor attitude to have. Joining the force isn't something you do lightly. We have a responsibility to the public, and we can't have officers with half-assed dedication to the cause."

"I intend to be the best police officer possible," I assured her, wondering if I was lying to her or myself. "But I didn't expect to be here."

"I hope that's true."

"What was the worst case you ever worked?" I asked, eager to change the subject. Everyone knew Carter was a beast. She brought in killers, drug runners, and ring leaders on a weekly basis. "Or I suppose which cases affected you the most?"

Carter chewed on her boba. "I saw some pretty

wicked shit when we broke up a human trafficking ring that was shipping 'product' through this area. But I have to say the animal abuse cases have the biggest effect on me. I was kicked off a dog fighting case a few years ago for being too emotionally involved."

"What happened?"

"I shot the guy who ran the fights." She checked my shocked expression. "Relax. He didn't die. I got him in the thigh. But I shot him after my superior told me to stand down. I shot him even though he had no weapon and wasn't threatening my life."

"Did you get in trouble for it?"

"Yeah, I got suspended from the force," Carter said. "But it was worth it. That ass deserved it for what he did to those dogs. Check the glove box."

Among a stack of clean napkins and an extra set of handcuffs, I found a picture of a Rottweiler mix with sweet, sad eyes and patches in her fur from where her battle scars would never heal. Her tail was blurry in the picture, wagging too fast for the camera to capture it properly.

"That's Jemima," Carter said. "When I found her, she was covered in so much blood that it looked like syrup."

I bit my lip to stop my anger from spilling over. "She's okay now?"

"Happy as a clam, but Marín redirects animal abuse cases to other officers these days." She winked at me. "Seeing as I can't be trusted not to shoot assholes."

I put Jemima's picture back in the glove compartment where it was safe. "I would have done the same thing."

"Oh, yeah? What's your story?"

"I don't have one."

We pulled up to a red light, and Carter whirled her straw around at the bottom of her cup to get the last few beads of boba. "Everyone's got a story, Ryder."

I blew a sigh out the open window. "You know when you see those stories on the Internet about women who have their baby in a toilet or an alley because they didn't know they were pregnant? That was my mom. I was born behind a Chinese restaurant in Brooklyn, and she left me there. I grew up in the foster system until I was six, at which point my mom came to collect me. She gave up trying to raise me when I was fourteen. I asked to be emancipated, and she signed the papers without looking at them. Then I moved across the country and I've been on my own ever since."

"Respect," was all Carter said.

"I went looking for my dad." Now that the floodgates were open, I couldn't stop talking. "He turned out to be a decent human being. Owned a non-profit to help at-risk youth in the city. Of course, when I finally tracked him down, he was already dead. Heart condition. Go figure. Anyway, his brother—the cop uncle—took pity on me."

"So you're a fighter," Carter commented.

"What do you mean?"

"You've been fighting to stay alive ever since your mother dumped you in that alleyway," she said, her eyes on the road. "And you haven't stopped since. Good for you. Be proud of yourself."

"Thanks, I guess."

The radio crackled, and dispatch came through. "Seventy-three at 3220 Horizon Way. Any units available?"

Carter handed me the radio. "Call it in."

I cleared my throat, heart pounding, and replied, "Uh, two-oh-three responding. En route."

The dispatcher confirmed, and I put the radio back on the dash.

"Next time, nix the 'uh,'" said Carter. "You remember what a seventy-three is?"

I fumbled for the cheat sheet of codes I had in my pocket. "Seventy-three, seventy-three—"

"Domestic dispute," she cut in. "How do we approach?"

"Quietly," I answered. "No lights or sirens in case the abuser is violent."

"You got it."

3220 HORIZON WAY was located in a quiet cul-de-sac of a nearby neighborhood with perfectly green lawns, neatly arranged landscapes, and moderately expensive cars in the driveway. As we pulled up to the house in question, nothing seemed to be out of the ordinary except the overgrown grass and weeds in the front yard. A middle-aged woman with plump lips and an impeccable brown-to-blonde balayage waved to us from the front porch of the house next door as as we pulled in.

"Oh," she said once Carter and I got out. "You're women."

"Did you call in a domestic disturbance at this address?" Carter asked.

"Yes, ma'am," the woman replied. "I'm Connie Carlton. I'm a member of the HOA. I heard some horrible screaming coming from next door, and we have noise restraints here. Of course, I was also worried for the safety of my neighbors."

All three of us looked at the house. It was silent.

"I swear I heard it," Connie said.

"Do you know the occupants?" Carter asked. "Do they have a previous history of domestic violence?"

Connie shook her perfect head of hair. "God, no. Dominique and Dustin Benson live there. Nice, sweet couple. Well, they were when they first moved in. I haven't seen either of them in a few weeks. I don't suppose you could remind them to mow the law when they get a chance? Their weeds are creeping into our yard."

"I'll do my best," Carter replied shortly. "Why don't you head inside, ma'am? Come on, Ryder. Let's check it out."

As Connie craned her neck from her front porch, Carter and I headed up the front walk of 3220. It was a nice house with a front porch swing and a summery wreath of sunflowers hanging on the front door. Carter knocked.

"This is Officer Carter and Officer Ryder from the Tampa Police Department," she called. "Is anyone home?"

No one replied. Carter knocked again and repeated her statement. Still no luck. I scanned the area around the door. Flyers for pool cleaning and lawn care services were strewn across the doorstep, the words and pictures faded from sitting out in the sun for so long.

"I don't think anyone's been here in a while, ma'am." I nudged the flyers with my boot. "There are a bunch of newspapers in the driveway too, and the mailbox is overflowing."

"Peek in that window over there. I'll check this way."

My footsteps crunched through decorative red lava rock as I stepped into the landscaping. I cupped my hands around my eyes and glanced into the front window. It was an at-home office. The computer on the desk was on. The screensaver bounced back and forth. Nothing suspicious caught my eye. I almost turned away but—

My stomach dropped. "Uh, Officer Carter?"

"What do you got?"

"I think it's a body."

Carter hurried across the lava lamps and peered inside. I hoped she would tell me I'd seen something else by mistake, but that wasn't the case. She took the radio from her belt. "We got a possible body at 3220 Horizon Way. Requesting backup." Dispatch confirmed, and Carter pulled her firearm. "Get ready. We're going in."

"W-what?" I said. "Shouldn't we wait for backup? What if the person who did that is still in there? We could—"

"What's rule number two, Ryder?"

"Do as you say."

"And I'm saying we're going in," Carter ordered. "There might be more victims in trouble, or that guy on the floor in there might not be dead yet—"

"But the blood—"

"This is the job, Ryder. This is *your* job. Get ready."

She waited until I'd pulled my own firearm and held it at the ready. Then she reared back and kicked the front door with all her might. The lock gave in to the power of her leg, and the door flew open.

I had to pee. Freaking boba tea.

Everything was dark. The vertical blinds on the sliding glass doors were pulled shut. None of the lights were on. I blinked away floaters as my eyes adjusted. The main room was clear of bodies but not of blood. A huge smear led from the kitchen to the office.

"Main room's clear," Carter said in a low voice. "Check the office. I've got the bedroom."

My hands shook around my gun as I followed the blood smear. Carter made me clear the office for a reason. A dead body wasn't going to attack me, and the perpetrator was more likely to be in a different part of the house.

I edged into the room, doing a visual sweep as I was taught. No movement. My eyes flickered to the body. The man was dead. He was propped up against the wall beneath the window, so people peeking in wouldn't see him. I'd noticed him from outside because of the bloodied sneaker he'd lost in the middle of the carpet. Someone had tied thin loops of wire around his fingers and toes, a slow and tortuous amputation method. His open eyes were glassy. He'd been here a while.

I backed out of the room. Carter emerged from the bedroom.

"Office is clear," I whispered. "Except for the dead guy."

"Keep moving."

We swept the living room and crept toward the kitchen. There were two ways to reach it, one through the living room and another through the hallway. Carter tapped her nose and pointed toward the hall-way. She would take that way. I would take the other.

I inched toward the archway that separated the living room from the kitchen. The vertical blinds rustled as I passed by, drawing my gaze. I caught a glimpse of the pool. The water was murky and gross. I craned my neck, stepping into the kitchen without realizing my attention had wavered—

A bloodied hand came down on my forearm and knocked my gun away. I stumbled after it, but the hand gripped me tight. Fingernails dug into my forearm. I fought to free myself before looking into the face of the hand's owner. Bloodshot eyes. Matted hair. Lacerations from head to toe.

"Please," she begged. "Get me out of here, and I'll tell you everything."

Carter blazed into the kitchen. "Don't move!"

The woman—blonde, twenties, brown eyes— cowered from Carter's gun, but she refused to let go of me. "Please! Help me. It wasn't me. I was held here. It wasn't—"

"Secure her," Carter ordered me. "Then help me sweep the rest of the house. Backup's on the way. They'll take care of her."

"Yes, ma'am."

Carter continued on, checking the other bedrooms on her own. I half-carried, half-guided the bleeding woman to a room we'd already cleared and helped her sit on the bed. Her fingers bore signs of wire torture too.

"Stay here," I told her. "I have to help my partner clear the rest of the house. Do you know where the person is who did this to you?"

She clutched my arms, spreading more of her blood

across my skin. Her lower lip trembled. "Please don't leave me. Get me out of here first, and I'll tell you everything."

"You have to stay here for now." I tried to pry her fingers off of me. "I'll come right back as soon as I check in with my partner. Other officers are coming. Just stay put—"

"No!" She threw her arms around my waist and threaded her fingers through my belt loops, securing herself to me. "You can't leave me! Get me out, get me out!"

"Shh." I glanced through the bedroom doors. Carter was nowhere in sight. "Okay, come on. I'll take you to the cruiser, but be quiet."

She crumbled with relief as I pulled her to her feet again and helped her from the bedroom. We were halfway to the front door when another person stumbled out of the master bathroom, fled across the living room, and barreled through a back exit so quickly that I didn't see whether or not the sprinter was a man or a woman.

"Hey!" I dropped the woman on the couch near the door and pursued the runner, picking up my gun from the floor as I did so. "Freeze! Carter, help!"

I stumbled onto the patio as the screen door to the backyard slammed shut. Carter bumped into me from behind as the runner disappeared into the thick swampy conservation land behind the house. Carter took off after the suspect. The screen door slammed again as she tore through it, then she too vanished in the palm trees and marshy weeds.

Sometime later—minutes but it felt like hours—Carter returned from the wild, sweating and covered in mud up to her knees. Backup arrived, red and blue lights flashing through the house. As the extra officers cleared the scene, Carter turned on me.

"Where the hell were you, Ryder?" she demanded. "I told you to help me clear the house."

"I was with the vic," I stuttered. "She wouldn't let me leave her alone—"

"I lost the perp," Carter said. "Because I didn't have my partner to back me up. Rule number two, rookie. Rule number freaking two." She jabbed me in the chest with her index finger, bruising my collarbone. "We lost a killer because of you."

Lieutenant Marín loomed over my shoulder. "What happened, Carter?"

Carter glared at me. "Rookie mistake, sir. Rookie mistake."

---

2

*T*hough I never remembered my night terrors, I could always tell when I had one in the morning. I woke up slick with sweat, sore from head to toe, and with a throat like sandpaper. They were different than regular nightmares. Normal people had a bad dream, jolted awake, realized it wasn't real, and faded off to sleep again. Meanwhile, I'd lost count of how many times my landlord banged on the door of my apartment because another neighbor had complained about the screaming.

I wasn't a rookie anymore. That day at 3220 Horizon Way was eight years ago. We never caught the killer, but my mistake motivated me to put all my effort into becoming the best cop possible. I was a detective now, but no matter how many murderers and abusers I put behind bars, I never forgot the one I let slip by. That one haunted me at night.

The sheets were cold, damp, and twisted into rat tails. I kicked them off and swung my legs off the edge of the bed. The chilly tile beneath my bare feet grounded me. As I pulled off my sweaty night shirt, I went through a list of affirmations.

"I'm okay," I muttered. "I'm in control of my emotions. I'm in control of my thoughts. I can let go of the past."

Sandy, my therapist, had prescribed affirmations as a way to prevent me from spiraling into anxious or depressed thoughts. At first, it felt like bullshit, but combined with daily mindfulness practice, it helped me relax. The key was constant maintenance. My mind was a rusty old pickup truck. Therapy made me change the oil and rotate the tires so I could keep hauling emotional baggage in the bed of it.

Sunlight streamed in through the glass balcony door. I'd chosen this apartment complex for its south-facing windows, so it was light inside all day. Vitamin D coerced me out of bed, ushered me to the electric kettle, and convinced me to pop a frozen waffle in the toaster.

As the kettle boiled and the toaster toasted, I pulled on a pair of easy-wash slacks and a men's button-up shirt. The women's ones were too short for my long torso. I tucked in the shirt and checked the mirror. Other than a slight flush to my cheeks that would be gone by the time I reached the station, no one would know I'd had another episode last night.

The toaster dinged. I frosted organic peanut butter and blackberry jam across the burnt waffle then dumped a spoonful of matcha green tea powder into a hot cup of water and stirred until froth bubbled on the surface. I went out on the balcony to eat and let the sun soak into my unprotected pores as I dialed the one person I could tell anything to.

"Hi, Dom," I said when she answered. "It's me."

"Uh-oh." Dominique had a sixth sense for when I was having more trouble than usual. "Bad night? You never call me before work."

I sighed into the phone and pressed the deck chair back to get it to recline. "Yet another eight hours of thrashing around and screaming in bed."

"Aw, I'm sorry to hear that, honey," she said. "You should take a vacation! If anyone in your department deserves a few days off, it's you."

"Maybe I'll come see you," I suggested. "Where are you at in your amazing nomadic travels these days?"

"Just arrived in New Orleans last night." She hummed a few bars of nondescript jazz music. "Parked the van at a gas station, busked on Bourbon Street for a couple of hours, made two hundred bucks, tried a beignet, got towed, and used the two hundred bucks to get the van back, so it was a pretty eventful evening."

I let out a chuckle and tasted my tea. The earthy matcha coated my tongue with a layer of comfort. "What a life."

"If you don't mind not having instant access to a

25

toilet at all times, you could come hang out for a few days," she said. "Or I could meet you in, like, Cancun. You can stay at a hotel while I park at the beach."

"No way. I want to stay at the beach too."

"There are hotels on the beach, Alex."

"Right."

We fell quiet. A breeze whistled through the palm trees. I chewed another piece of my open-faced peanut butter and jelly sandwich. On the other end of the line, Dominique played a light fingerpicking rhythm on her guitar. I closed my eyes and imagined laying on a beach in Mexico.

"So," Dominique said after a while. "How's Sandy?"

"Crazy," I told her. "Do you think therapists go to therapy?"

"They're probably more screwed up than the rest of us," she answered. "But I wasn't asking about Sandy's mental state of mind."

I let the lounge chair come up on its own. "I know. I was going to call her."

"Before or after you called me?"

"After," I declared. "I'm not avoiding Sandy. Sometimes, it's easier to talk to you. You were there. You know why I can't sleep at night."

Dominique stopped playing her guitar. The line was quiet except for her breathing.

"Sorry, I didn't mean to remind you of it," I said. "I know you don't like thinking about it."

"And I know you're the opposite." The guitar began

a haunting tune. "So it's fine. It's hard for me too. I still have the scars from that maniac."

I finished off my toast and dusted the crumbs off my hands. "You don't remember anything else? Where the perp might have gone after she ran off?"

"We've been over this a million times, Alex," she said. "I never knew her real name. She told me she was Sydney Mallone."

"We never found records of a Sydney Mallone," I mused. "She created an entire identity for herself."

"You're doing it again."

"Doing what?"

"Brooding," Dominique said. "Getting stuck in the past. Doesn't Sandy want you to move past all this stuff? Focus on your current cases?"

I collected my plate and headed inside. "I am focused. I'm one of the best detectives in the City of Tampa. I was honored last year for the Bleeker case, remember? Besides, it's been slow at work."

"You don't have to prove anything to me," she replied. "I knew you were going to be a great cop as soon as you charged into my house all those years ago."

"Crimes of passion," I said. "That's what they call my speciality. Isn't that nuts? How can you be passionate about murder?"

"Aren't you?"

"Not in the same way," I muttered.

"Call Sandy," Dominique ordered. "I'm not trying to write you off and redirect you to your therapist, but this isn't going to be a productive conversation between you and me. We need different things, things that neither one of us can give to the other."

I set my plate in the sink and stirred my tea again. The matcha powder had settled at the bottom of the cup. "You're right. I'm sorry."

"Don't apologize," she said. "Call me back later, okay? I want to hear about your day."

"Okay. Don't get towed again."

"I'll do my best. Love ya."

"Love you too."

The phone clicked as she hung up. I scrolled through my contacts until I found Sandy's number. I didn't keep her in my favorites. There was something pathetic about having your therapist in your favorites list. I hesitated before tapping her name. Did I need Sandy for this or could I deal with it myself?

Dominique's face flashed in my mind, her eyes wide and terrified. Bloody marks around her fingers. Fresh bruises across her face. When we first interviewed her, she wouldn't talk to anyone but me. She jumped at the slightest noise, and she was more scared of Officer Carter than any of the rookies in my division that year. It wasn't until I got her out of the interrogation room and into a safe apartment that she started talking. I promised her I'd bring in the person responsible. Later, Carter told me never to make a promise in this line of work.

I called Sandy. "It's Alex. Are you free?"

"I've got five minutes," Sandy said, brusque as always. "Is this an emergency?"

"No. I had another night terror."

A horn beeped through the phone.

"Screw you!" Sandy said. "Sorry, Alex. Some idiot cut me off then had the nerve to flick *me* off. Do you want to make an appointment? It's been a while."

"I've been busy with work."

"Everyone's always busy with work," she said. "You have to make time for yourself. That's the thing about self-care, especially when you're working with a mental illness."

"I'm not mentally ill," I argued.

"You've been diagnosed with anxiety and PTSD," she reminded me. "You don't have to let it define you, but you do have to face facts. Don't let your treatment go by the wayside. Do you want to relapse again?"

"No."

"Good. How's this afternoon?" Tires squealed, and Sandy beeped her horn again. "You son of a—! Two o'clock, Alex? I had a cancellation."

"Sure."

"Great. See you then."

She hung up on me. A second later, the phone rang. It was the station.

"Ryder," I answered.

"It's Carter. Got a case for you."

In the years since my rookie days, Marín had retired and Carter was promoted to Lieutenant. She was the first woman to hold the role, and she made damn sure everyone knew she was up to the job.

I poured the rest of my tea in a to-go thermos. "I'm on my way in. Details?"

"You can see for yourself," Carter said. "I'll text you the location. This one's right up your alley, Ryder."

Sandy and Carter had one thing in common. They hung up the phone without saying goodbye. After the call, my phone chimed. I looked up the address Carter had sent me. It was a yoga studio called Day Moon not far away from my apartment complex.

I changed my shirt. A button-up was fine for the station, where custodial cranked the air conditioning up to full blast. Crime scenes, on the other hand, made me sweat. I pulled on a dark green T-shirt and loose, light wash jeans instead, grabbed my sunglasses and keys from where they hung by the door, and headed out.

DAY MOON WAS LOCATED in a cute shopping center smack in the middle of suburbia. Mid-priced minivans and crossovers littered the parking lot while the soccer moms who owned them craned their necks to see over the blockade of cop cars around the yoga studio. The entrances to the bakery and the boutique on either side of Day Moon were closed off too.

I parked as close as I could and approached the scene. For anyone else, the flashing lights and crowds of officers might be overwhelming, but a sense of calm stole over me whenever I got a new case. It reminded me I had a purpose.

As I ducked under the crime scene tape, a county officer stepped in my way. "Whoa! Excuse me, miss. This is a crime scene. You can't be here. It's not safe for civilians."

I flashed my badge. "Detective Alex Ryder. I'm working this case. Mind stepping out of the way, Officer?"

He tripped getting out of my way. "I'm so sorry. You don't look like a detective. You kind of look like one of the moms who keep trying to get in here to see the yoga schedule."

"Wow, thanks. Keep it tight, Officer. I'm going to go inside and do my job."

"Yes, sir. I mean—yes, ma'am."

An argument broke out between Day Moon and the neighboring bakery. Angela, still a part of our patrol division, was attempting to calm down a woman with flour in her pores and batter on her arms.

"I understand your concern, Miss Bailey," Angela was saying, "but I'm afraid we can't let anyone into this area until we sweep and clear the crime scene."

"My bakery isn't a part of your crime scene." Miss Bailey's arms flung flour and dough like vanilla-scented fireworks as she gesticulated her frustration. "I'm losing time and money here. My customers can't

31

come inside because of all this hubbub. All I'm asking is for you to move the crime scene tape."

Angela assumed resting cop pose. Shoulder-length stance, hands on her belt, and a practiced air of nonchalance. "I can't do that, ma'am. I'm sorry, but we have rules."

Miss Bailey crossed her arms. "Do you plan on reimbursing me for the business I'm losing due to this investigation?"

I stepped between the two women. "I have an idea. When we catch the person responsible for the crime, we'll bill them for your lost business. Sound good, Miss Bailey?"

She looked me up and down. "Who are you?"

"Detective Alex Ryder," I said. "You're officially interfering with a homicide investigation. I could have Officer Pennacchi here arrest you for that. Or would you rather step back inside and let us do our jobs so we can make sure your business isn't interrupted by other murders in the future?"

Miss Bailey clapped her hands together and sent a cloud of flour up as she disappeared into the bakery like a confectionary magician. Angela let her shoulders slump.

"Thank you," she said. "I hate working homicide, man. It's worse than a customer service job."

"Speaking of which, how's Jess?"

"She's *fine*," Angela answered. "She only took that

call center job because of the baby. Working on the force was too stressful."

"Stressful. Sure."

"I wish I didn't have to play referee between you and my wife," she lamented. "When is this dumb competition of yours going to be over? You've been at each other's throats since we met as rookies. We're having a dinner party tonight with some of the other officers, and I'd love to be able to invite you without starting a war."

"The competition is over," I told her. "I won. I made detective before her. By the way, I wouldn't say no to dinner."

Angela bumped my shoulder. "Don't you have a job to do, *Detective* Ryder?"

I waggled my eyebrows and left Angela to ward off more mommies and store owners. I was happy Angela had found her soulmate in Jess, though I didn't understand it. Angela was a positive ray of sunshine while Jess was a cocky cynic. Nevertheless, they made it work. When I saw them together, jealousy colored the world in green. Dominique was the closest thing I had to a soulmate, and I hadn't seen her in person since her testimony eight years ago. It wasn't the same as having a partner who understood your every quirk.

Day Moon was crawling with officers, crime scene investigators, and photographers. The studio itself was hip and cute. One wall showcased local artists' works while the other sported a giant, room-length mirror for yogis to check their alignment during class. The wood floor creaked underfoot and bounced back after every step. The studio was small and crowded, so much so that I couldn't spot the victim.

Carter stood nearby with a woman in flowy yoga pants and a loose tank top. I caught Carter's eye, and she waved me over.

"What do we got?" I asked Carter. "I can't see."

"Female. Thirties. Lacs—" Carter glanced at the yogi beside her. "I'm sorry. This is Lacey Braham. She's the owner of the studio. Miss Braham, this is Detective Alex Ryder. She's our go-to for homicide."

"Call me Lacey," she said and shook my hand. She sniffed and wiped her nose. "Thanks for being here, Detective."

I offered her a travel pack of tissues. "Absolutely. I'm sure we'll talk later."

"Do you mind excusing us, Lacey?" Carter asked. "You can wait outside with Officer Pennacchi. Someone will take you to the station in a little bit."

Once Lacey was out of earshot, I turned to Carter. "Well?"

"It's a good one," she said. "Lacerations on the skin above every chakra point."

"You're kidding."

"Take a look."

Carter carved a way through the crowd. As the photographer stepped aside, I saw the body for the first time. No matter how many homicides I worked, a rush of adrenaline hit me every time I beheld a crime scene. Over time, I'd learned to channel the onslaught of energy into examining every inch of the scene in excruciating detail.

The victim was a pretty blonde woman. She and I had a similar haircut, chin-length and angled forward. She was laid out on a yoga mat in the middle of the studio with her arms and legs at her sides. Were it not for the blood, she could have been finishing up a session and resting in—

"Corpse pose," I said.

"Appropriate, isn't it?" Carter replied. "Want to take a closer look?"

"Did CSI clear us?"

"Yup. We're good to go."

I stepped out of the throng and knelt beside the body, as close as I could get without stepping into the puddle of blood. As Carter mentioned, the victim had wounds down the center of her body, each one correlating with one of the seven chakras. All but one were shallow lacerations.

"Obvious cause of death." I pointed to the victim's stomach. An enormous knife wound had opened the area, and the woman had bled out from there. "Which chakra is that?"

"No idea," Carter said. "Anything else stand out to you?"

I pulled the flashlight from my belt and illuminated the other lacerations. "These knife patterns look familiar, don't they? I feel like I've seen them before."

"Mm-hmm. What else?"

It took me a good minute to spot it. When I did, the flashlight dropped out of my hand and rolled through coagulated blood.

"Watch it!" one of the crime scene investigators called.

My breath stuck in my lungs. I couldn't tear my eyes away from the victim. Carter thumped me on the back.

"Easy," she murmured. "Focus. I put you on this case for a reason. What do you see?"

On the victim's left hand, in the place of her wedding ring, was a loop of gold wire. The finger beneath it was blue, as if the wire had been there for hours or days, cutting off circulation.

"Wire torture," I said at last. "Similar to the methods used on Dominique and Dustin Benson eight years ago."

"Wire torture, matching knife patterns, similar victims," Carter listed. "What does that tell us?"

I swallowed hard, fighting against the lump in my throat.

"Our killer's back."

3

_____

*T*he station was business as usual. Officers bustled to and fro across the bullpen. Detectives fed coffee to the dark circles beneath their eyes. Rookies answered phones and complained about the latest petty criminal who had passed through booking. The AC pumped a draft of cold air right across the back of my neck as I sat at my desk. The red light on my phone blinked. I had six messages from that morning. I put the receiver to my ear and hit the playback button.

"Detective Ryder?" a tearful male voice said. "This is Alan Spitz. I'm so sorry to call you this early, but I heard you were assigned to my wife's case. I was wondering if you had leads yet. Call me back when you get a chance."

I jotted Alan Spitz's name and number on a sticky note. The phone beeped and played the next message.

"It's Alan Spitz again. It's been about an hour, and I haven't heard anything about my wife yet. I'm sorry, Detective. I've got three kids, and I don't know what to tell them. Any information would be helpful."

Another beep.

"Detective? It's Alan—"

The next three messages were replicas of the first few, though Alan grew desperate and teary with each reiteration. I made a mental note to call him later. I had nothing to tell him yet, and the family of murder victims needed more than common consolation.

Carter stopped by my desk to hand me a manila envelope. "Photographs from the scene. How are you making out?"

"Got a name and address," I told her. "Jenn Spitz of Pelican Point subdivision. That's about all I got so far. Is the owner of the yoga studio here?"

"She's waiting for you in the interview room. You should get in there before she gets too emotional." Carter planted her hand on my desk to stop me from getting up. "You can handle this one, right? I figured you were the best woman for the job, but if it's too hard on you, I can hand it off to another detective."

I pushed my chair away from the desk to evade Carter's offensive stance. "Don't worry, Lieutenant. I got this. No rookie mistakes this time."

My blood sugar was low. Examining the crime scene had taken all morning, and my breakfast had long since made its way through my digestive system.

I needed lunch, but the case took first priority. I ignored the gnawing pains in my stomach and grabbed two coffees on my way to the interview room.

Lacey Braham paced the small dimensions of the room. She eyed the two-way mirror with suspicion.

"Don't worry," I said, making her jump. "No one's watching you."

Lacey rested her hand over her heart. "Is that what you say to everyone who comes in this room?"

"Nah." I offered her one of the coffees. "You're not a suspect or a criminal. If you were, I would have let you think someone else was behind that glass. Adds a certain level of intimidation, you know?"

She accepted the coffee and held out her palm for the sugar and powdered creamer packets. "So I'm not a suspect?"

"Not yet," I told her. "Why? Should we put you on the list?"

"No, of course not. I wouldn't murder one of my own customers."

"Good to know." I pulled out the metal chair for her. "Sorry, it's not the most comfortable situation, but we don't have anything cozier for interviews."

Lacey sat in the chair, crossed one leg over the other, and began dressing her coffee. "It's fine. I don't suppose you could throw some sedatives in here? I'm kind of freaking out." She chuckled weakly to make sure I knew the drug comment was a joke.

"I could check evidence," I said. "I'm sure we have something back there."

She cracked a small smile, but it fell shortly after. "I can't believe this is happening. I can't believe I saw a dead body!" She covered her face with her hands.

"Lacey, I know it must be hard for you to know that this kind of violent crime could happen in your place of business." There was an unofficial script to stick to when talking to possible witnesses. I found it successful in most cases, and it helped me distance myself from the emotional aspect of my job. "But it's important for me to take your statement as soon as possible so the details don't get lost in the chaos. Can I ask you some questions?"

Lacey produced the travel pack of tissues I'd given her earlier and wiped the table beneath her coffee cup. "Okay. I'm ready."

I took the seat across from her so she wouldn't feel as if I were towering over her. "Is it okay if I record this conversation so I can refer back to your notes later?"

"I suppose so."

I clicked on the recorder. "This is Detective Alex Ryder with Lacey Braham, owner of Day Moon yoga studio, at which a homicide occurred earlier this morning. Lacey, can you tell me what you found at the scene when you entered the studio this morning?"

Lacey pressed her fingers to her throat and coughed. "Well, I saw Jenn's body—"

"Start at the beginning, please," I instructed. "From the moment you pulled into the parking lot."

She cleared her throat and tried again. "I pulled into the parking lot shortly after six. Our sunrise yoga class is at 6:30, so I get there early to set up the studio. I usually go through the back door, but there was some maintenance going on behind the shopping center, so I couldn't get through that way. I entered through the front, put my bag behind the counter, and went to turn the lights on. That's when—" She faltered, the words getting caught in a vocal gurgle. She stared into her coffee.

"Take your time," I said softly. "There's no rush. Be as detailed as possible."

She sipped her coffee, the best liquid courage when no booze was available. "The light switch is at the back of the room. That's when I saw her. Actually, I practically stepped on her. She was right in the middle of the floor, and my studio isn't that big."

"What did the victim look like?"

"She was lying in Savasana," Lacey said. "For a second, I thought maybe I'd forgotten to lock up the night before and she had come in early. Then I saw the blood." The tears started flowing. "S-she was covered in it."

"Did you see anyone else come or go from the studio? Was anyone else at the shopping center?" I asked, trying to divert her attention from the body bag aspect of everything. "While you were parking or walking in?"

She drew another tissue and blotted her eyes and nose. "The only person who gets there earlier than I do is Becca Bailey, the woman who owns the bakery next door. I didn't see her, but I could smell her baking, so she or one of her assistants had to be in there."

"But no one else in the parking lot?"

"Um, there was a male cyclist passing through, but I don't think anyone else was around."

My knee bounced up and down, a bad habit I couldn't help, especially when I was gaining intel on a case. "What do you know about Jenn? Was she a regular? Would you consider her a friend of yours?"

"I try to make all of my regulars feel like friends," Lacey said. "We're all connected through yoga. Jenn came every Monday, Wednesday, and Friday mornings. Sometimes, she came Saturday afternoons."

"What was Jenn's usual demeanor like?"

"She was always friendly," she replied. "But for the last couple of weeks, she seemed to be having more trouble than usual. She was distracted in class, skipping postures or ignoring her alignment. She stopped coming about a week ago."

I leaned on my knees to keep the left one from bouncing. "She stopped coming? Which day?"

Lacey gulped on her nerves. "I saw her last Monday. She hasn't come in since then. She hasn't paid her monthly membership fee either. I thought maybe she wanted to quit, but it was so out of the blue. My regulars don't skip out like that."

"Did you notice anything else different with Jenn in the last few weeks?"

"She stopped talking to her friends," Lacey said. "The other women in class."

"Do you have their names?"

"I gave my entire client list to your lieutenant," she told me. "I'm not sure what good it will do. Jenn didn't hang out with my other clients after class. They all lived in different neighborhoods, and Jenn always had some errand to run."

"Do you know of anyone who would want to hurt Jenn?" I asked. "Anyone who might have had a quarrel with her? The perpetrator has a knowledge of yoga and chakras, so it could be someone in or around your establishment."

Lacey shook her head and traced the lip of her coffee cup. "No. You should ask her husband. Sometimes, she walked to class, and he would come pick her up. Perpetually late. Can I go? I'm exhausted, and someone told me there's all this stuff I have to do before I can reopen the studio."

I pushed my chair away from the table. "You're not obligated to stay, but it would help if we have a way to contact you in case we find or need more information."

"I can leave you my number."

. . .

AFTER I GOT her contact information, I passed Lacey off to an officer so she could figure out how to progress with her business. Day Moon wasn't likely to open for a while, not with all that blood soaked into the bouncy wood floor. Hunched over my desk, I looked up everything we had on Jenn Spitz, something I should have done before I interviewed Lacey. It didn't help much. Jenn had a couple of speeding tickets, but that was it. No dirty laundry a murderer might have taken offense to.

As I hunched over my computer, Carter came up behind me. "Did the studio owner give up anything?"

I stretched over the back of the chair and all of my joints popped into place. "Not much. The owner of the bakery might have seen something though. She was arguing with Angela this morning, pretty adamant that her shop wasn't involved with the murder."

Carter rested her elbow on the divider between my desk and another detective's. "Hmm. You thought it was an act?"

"Could be. I don't have any other suspects at the moment." I scrolled through a list of Day Moon's clients on my computer. "Other than some random cyclist passing by."

"Do you have security footage from the yoga studio?"

"Yup, the front door's clear, but—" I pulled up the videos from the studio that morning and played a segment of interest for Carter. "Here's the view from the back."

Carter squinted at the screen. "I don't see anything."

"Exactly. Lacey said there was maintenance going on behind the shopping center," I said. "This big ass truck is parked right in front of the camera that monitors the back door. Guess when it moves?"

"Right after the estimated time of murder?"

"You got it."

She tapped my desk with her knuckles. "Call the maintenance company. See if that's a coincidence or not."

"I'm on it." I switched to another page on my desktop. "I've got something else too."

She leaned over my shoulder to look. "'Know Your Solar Plexus Chakra?' Is this some Gwyneth Paltrow shit, Ryder?"

"The victim had knife wounds over the site of every chakra," I reminded Carter. "But she was stabbed through the stomach. The third chakra."

"So?"

"So each one represents something," I said. "One of the meanings associated with the solar plexus chakra is taking control of one's life. A blocked third chakra might mean the inability to do so or a lack of confidence in oneself."

Carter crossed her arms. "You really think we're dealing with a yogi killer? Murder doesn't exactly mesh with that whole spiritual awakening thing."

"Gotta exhaust every avenue, right?"

"You're right. Keep me posted."

Carter left me to contemplate the meanings of the third chakra on my own. It might have been a stretch to focus on the location of the wound, but it seemed too pointed to ignore. Something gnawed on my stomach, either instinct or discomfort. One of the things I often talked to Sandy about was taking control of my life and my emotions. The third chakra also had to do with force of will, self-assurance, and personal power. This case had punched me where it hurt: right in the stomach.

I opened the manila envelope and shuffled through the photographs on the crime scene until I found one of Jenn's full body. The killer had carved the sign for each chakra in its corresponding location except for the stomach. The wound there wasn't graphic or attention-seeking. It was a quick, short jab, deep enough to penetrate the vital organs and ensure Jenn's death. The killer wanted to be seen for the method of murder, not the violence of the murder itself.

"They wanted to send a message," I murmured.

"You're doing it again, Ryder," Angela called, passing by behind me. "Talking to yourself. I told you. It's creepy."

I whirled my chair around and held up the picture of Jenn. "What do you see here?"

Angela wrinkled her nose but stepped closer for a

better look. "A dead yogi. I don't work homicide for a reason, Alex. It makes me want to barf."

"Did the bakery owner seem legit to you?" I tucked the photo into the envelope. "Becky—whatever her name was?"

"Becca Bailey," Angela corrected. "What do you mean?"

"She made quite a case this morning."

"With good reason." She unbuttoned the top of her uniform shirt and used a recruitment brochure to fan herself. "She was mad about losing business because of us this morning."

"Someone was murdered next door to her bakery," I pointed out. "You think she'd be more worried about the fact that the killer wasn't apprehended."

"You think she had something to do with it?"

"Lacey Braham said Bailey's the only one who gets to that shopping center earlier than she does," I said. "If anyone saw something, it would be her."

"So go check it out."

"Nah, I need more before I do that."

"Such as?"

I spun my chair back and forth. The open tabs on my computer screen bombarded me with choices. Jenn Spitz's limited file. Security footage from the shop. Research on chakras. Day Moon's yoga schedule.

I clicked on the window that displayed the security footage. In the top right corner of the screen, a tiny triangle of space wasn't blocked out by the construction vehicle. The upper part of the bakery's back door was visible. As I watched the tape over again, the door opened and shut.

"Did you see that?" I rewound the footage and played it for Angela. "Someone went into the bakery."

"So?" Angela said. "It was probably Becca."

"It's time-stamped 5:47," I said. "CSI said the victim was most likely killed around oh-six-hundred. The truck moves out of this frame at 6:06. Becca Bailey was there during the murder. I gotta check this out. You want to come?"

"Nope. But bring me back a donut."

"No promises."

I grabbed my keys and sunglasses and headed for the door, but Carter caught my arm on the way out.

"Whoa, where are you going, rookie?" she asked.

"I'm not a rookie anymore," I reminded her.

She stirred a cup of tea with a toothpick. "You'll always be my rookie. You got something?"

"I think the bakery owner was at the scene of the crime." I perched my sunglasses on my head so they tucked my hair behind my ears. "I'm going to over there and question her."

"Nope."

"What?"

Carter nodded toward the front desk. A few civilians waited by the brochures for officers to assist them. They paced back and forth, instinctively nervous about being surrounded by cops, except for one guy. Early forties. Thinning brown hair and brown eyes. The dad bod that women these days were proud to settle for. He stared at the ceiling and blinked like his eyelids were on a timer to remind him when his eyes needed moisture. He carried a woman's raincoat patterned with lilies.

"Let me guess," I said to Carter. "That's Alan Spitz."

"You got it." Carter took my car keys and booted me toward the forlorn husband. "If you'd answered his hundred messages earlier, maybe you wouldn't be in this situation."

I sidestepped her boot. "Can't you get one of the officers to fill him in? How about Angela? She's good with the crying and emotions. I'm not—"

"It's your case, Ryder."

"But I have a lead—"

Carter put herself between me and the path to freedom, then lowered her voice to a dangerous level. "You also have a responsibility to that gentleman. His wife has died. His whole world has flipped upside down, and the only way he's going to get any kind of closure is if we can figure out who did this. I don't understand why I have to have this conversation with you for every homicide. Get some fucking feelings, Ryder."

She gave me back the keys and got out of my way. A bubble of air got stuck in my throat as Carter walked back to her office. I knew she'd be watching me for my decision. If I walked out of the station to interview the bakery owner, it would mean an automatic lack of respect for an indefinite amount of time to Carter. I had to deal with the husband first.

Carter didn't understand the situation. It wasn't that I didn't have any feelings. It was that I had too many. With every case I took up, I separated myself as much as possible from the victim's family and friends. If I got too close to them, it clouded my judgement. I made mistakes. If I wanted to be a successful detective, I had to keep things cold and objective. It was the way I worked best. Unfortunately, it wasn't the way Carter expected me to work.

I approached Alan Spitz and cleared my throat. He took a second to orient the bones in his neck, pulling his head up from the back of the waiting chair.

"Mr. Spitz?" I clasped my hands behind my back. "I'm Detective Alex Ryder. Would you like to go somewhere quiet so we can discuss what happened to your wife?"

His eyes were red but dry. He hadn't cried yet. He lifted the raincoat from his lap. "This is hers," he said. "She forgot it at home this morning. I keep telling her 'Don't forget your raincoat. You never know when it's going to rain.' She doesn't like getting caught in the rain. Or piña coladas."

I didn't react to his empty laugh. "Why don't you come with me, Mr. Spitz?"

He lifted himself from the chair with a heavy, drawn-out groan and clutched his low back. I led him to the break room, where a few officers mingled and ate snacks.

"I need the room," I announced. "Clear out, please."

The officers did as told, eyeing Alan Spitz as they passed him. Alan took a seat on the old sofa next to the water cooler and smoothed the raincoat across his lap.

"This isn't how I imagined being questioned." He gazed around the break room, taking in the half-eaten box of donuts, the dirty fridge where we kept our lunches, and the gurgling coffee pot that hadn't been washed in days. "Don't you have some kind of interview room?"

"It's not as comfortable." I closed the door to the room, cutting off the chatter in the bullpen. "You've been through enough this morning. The atmosphere in the interview room is a bit cold. I didn't want to subject you to that."

Truth be told, I was more comfortable in the interview room than anywhere else because it had nothing for my interviewee to hide behind. People felt all sorts of things in the interview room—nerves, guilt, innocence, euphoria—but to me, it was a clean gray slate.

"What happened?" Alan asked. "Where's my wife?"

I leaned against the coffee table and folded my hands in front of me. "How much do you want to know? You should ask me to sugarcoat it. From experience, I know how difficult it is to hear these things."

Alan patted the raincoat, taking the sleeves between his hands as if he had the power to make her magically reappear in it. "I want to know everything. I have to know."

I gave him ten seconds to change his mind. Then I said, "Your wife was found at approximately 6:15 this morning at Day Moon yoga studio. She had knife wounds to her head, face, and body, including one in her abdomen that caused fatal damage. As of right now, she is most likely on her way to the morgue for a medical examiner to officially determine cause of death."

Alan keeled over the raincoat. He was silent for a few moments. Then his lungs protested the lack of oxygen, and he gulped a panicked gasp and started hyperventilating. I opened the fridge and upended someone's lunch. Half of a sub and a bag of chips fell out. I handed the empty paper bag to the grieving husband.

"Breathe into this." I showed him how to hold it. "Take it easy. This happens all the time. Just breathe."

Alan's eyes watered as he gasped into the bag. After a few minutes, his breathing slowed, and he began to calm down. When he was ready, he set the bag aside.

"I can't do this alone," he said. "We have three kids all under the age of ten. I work full-time. Jenn is the one who knows which bedtime story Trevor likes the best and what kind of cheese Shelby will actually eat with her macaroni. She's the one who washes the one pair of socks Danny doesn't refuse to wear. I can't do this—I can't raise them—without her."

I stepped out of reach when he groped for physical comfort. "Mr. Spitz, I tell this to every person affected by the death of a family member or friend. Seek therapy. A professional will be able to help you sort through all the complications that come with this shock to your life."

Alan glanced up at me. "That's your advice? Go to therapy? My wife was murdered!"

"I'm sorry, sir. Professional help will help you come to terms—"

"I don't want to come to terms with this." He stood up, and the raincoat dropped to the floor as he thrust his index finger toward my face. "I want *you* to tell me how this could have happened. We live in a nice neighborhood. When Jenn first got pregnant with Danny and we decided to move, I researched the place with the best schools and the lowest crime rates. Murder shouldn't happen here, so why don't *you* tell *me* why your damn department couldn't keep my wife alive?"

"I'm sorry, sir. It's common in situations like this to place blame on guiltless parties—"

"Are you a fucking robot?" he demanded. "Can you say something other than 'I'm sorry, sir?'"

Alan took a heavy step toward me. My hand drifted to the travel pepper spray in the back pocket of my jeans. This wasn't the first time a victim's family member reacted like this. For some people, rage was the default emotion.

"I understand how you're feeling," I told him, "but I

need to ask you a few questions about your wife and her life at home. If you could take a seat, sir—"

"You don't understand anything."

"Sir, please sit down."

"No!" he hollered. "Get me someone else! I want to talk to someone with half a brain."

"Mr. Spitz, I'm the detective assigned to this case—"

The door to the break room flew open in the middle of my sentence, and Carter walked in. She took one look at my hand, buried in my back pocket, and the utter rage on Alan's face, and said, "Detective Ryder, someone at the front desk has a tip for you. Why don't you go take care of that while I answer Mr. Spitz's questions?"

"Lieutenant, I was—"

"Out," she ordered.

I had no choice but to leave. There was no one waiting for me at the front desk. It was all Carter's doing to get me out of the room with Alan. I stormed out to my car, got in, and slammed my fists against the dashboard. I only stopped when a passing officer glanced my way. I checked my hands. They were red, sore, and would probably bruise later, but at least my head felt clear. That was all that mattered.

4

My therapist ran her own private practice and rented her office out of a coworking space near the university. I drove out to the USF area early and waited in the parking lot until it was time to go in. College students hurried in and out of the nearby bookstore, coffee shop, and burrito place. Everyone who passed by was decorated with damp sweat spots across their T-shirts. The sun beat through the tinted windows of my car and burned its way into my brain. By the time two o'clock rolled around, I had one hell of a migraine.

The main area of the coworking space was set up like a common room in a dormitory with added desks, power bars, and rolling chairs. Everything was painted an alarming shade of white that reflected the light from outside. Somehow, the air-conditioned room was hotter than the parking lot. Students hunched over textbooks and laptops, though it was hard to tell who was actually studying. Half of them were snacking and browsing through social media, and at least three of them were asleep.

"Yo, Detective!"

Sleepy heads turned in the direction of the voice, and one of the students flagged me down. I headed toward his desk.

"What's up, Roark?" I asked, high-fiving the kid. He was a senior studying criminology at USF. The first time I'd met him, he'd stopped me in my tracks because I was wearing my uniform. Since then, he made a point to say hi whenever he saw me.

"Not much." He swept his long blond hair out of his eyes and tied it up in a bun. "One more year until I graduate. Then I'm coming to work with ya."

"You know you could've been a cop all this time," I told him. "Right out of high school. Besides, you gotta think bigger. You could work for the FBI if you wanted."

"Nah, I want to stay local," Roark said. "My mom lives in this area. I want to keep her safe. So what do you got for me? Anything good?"

Roark and I liked to play a game when we saw each other. Before my appointment, I'd give him the details of the last case I cracked. He had the hour to figure out who the perpetrator was. On my way out, I'd tell him if he was right or wrong and explain how the rest of the case panned out. He was a decent kid with a great brain for what he wanted to do. I told myself it wasn't illegal to share details of a case with him if the case had already been closed. Today was different though. I needed someone else's perspective.

I checked the clock—five minutes until two—and leaned over Roark's chair to whisper: "38-year-old female killed with a knife wound to the third chakra in a yoga studio. Her body was staged. The owner of the studio found her, there's no surveillance footage, and supposedly no witnesses. However, the chick who owns the bakery next door was already at work when the murder occurred. Who did it?"

"Whoa, hang on," Roark called as I started walking away. "That's all I get? You usually give me more to go off of."

"That's all I got. See you in an hour."

Sandy's office was situated in the back hallway of the coworking space. I knocked lightly on the door.

"Come in, Alex!"

Sandy sat in an ergonomic chair by the window, fiddling with one of those puzzles with two pieces you were meant to figure out how to take apart and put back together again. After another minute of playing with it, she hurled the puzzle across the room. It hit the opposite wall and fell to the floor—in two pieces. She smiled peacefully at me.

"Early as always," she commented. "Take a seat. What's been going on?"

Sandy's office didn't feel like it belonged to an

actual person of science. She didn't have her degrees and certifications hanging on the walls. They were stuffed in one of the drawers of her file cabinet. On a small table in the corner, Sandy had one of those at-home espresso makers that cost about a thousand dollars. The office smelled of fresh beans, and if I was lucky, Sandy had also run to the local café that morning for a batch of croissants.

"I only share them with my favorite clients," she'd told me on the first day she offered me one. "The ones who actually have the drive to make progress."

There were no croissants today. That's what I got for scheduling so late in the afternoon. However, Sandy was more than willing to fire up the espresso machine.

"Coffee?" she asked. "I finally learned how to make a cat out of the milk foam."

I settled myself on the leather sofa across from her and kicked my feet up. "As much as I'd love to see you try that, I've gotta keep this quick. I picked up a huge case this morning, and my boss is probably going to call me in ten minutes."

Sandy crossed the room to the espresso machine anyway. It gurgled as she turned it on. "This thing's got a three-second heat up feature." She snapped her fingers as the green light lit up to indicate the machine was ready to brew. "Isn't that amazing? Totally worth the cash. Anyway, what have I told you about that?"

"About three-second heat up features? That it's totally worth the cash."

She crumpled up a paper cup and tossed it across the room at me. "About making time for your self-care. Your boss isn't going to appreciate it if you flip out due to sleep deprivation because you haven't tended to the emotions causing your nightmares."

"That was a bit of a long sentence. Can we back up to my boss flipping out?" I unfurled the paper cup and began folding it into a new shape. "She already did that this morning because I was tactless with the victim's husband."

Sandy flipped on the bean grinder and yelled over it, "I don't want to talk about your case. Tell me about your night terror!"

"The case is related to the night terror! It's a repeat —!" The bean grinder cut off, leaving me yelling over nothing. I tried again. "I think I had a premonition. You know I haven't had a night terror in ages. That's why I haven't been to see you. But this case is exactly like the one I screwed up all those years ago. The knife patterns are the same, and the victim is—"

"Hold up." Sandy tamped the ground beans until they formed a perfect puck. "You know I don't like cop shop talk in here. Tell me about the case in layman's terms."

I stood up and reached for the puzzle toy on the floor. Sandy, unlike others, didn't care how her patients moved during the session. One time, she'd let me juggle the weird crystal ornaments she kept on her bookshelf to make me more comfortable as I recounted a particularly hard day at work. I'd broken one, but she'd kept the pieces of it up to this day. The metal puzzle was at least meant for worried hands.

"I woke up sweating," I told Sandy. "I knew today was going to be hard. Then Carter—my lieutenant—called. She said she had a case for me." I explained the day's events so far, ending with Alan Spitz's freakout in the break room at work. "Anyway, I guess I didn't handle it well enough, and Carter's probably going to kick me off the case."

Sandy resumed her mission to create the perfect cappuccino. The milk frother screamed and bubbled. "Maybe that's for the best."

"Are you kidding?" I said. "It's my fault this person got away in the first place eight years ago. This is the only chance I have to redeem myself. If I don't solve this case, I might as well retire from the force now."

"You're talking in extremes," Sandy said, a phrase I'd heard from her mouth countless times over the years. "Your career won't end because of one case."

"It *could*. It's happened before."

"Stop playing the what-if game." Another familiar command Sandy often repeated to me. "Focus on the here and now. First of all, do you have any confirmation that this killer is the same one from your first day on the job?"

"All the evidence points to the same perpetrator."

"Yes, but do you have confirmation?"

"No, I guess not."

She turned off the milk frother and banged the steel warming cup against the counter. "Then you're already sabotaging yourself by not keeping an open mind. Yes, there are similarities in these murders, but what if they're not the same killer and you've pinned yourself into a hole you can't get out of?"

"You don't understand," I said. "My job is to study patterns like this. I work so closely with forensics because of cases like this, so that when a killer comes back around, we know what to look for."

"Maybe you're right." Sandy lifted the mug of espresso and the milk cup to make sure I was watching. "Maybe I don't know enough about your job, but I do know enough about you to see you're immersing yourself in a case that you might not be able to handle. Your boss has given you the option of handing this off to another detective. She knows this is difficult for you. Why not take her up on the offer?" She poured the milk then shaped the foam with a twist of her wrist. "Eh? Not bad, right?"

I glanced into the cup. Sure enough, instead of the classic cappuccino heart, Sandy had managed to erect a two-dimensional cat's head in the coffee. She shoved the cup into my hands.

"You drink it," she ordered. "I've had five already."

Knowing it was a lost battle, I took a sip. "I'm not giving up this case. If I hand it to another detective,

Carter will never stop asking me why I couldn't handle it. She won't trust me with similar cases in the future. I can't risk that."

"Here's an idea," Sandy deadpanned. "Why don't you tell Carter you have PTSD because of the first case?"

"Do you know what happens to cops who have PTSD?" I said. "They get phased out or declared unfit for the job. I'm handling my shit. I *am* fit for the job, and I won't have Carter thinking otherwise."

Sandy rinsed the milk cup in the sink of the adjoining bathroom. "There are also plenty of cops who have PTSD and handle their workload because their bosses know not to weigh them down. All I'm saying is to let Carter know you have limits."

I frowned at the cat face in my coffee. "What if I don't want to have limits?"

"Everyone has limits," Sandy said. "What matters is how you deal with them. Have you spoken with Dominique lately?"

"I called her this morning when I woke up," I answered. "She didn't want to talk about it."

"Can you blame her?"

"No, I guess not," I said. "But she's the only person who understands the situation. She was there. She was directly affected by what happened."

"You need to consider her feelings," Sandy said. "She was tortured and almost killed. Her husband was murdered. You can't expect her to hear you out every time you have a night terror."

"What am I supposed to do then? I can't talk to anyone else."

Sandy settled in her ergonomic chair and adjusted the blinds to keep the sun out of her eyes. "First of all, you have me. I think you should consider coming in for weekly appointments again, especially if you don't plan on relinquishing this case."

"I don't have time—"

"Ah, ah, ah." She held up a condescending finger. "Make time. I have another homework assignment for you as well. Hang out with someone outside of work. It sounds like Dominique is the only person you ever express your feelings to, and she doesn't live in this state. As human beings, we need physical support as well as emotional support. Go out. Be social, and when you do, don't talk about your problems non-stop. The people around you are not your therapist. I am. Alternatively, I am not your friend. Make a distinction between the two. It's important for your health."

The metal puzzle pieces clicked in my brain. With a swift, smooth movement, I attached the two of them together and pulled them apart again.

"If only everything was that easy," Sandy remarked.

On my way out of the coworking space, Roark

bounded to my side. He shook chip crumbs out of his shirt as he hurried along next to me.

"This is an open case, isn't it?" he asked in a hushed tone. "That's why you don't have any more information yet."

"Shut up," I muttered. "You know I can't give you details on an open case."

Roark grinned with excitement. "I'm right, aren't I? When did it happen? Do you have any research on the victim? If her body was posed, it means the murder was premeditated, right? Someone planned it. Did the victim have beef with anyone? Do you think—?"

"Roark!" I stormed out of the building and into the parking lot. The hot sun hit me like a death ray, frying my retinas. I shielded my eyes with my hand as I put on my sunglasses. "I gave you what I had in case you had any ideas of your own. If you don't, this conversation's over."

Roark followed me to my car. "It was a woman."

"How do you figure?"

"You think a dude would go to the trouble of learning about chakras to murder someone?" He grabbed the door of my car to stop me from closing him out. "She was killed in a yoga studio. Yoga is a chick's sport now. Not a lot of dudes practice because they don't consider it manly. I'm not one of them," he added hastily. "I think yoga's cool, but I'm telling you. Check the client list at that studio. It's gonna be like ninety-five percent woman. Your perp knows the area, the studio, and the victim. Hell, her name's probably on that client list."

As Roark awaited my confirmation or approval, my phone rang again.

"Ryder," I answered.

"Where are you?" Carter demanded so loudly I had to hold the phone a foot away from my ear to avoid hearing damage. "You think because you blew an interview with the victim's husband that you can avoid work for the rest of the day?"

"Actually, I had a prior appointment."

"I don't give a rat's ass about your prior appointments," Carter replied. "Get your ass over to Crescent Cakes Bakery. I got the owner to agree to a casual interview with you, but she refuses to come to the station. Do me a favor, Ryder? Don't piss this one off. She's already upset about the business she lost this morning because of the crime scene."

She hung up on me.

"Trouble in paradise?" Roark asked.

"Shut up." I yanked the door out of his grasp. "Go inside and do your homework. You look like you're about to melt into a puddle."

He wiped sweat from his forehead. "Hey, come back when you figure it out. I want to know what happens."

I shut the door and rolled the window down. "I'll keep you posted. Good luck with school. Pay attention. Don't procrastinate. All that bullshit."

Roark saluted me and hastened to get out of my

way as I pulled the car out of the space. I watched him in my rear view mirror, waiting at the stop sign until he was safely back inside.

ON MY WAY to Crescent Cakes Bakery, I phoned Lacey Braham.

"Hello?" she answered in a small voice. It sounded like she was expecting more bad news.

"Hi, Lacey. It's Detective Ryder," I said. "I know you already gave your client list to my lieutenant, but I was wondering if you could email me a copy as soon as possible."

"Oh! Sure, of course."

"Could you do me a favor?" I asked. "Can you high-light all the names of the people who went to the same classes as Jenn? I'm wondering who else might have been around Day Moon this morning."

"Yes, I'll do that right away," Lacey said. "Do you need anything else?"

"Not at the moment," I told her. "I'm heading to the shopping center now. I'll check on the clean-up process at the studio and give you an update later."

A few short minutes after I hung up with Lacey, I got an email notification on my phone. She'd already sent me the client list. At a red light, I opened the attached document to scroll through it. Lacey had highlighted at least twenty names. It would take all afternoon to look up each and every client.

The sun retired behind a nasty storm cloud as I pulled into the shopping center's parking lot. Fat droplets of rain pattered on my windshield. I grabbed the raincoat that remained stashed in my trunk, tossed it over my head, and ran into Crescent Cakes Bakery right as the heavens opened up. Within seconds, the sidewalk and everyone unlucky enough to be caught outside were drenched. The breeze kicked the rain against the bakery's glass windows as I shook off the excess water over the doormat.

Crescent Cakes Bakery was quaint and cozy. Most of the patrons sat alone, working on laptops or reading books as they munched on whatever delicious delight they'd ordered at the counter. It smelled sweetly of confections and fresh coffee. The café had a vague Parisian feel to it with tiny tables, striped padded chairs, and a decorative awning over the counter. Becca Bailey wasn't in sight, so I approached the barista instead.

"Hi, I'm Detective Alex Ryder."

I flashed my badge, aware of the other patrons' eyes on me. The fiasco next door was still in full swing, and everyone in the bakery would have seen the four cop cars, CSI van, and yellow tape around the yoga studio. They already knew why I was there, but it didn't stop them from trying to casually eavesdrop in on my conversation with the barista.

"Oh, about the murder?" the barista said. She was college-aged with braided brown hair and fat round glasses. She manned the espresso machine behind the counter with a swiftness Sandy would envy. "I don't know anything about it. My shift started at noon. Who died anyway?"

The café's customers collectively leaned in to catch my answer.

"That information hasn't been released to the public yet," I said. "Is the owner around? She should be expecting me."

"She's in the back. Becca!"

The owner stuck her head out of the food prep room. She was covered in flour, same as this morning, except now it had made its way into her hair like an odd, newfangled type of dry shampoo. When she saw me, she frowned.

"Five minutes." She held up her hand with her fingers spread apart to make her point. "That's how much time I have left for the macarons to set. Any longer and they'll be chewy."

"Five minutes is all I need," I assured her.

"Let's talk out back." She dusted her hands on her apron and sent a cloud of flour up. "Come on, what are you waiting for?"

I made my way through the crowded shop and followed Becca through the kitchen to the back entrance. We emerged in the loading area behind the shopping center. Thankfully, a short overhang shielded us from most of the rain, but it didn't stop the wind from slapping against my shins like a wet towel. I squinted through the gray sheets for a look at the camera that kept watch over Day Moon Yoga's back side. Next door, a few officers guarded the studio, swathed in ugly yellow ponchos.

"Detective," one of them said, nodding in my direction. "Any leads?"

"Working on it."

The officer—a guy named Peck who'd been with the force for about three years—smiled. It was a charming and disarming smile, the kind that could knock you off-balance if you weren't ready for it. "You wanna trade socks?"

I glanced at his soaked boots. "No chance. I'll bet your toes are like raisins."

"Excuse me, Detective?" Becca said. "I thought you were to interview me, not flirt with your co-workers."

"Oh, I wasn't flirting," Peck said. "That would be inappropriate."

"Just a friendly exchange," I added. "Get back to work, Peck."

"Yes, ma'am." He assumed a dramatically severe watchdog posture and winked at me. "Doing my job."

I intentionally turned to keep Peck's distracting aura behind me. "Okay, Becca. My lieutenant said you might have something for me. By my watch, you've got four minutes and twenty seconds until your macarons get chewy, so let's get to the point. What time did you get to the bakery this morning?"

"About a quarter to six," Becca said. "And before you

ask anything else, I didn't hear or see anything next door."

"Then why did you agree to have this conversation?"

"To make sure you people don't think I have something to do with it," she replied. "I realize I was antagonistic this morning with Officer what's-her-name."

"Pennacchi."

"Right," Becca said. "I didn't mean to give her a hard time, but you don't understand what it takes to keep a small business like mine running. This murder next door is going to kill my sales. I can't have you and your buddies wasting my time like this in the future."

I shuffled closer to the building as another gust of wind blew cold rain in sideways under the overhang. "Unfortunately, that's not the way things go during a homicide investigation. I'd love to be able to keep you out of it, but you were present when the murders happened. We have it on tape."

"What do you mean?"

I pointed to the camera that monitored the back door. "We have the footage from that camera. It shows you entering the establishment at 5:47 this morning."

"Yeah, exactly," Becca said. "I was inside the entire time. I didn't go out back until a quarter after to take out the trash. By that time, I already heard sirens pulling into the parking lot out front."

I scrawled the information in a pocket notebook, trying to keep the pages dry from the relentless rain.

"Did you happen to see a maintenance van out here when you took out the trash?"

"I saw it when I came into work," she said, "but it was gone by the time I went out back again."

"Did the van have a logo on it?" I asked. "Something to identify the company?"

"No logo." Becca lifted her apron to wipe condensation from her eyelashes. "But the company had the initials MMS. Something Maintenance Services. It was a last name. Miller or Morris or something like that."

"Did you see anyone actually performing any work out back?"

"There was a woman in a gray coveralls looking for something in the back of the truck when I pulled in," Becca said. "I didn't see her face, but she had platinum blonde hair tied up under her hat."

I wrote it all down and checked my watch. "Your five minutes are almost up. Go check on your macarons. Thanks for taking the time to talk to me."

"It's not a problem," she said. "Do me a favor? Keep me posted on all of this. I'm scared of what could happen, and if I need to move my business, I'd rather prepare for it sooner rather than later."

"I'll do my best," I assured her. "But you have my word that we're doing everything we can to keep this community safe, including your bakery."

"That's all I needed to hear."

5

---

*B*ack at the station, the day crew was starting to wind down. Around four o'clock, the energy changed at the station. People became sluggish and succumbed to the power of Tampa's afternoon showers. They slogged in and out of the station with bowed heads and wet shoulders, lugging raincoats and umbrellas with them. The phones rang incessantly, overwhelming the rookies who had been sentenced to desk duty for the day. Rain meant car accidents, from fender benders to full-on fatal crashes. Summer afternoons were the worst. They were hottest, wettest, and busiest. I was never more grateful to be a detective than on a day like today.

I tracked Carter down in her office and stuck my head in. "Got a lead from the bakery owner. I'll let you know how it pans out."

"Whoa!" Carter called after me as I tried to sneak off to my desk. "Get back in here, Ryder."

I framed myself in the no man's land between her office and the hallway. "Yes, ma'am? Can I do something else for you?"

"Come in and shut the door."

My pulse skyrocketed as I did as asked. This was it. One day into the biggest investigation of my life and Carter was ready to boot me off the case. Maybe Sandy was right. Maybe it was better to come clean about my PTSD and go down with a solid excuse rather than get fired for something stupid.

Carter scribbled notes on a file. "The husband's giving me some red flags. Did you get anything from him before his Mount Vesuvius impression?"

"I'm sorry, ma'am?"

She looked up from her notes. "Alan Spitz, the victim's husband. He doesn't have his story straight. Earlier, he told you Jenn drove to the studio herself this morning. After I calmed him down, he told me that one of Jenn's friends picked her up."

"Well, where's Jenn's car?"

"Mysteriously missing."

"So what?" I sat in the chair across from Carter's desk. "The killer stole it? That doesn't make any sense.What would she have done with the victim's car?"

"She?"

"Just a hunch."

Carter closed her file and tossed it aside. "The

husband doesn't know where the car is either. It's a blue 2016 Chrysler Town and Country. I already put out a BOLO. Anyway, put Alan Spitz on your suspect list if you haven't already and have an officer cruise by his house every so often to keep an eye on him."

"What else happened when you talked to him?" I asked. "He barely gave me anything."

"He walked me through Jenn's daily schedule," Carter answered. "It wasn't helpful, though he admitted Jenn started acting odd about three weeks ago."

"Change in medication? Big life event? Added stress?"

"According to Alan, none of the above." She stretched her arms over her head and groaned. "There had to be something going on. I want you to find out what it was. Interview everyone. Friends, kids, neighbors. Whatever it takes. What did you get from the baker?"

"The name of the maintenance company that was working behind the shopping center this morning," I said. "And a possible witness."

"Details."

"Blonde woman in protective coveralls and a hat."

"Not much to go on."

"I'll figure it out." I paused halfway out of my chair. "Can I go?"

Carter waved me off. "Sure, get out of here. Oh, and Ryder? This case is important, but so is your health.

This shit gets to the best of us. If you're struggling, let me know."

"Uh, thanks."

I swallowed a hairball of anxiety in my throat as I walked to my desk. Discreetly, I patted myself down, checking for a wire. It was pure paranoia to think Carter might have mic'd me, but her statement was too well-timed after my session with Sandy to ignore. Doubts piled up and whirled around in my head as I rode the tilt-a-whirl of anxiety. One thought after another bombarded me. I couldn't do this. The case hit too close to home. I wasn't smart enough to solve it. I wasn't a good detective. The killer would go free, just like last time—

"Ryder!" Angela bumped the back of my chair and jolted me out of my rabbit hole. She recoiled when I made eye contact with her. "Whoa. Are you okay? You look a little…" She made a little spiral with her index finger near her ear.

I pasted a smile on my face and worked to set my eyelids at a normal width. "Yeah, sorry. I guess I got lost in thought. What's up?"

She sat on the edge of my desk. "Just thought I'd check in on you. See where you're at with the case. Any luck?"

"So far, it's all branches and no roots."

"What?"

I spread out my files, notes, and crime scene photographs to get a better look at all of them. "I've got a ton of different things to look into, but none of them are quite as promising as I'd hoped. Carter's got a gut feeling something's up with the husband. The victim's car went missing this morning. I have a possible witness but no way to contact her yet, and a giant list of women who enjoy yoga or murder or both."

Angela sucked in air through her teeth. "Sounds like a busy evening. I'll take it that's a no on the dinner party tonight then?"

"You were serious about that?"

"Uh, yeah," she said. "You're one of my good friends at work, but I've never seen you off the job. You never come with the rest of us to grab a beer or check out a food truck event. Do you have a secret second life or something?"

"Sorry. I'm not the best socially."

"That's totally cool," she said. "But you know how you get better at socializing? You practice. How's eight o'clock?"

I gestured to the mess across my desk. "I don't know. I've got a lot of work to do, and Carter's counting on me to get this perp behind bars as soon as possible."

"You're not gonna solve a murder in one night," she reminded me. "At least think about it. Come late if you have to. People don't start leaving until eleven."

Sandy's advice from earlier that afternoon echoed in my head. I needed people other than Dominique to talk to. "Okay. I'll do my best to make it."

"Great!" Angela hopped off my desk. "I'm out of here early. If I don't get home to help Jess prep for the party, I'll never hear the end of it. Wish me luck!"

"Good luck."

Once she'd gone, the smile dropped off my face. I didn't feel like going to a dinner party anymore, but therapy homework was never easy. Without Angela to distract me, the anxiety and doubt trickled back in. I closed my eyes and counted my breaths. Sometimes, it helped to give myself permission not to think of anything for a minute or so. After my miniature meditation, my head was clear enough to start working again.

I followed up on the van lead first and searched for a Miller or Morris Maintenance Service in the Tampa area. Neither one turned up an exact match. Not knowing what kind of maintenance the company performed didn't help either. I scrolled through pages of potential businesses before I came across Mason Maintenance Services. According to the website, they closed at five o'clock, which was in less than six minutes. I dialed the number.

"Mason Maintenance Services," a harried female voice answered. "This is Marissa speaking. We're in the process of shutting down for the day. Can I ask that you call again tomorrow?"

"Actually, Marissa, this is Detective Alex Ryder of the Tampa Police Department calling," I said. "One of your employees might have been on site of a homicide that occurred this morning, and I was hoping you could clear up a few questions for me."

A beat of silence passed as Marissa adjusted her attitude. Then:

"What can I do for you, Detective?"

I scrolled through MMS's website as I spoke. "I see here that your main services include screen repair, pressure-washing, and pool tiling. Is there any reason one of your vehicles might have been dispatched to Day Moon Yoga Studio or any of the surrounding businesses in that shopping center this morning?"

"Let me check for you." Computer keys clacked over the phone as Marissa searched her records. "Detective? We don't have any record of a visit to Day Moon. We mostly work in residential areas. The closest truck to that location was in a neighborhood about two miles away. Do you have a time frame?"

"Around six o'clock this morning."

"We don't even open until nine."

I wrinkled my nose. Maybe I didn't have the right MMS, but this one was the only active business with that name in the area. "Would you happen to know if you have any women with platinum blonde hair working for your maintenance team?"

"All of our maintenance workers are men," Marissa answered. "It's a team of three brothers. Do you need their names?"

"No," I said. "Thanks for your time, Marissa."

I hung up and checked the clock. 4:59. Marissa

would go home on time. I, on the other hand, was stuck at the station until I made some headway on this case. I pulled up the email from Lacey Braham that contained her client list and skimmed through the highlighted names. One by one, I looked up the yogis in the system. Eight-five percent of them were clean. The other fifteen percent had minor infractions like speeding tickets and public intoxication from their spring break in college years. None of them had a feasible reason to strike one of their own down.

"Crimes of passion," I muttered to myself as I packed up my desk. I had nothing else to go on for today. Tomorrow, I would have to take Carter's advice and start combing Jenn Spitz's neighborhood for clues. "What a load of bull."

Carter was gone for the day, so at least I didn't have to update her on my lack of progress. I waved goodbye to the officers on night duty and headed out to my car. Thankfully, the rain had died down to a drizzle. I was out of work in plenty of time to make Angela's dinner party tonight, so I dialed Dominique's number to let her know I wouldn't be able to make our nightly chat.

Footsteps splashed through a puddle behind me. I caught the reflection of a man's face in the window of my car as he thundered toward me. I ducked into the front seat, grabbed my baton, and whirled around.

It was Alan Spitz, red-faced and drunk off his ass. He smelled like vodka, pickle juice, and cigar smoke.

When I raised my baton, he wobbled to a stop and held up his hands.

"Corrine Corral," he said.

"What?"

"Your boss," Alan sputtered. "Loo-ten-aunt Carter. She asked me if Jenn had started hanging out with anyone new in the past couple of weeks. I didn't remember until now. Corrine Corral."

I lowered the baton. "Mr. Spitz, where are your children? Are they safe?"

"They're with their aunt," Alan replied. "Because I can't do it. I told you before. I can't raise kids on my own. I can't have a dead wife, Detective. It's not my thing."

I took the risk of patting Alan's sweaty forearm. "It's no one's thing, Alan. Are you sure you want to talk about this now? I need the information, but it's better if you're sober when you give it to me."

Alan collapsed over the trunk of my car and propped his chin in his hand. "I think I drank too much."

"Yeah... Do I have to book you?"

He waved a desperate hand. "No, I walked here! You can call the guy at the bar. My car's still there and everything. But I have to tell you—*Corrine Corral*. Please, before I forget about her."

"Okay, take it easy." I tucked my baton under my arm and got out my notebook. "Who exactly is Corrine Corral?"

"She's a woman who moved in around the corner," Alan said, struggling to keep his syllables from stringing together. "Her husband's name is Joe. They got here about a month ago. Jenn brought them a key lime pie to welcome them to the neighborhood, and—boom—they were best friends. Jenn was always hanging out with Corrine, and I thought it was weird because it seemed like they didn't have anything in common. They started a book club together with a few other women in the neighborhood. Jenn never read, not unless it was an article on her Pinterest board."

I scribbled at warp speed to get all of Alan's information recorded. "What does Corrine do? Does she work?"

"She sells jewelry," Alan said. "One of those ponzi—no, that's not what it's called—pyramid! It's a pyramid scheme. It's all cheap junk. Fake diamonds and pearls for housewives that pretend they don't know otherwise. I told Jenn not to buy that crap, but she didn't listen. She's got a whole drawer full of Corrine's crappy earrings and necklaces."

"Does Jenn usually buy stuff like that?"

"No! She thinks it's a waste of money," Alan told me. "You should see her when one of those commercials come on for new weight loss or cleaning products. She goes on a rant about how consumerism is ruining our culture. Then Corrine shows up, and all she wants to do is collect shitty jewelry."

"So you'd say Jenn wasn't acting like herself after she met Corrine?"

Alan's feet got tangled up, and he stumbled off to the side. I grabbed his arm to keep him upright. "Yes," he said. "Definitely not herself. She came home late every night. Half the time, I had to tuck in the kids, and they'd ask me where Mommy was." He gave a hearty sniff. "Oh, God. What am I supposed to tell them now?"

"Do you have Corrine Corral's address?" I asked. "Or a contact number? I'd like to check this out as soon as possible."

"Give me your notebook. I'll write it down."

I ripped out a fresh page and handed it to Alan with my pen. He widened his eyes and swayed to and fro as he painstakingly wrote something down. It took him a solid two minutes, and when he handed the page back, his writing was close to illegible.

I squinted at the paper. "Is that a seven or a one?"

"A seven," Alan said. "I gotta get back to my kids. You're gonna check it out, right?"

"Yeah, I'll go right now." I took hold of Alan's wrist and elbow. "But you've gotta spend an hour or two here."

"What? No!" Alan tried to free himself, but I pushed his elbow in. He winced and gave up. "Please, Detective. My wife just died. I'm mourning. I didn't do anything wrong."

"I'm not booking you," I said as I led him into the station. "It's just until you sober up. Believe me, you don't want your kids or their aunt to see you like this. The night officers will watch over you, and when you're ready to go home, you'll be free to do so. Hey, Jack?" One of the night duty officers, an older guy with salt-and-pepper hair, glanced up from his desk. "Could you take Mr. Spitz to the drunk tank?"

"Sure thing." Jack patted Alan on the shoulder. "Come on, bud. Let's get you settled in."

I mouthed a thank you to Jack and left the station for the second time. In the car, I stared at the raindrops that had come to rest on my windshield, colored red, green, and silver by the moon and the nearby stoplight. I clicked the wipes, and they swept across the glass, clearing everything off in one fell swoop.

The piece of paper with Corrine Corral's phone number on it watched me from the dashboard. It wasn't too late yet. I could still call tonight and ask to swing by, but I would definitely be late for Angela and Jess's dinner party if I did.

"Whatever," I muttered, and dialed the number.

It rang then went to voicemail. Whatever Corrine Corral was doing, she didn't have her phone on her. I checked the address again. Pelican Point. The upscale, middle-class neighborhood was on the way to Angela and Jess's house. I decided to cruise by.

Pelican Point wasn't quite bourgeois enough to join the ranks of gated communities, but it checked all the other boxes. The mailboxes matched, as did the trash and recycling bins placed three feet on the curb for pick-up tomorrow. Each front lawn was landscaped with palm trees and and hibiscus bushes to give the houses the most Floridian look possible. The streets were clean, well-lit, and freshly paved. Teenagers rode bikes, moms jogged, and dogs walked happily alongside their owners. Any time any of the neighbors crossed paths, they waved to each other. Did everyone know everyone else, or was it fake consideration to keep the neighbors from reporting a single thing to the HOA?

On my way to Corrine Corral's address, I stopped by Jenn and Alan Spitz's house. The driveway was empty. The windows were dark. A deflated basketball sat in the gutter. But the house was just like all the others on the block. No one would suspect a housewife in Pelican Point to be murdered. A cop car was parked out front, but the officer tasked with watching the house didn't recognize my unmarked vehicle from the station. I kept driving.

Corrine Corral's house was a minute's drive from the Spitzs' home. One car—a pristine white Jeep Cherokee—was parked in the driveway. The mailbox was overflowing with advertisements and jewelry cata-logs. The blinds on the front window were open, so the whole neighborhood could see into the kitchen. A skinny guy in an unbuttoned Oxford shirt manned a pot of pasta on the stove. From the way he jumped around and waved the ladle, it wasn't going too well. I parked on the curb, headed up the front walk, and knocked.

The skinny guy answered a moment later. He looked me up and down, then said, "Sorry, we don't want anything."

I planted a hand on the door to keep him from shutting it in my face. "I'm not selling anything, sir. Are you Joe Corral?"

He narrowed his green eyes at me. "Who wants to know?"

I stuck my hip out so my shiny badge reflected the patio light into his face. "Detective Alex Ryder. I assume you've heard what happened to your wife's friend, Jenn Spitz, this morning?"

Joe shrugged off his sweaty work shirt and tossed it aside. Thankfully, he wore a white T-shirt underneath. "The whole neighborhood's talking about Jenn. I don't know what to believe."

From the kitchen, water sizzled as it overflowed the pot and hit the burner.

"Shit, not again!" Joe ran off to the kitchen, calling behind him. "Come on in, Detective, but if you don't mind, can you take off your shoes?"

Against my better judgement, I left my sneakers near a pile of sparkly heels and men's loafers and followed Joe into the kitchen. It was rice, not pasta, on the stove, and he was having one hell of a time getting it to cook.

"Thanks," he said, nodding at my socks. "It's my

wife's rule. She thinks wearing shoes in the house is equal to smearing crap across the carpet. Is there something I can help you with?"

"Actually, I was hoping to talk to your wife," I told him. "Corrine, right? Alan Spitz said she and Jenn have gotten pretty close in the past couple of weeks."

He turned the burner up, then hastily turned it down again when the water bubbled ominously to the top of the pot. "Corrine has a ton of friends. I haven't met them all."

"Jenn brought a key lime pie over to welcome you to the neighborhood," I told him. "Ring a bell?"

He moved the pot off the burner, hissing as his bare skin touched the metal handle. "Uh, yeah. Jenn. Key lime pie chick."

"There's too much water." I stepped between Joe and his nemesis and used a handmade crocheted potholder to grab the boiling water. As I poured out some of the water and swirled the rice around, Joe wiped his sweaty forehead with a dish towel. "Pro tip," I said. "If you stick your middle finger in and touch the rice, the water should be no higher than the line of your first knuckle. See?" I demonstrated for him then put the rice on the burner and turned up the heat. "If there's too much water, it won't get absorbed and you'll have gross, mushy rice."

Joe ran his fingers through his damp, ashy-blond hair. "God, I can't even make rice. Corrine used to do this stuff for me. I know it's shitty of me. I'm the classic dude who can't do anything without his wife, but she kinda pulled a one-eighty on me, you know?"

I ran Joe's dish towel under cold water and made him wrap it around his burned hand. "In what way?"

"Ever since we moved here, I hardly see her," Joe said. "She's always working on her 'business,' if you can even call it that."

"Are you talking about the jewelry she sells?"

"How'd you know?"

"Alan mentioned Jenn had bought quite a few things from Corrine," I told him. "So your wife's been pretty focused on it?"

Joe sat at the breakfast table in front of the window and checked his wound. "Focused is an understatement. She's obsessed. All she does is order more of that crap and parade it around to all her friends."

"Do you mind if I have a look around?" I asked him. "Nothing official. Just a quick peek."

"Yeah, whatever. But what about the rice?"

I glanced into the pot. "It'll take another fifteen minutes or so. Keep an eye on it. If you want a challenge, you could try making that package of chicken tenderloins. You can never go wrong with olive oil, salt, pepper, and garlic. Easy peasy."

I left Joe to contend with the raw meat and took a quick look through the Corrals' house. The search wasn't exactly legal. I didn't have a warrant or a cause to go snooping through Corrine's stuff, but Joe at least had given me permission to look around. The house had three bedrooms. The first belonged to the couple, the second was empty, and the third housed Corrine's office space.

Piles of jewelry took up every spare inch. Earring trees decorated the windowsill and the bookshelves. Necklaces and bracelets were spread out across the flowery futon. Velvet cases of all shapes and sizes were stacked in the closet. Catalogs from the company—Forever Beautiful—were heaped everywhere, dating up to six months ago. As I shuffled a few aside, I uncovered Corrine's laptop.

I checked over my shoulder to make sure Joe hadn't wandered away from the kitchen then opened Corrine's laptop. It was password protected.

"Hey, Joe!" I called. "How's the rice coming along?"

"Uh, I think it's okay!"

"Great! Do you happen to know the name of your wife's first pet?"

"Bunny," he shouted. "It was a friggin' cat."

I typed "Bunny" into the password box and hit enter. No dice. I tried "Bunny123" instead, and the password page disappeared to allow me access to Corrine's desktop.

"Sheesh," I muttered. "Try harder, lady."

Corrine's computer contents were boring. All of her emails were five to ten threads long, each one arguing about the price of a piece with a customer. Corrine seemed to think her junky jewelry was worth way more than her customers did. I couldn't believe people were paying hundreds of dollars for fake rubies and pearls.

"Uh, Detective?"

I slammed Corrine's laptop shut and straightened up as Joe came into the spare bedroom.

"I think the rice might be done," he said. "The water's all gone."

"I'll be there in a second."

Joe showed himself out, but as I made to follow him, the corner of a bright yellow flyer sticking out of the desk drawer caught my eye. It didn't match the pastel patterns of Corrine's catalogs. I pulled on the corner and drew out the flyer. It was an advertisement for a luxury cruise line launching from the Port of Tampa. On the front, Corrine had written the date of departure in permanent marker and circled it.

"Leaving tomorrow, eh?" I murmured as I took a picture of the flyer with my phone. "Right after the death of your best friend? That's a little suspicious, Corrine."

"Detective, the chicken's burning!"

"Coming!"

6

_T_he blare of a train horn pushed me out of bed the following morning. My cell phone vibrated angrily as my brain wrenched itself out of sleep and put me in fight-or-flight mode. I freaked out, rolled off the edge of the bed, and smacked against the floor. I groaned and rubbed my shoulder. The phone fell off the side table and hit me in the face.

"I gotta change my ringtone." I swiped to answer. "Hello?"

"Are you okay? Are you hurt? You never called me last night."

"Everything's fine, Dominique." I pulled myself upright and disentangled my legs from the blankets. My dry lips cracked as I spoke, so I reached for a tub of petroleum jelly and slathered a dab across my mouth. "Other than the fact you woke me up out of a dead sleep."

"You were actually sleeping?"

I took note of my current state. Other than the dry lips, I also had a bruise on my hip that hadn't been there yesterday when I fell into bed. "I'm not sure. What's up?"

"I wanted to check on you," Dominique said. "You sounded like you were having a rough time yesterday. Is everything okay?"

"Something weird happened." I used the side table to lift myself from the floor and checked myself for other signs of night terrors. If I'd had one last night, it wasn't as bad as they usually were. "Carter assigned me this case, and I'm pretty sure the killer is—never mind."

"No, what? Who's the killer?"

I chewed on my bottom lip. "I don't want to upset you. I shouldn't be talking about it anyway. It's police business."

She scoffed into the phone. "Oh, please. When was the last time you cared about keeping your cases quiet from me? This must be a big one. Come on, tell me!"

"Are you sure you can handle it?"

"Yes! What happened? Did someone get maimed?"

"Yeah, we turned up a body at a yoga studio," I told her. "The woman was all sliced up like a piece of prosciutto."

"Ew," Dominique said. "I don't get it. Why wouldn't I be able to handle that?"

I put the phone on speaker then rinsed dried sweat from my face in the kitchen sink. As I patted it dry, I said, "Because the person who did it used similar torture methods as the person who tortured you. Exactly the same."

Were it not for the sound of her breathing, I would have guessed she had hung up. She didn't speak for several long moments.

"Dominique?"

"I'm okay."

"I knew I shouldn't have said anything."

"No, it's fine," she assured me. "We knew this was a possibility, right? The killer got away. We should have expected them to come back at some point."

I leaned against the kitchen counter and rubbed my eyes. "The body was staged. It wasn't like last time, where the killer tried to operate under the radar. This time, she wanted us to see it."

"You really think it's the same person?"

"The victim had a loop of gold wire around her ring finger."

"Oh, God. What am I supposed to do?"

I forced myself to put on a pot of coffee. My body ached and my head throbbed. "You're in New Orleans, right? Stay there. Or go somewhere else, but don't come here. I don't want you anywhere near this thing."

"What if I can help?"

I accidentally poured a heap of coffee grounds onto the counter instead of the paper filter. "You want to help? It's not too much for you?"

"I want you to catch this asshole," Dominique's

voice hardened. "I want you to put everything you've got into this case, no matter where it takes you. Are you going to do that?"

"You bet your cute little travel van on it."

"Then hell yeah, I want to help."

I abandoned the coffee, opened the balcony door for some fresh air, and sank into an armchair. The rain from yesterday had cleared away some of the humidity, but the hot, wet air would return soon. Best to enjoy the breeze while I had the chance.

"Walk me through how you met Sydney Mallone." I took out my notebook for this case and flipped to a fresh page. "Tell me everything you can remember."

WHEN I GOT to the station, I was caffeinated and ready to bring a fresh perspective to the murder of Jennifer Spitz. It was a busy morning. One of the narcotics detectives had made a huge bust. They hauled criminals through the bullpen for questioning while the narcotics team moved out to confiscate whatever the gang had been selling. Desking officers made the usual jokes.

"Y'all, I got a kilo of cocaine in the evidence locker," Miller stage-whispered. "Who wants to make it snow later?"

I knocked Miller on the back of the head as I passed his desk. "Don't you have paperwork to do, Officer?"

"Yes, Detective."

Miller's friends did a poor job of concealing their sniggers.

"Shut up!" he growled.

At my desk, the red light on my phone blinked with three new messages. I unlocked my files and tossed them next to my computer to study. With the notes from my call to Dominique that morning, I hoped to find a correlation between the unresolved Benson case and the murder of Jenn Spitz. Before I sat down, Angela bumped my shoulder. Her radio mouthpiece clipped my clavicle in an unpleasant way.

"Ouch," I said, rubbing the bruised bone. "What was that for?"

"You bailed last night," she said.

"Last night?"

"The dinner party?"

My mouth dropped open. "Oh, man. I completely forgot."

Angela rested her hands on her belt. "Mm-hmm. Sure you did. If you didn't want to come, you could have said so. I convinced Jess that things were going to be different, but you had to go and prove me wrong. What's with you, Ryder?"

"Seriously, Angela," I said. "I was working on my case until nine o'clock at night. By the time I finished, I was beat. I went home. I didn't mean to blow you guys off. I promise."

She clicked her tongue. "You're a hard person to be friends with. Did you know that?"

"So I've been told."

"What's up with that?" she asked. "Everyone needs someone. You don't ever talk about friends or family, so who do you go home to at night?" The lines around her eyes tightened inward like she was focusing a laser beam on my reaction to gauge if my answer would be truthful or not.

"Myself," I said. "I'm a bit of a loner. So what?"

Angela looked over my desk. She shuffled through my notes and the photos of the crime scene. "If all you have is work, it will eventually consume you. It's okay to take a breather every once in a while, Ryder. It clears the mind. Hell, if you gave yourself some slack, maybe you'd have an easier time getting through the day."

"What are you talking about?"

"I'm not blind," Angela said. "You've got bags under your eyes the size of Texas, and don't think I haven't noticed when you come in all covered in bruises and scratches."

I pulled on my shirt to make sure the most recent evidence of my night terrors was covered up. "Angela, I really don't know what you mean."

"I think you do," she pushed, "and I think you're too scared to talk to anybody about it. If you need some- one, I'm here for you. But if you don't tell me what's going on and I see you do something that jeopardizes your career or compromises any of your cases, I'm obligated to report that to Lieutenant Carter."

"You'd be snitching on me for a non-event," I said.

"You want to be friends? Don't threaten to report me for something you can't begin to understand. Get away from my desk, Officer. I have work to do."

Her shoulders drooped. "Come on, Alex. I didn't mean to upset you. I'm worried about you."

"Worry about your wife." I sat down and spun around so she could only see the back of my chair. "I can take care of myself."

"You know what? Fine. Good luck with your case."

I waved a petty goodbye without watching her leave. A gnat buzzed into my ear, and I smacked it so hard that my head rang. Another officer gave me a weird look then went back to his work when I glared at him.

I was stupid to think no one in the division had noticed the evidence of my night terrors. Angela was especially observant, but at least her determination to take care of me was rooted in compassion. If it was Jess, she would have done it to take out the competition. Would Angela actually report me? The only silver lining—if you could call it that—was that she didn't know what she was reporting.

I stared at my notes without seeing them. I read the first clause of the same sentence five times before I actually processed it. My jaw twitched, and I unclenched my teeth for the first time in several minutes. I hadn't realized I was holding tension there. I closed my eyes, took a deep breath, and rubbed my jaw. This wasn't about me. It was about the case. It was about honoring my promise to Dominique, and nothing would get in the way of that.

I pulled up the photo I'd taken of Corrine Corral's cruise brochure last night and shook the mouse of my computer to wake it up. I typed in *Emerald Cruises* and checked their bookings for the day. Their ship, the *Emerald Adventure*, was due to leave the port of Tampa Bay that afternoon at four o'clock. In a few hours, Corrine would disappear for five days at sea. If I didn't catch her for an interview before then, it would impede my case.

"Ryder!"

Carter's voice cut through the rabble of the bullpen. She sounded pissed. I checked over my shoulder. She *looked* pissed. She usually did a better job of obscuring her emotions, but today she let her eyebrows furrow and her lip curl like an angry Rottweiler. When she caught my eyes, she beckoned me into her office with one finger.

"What's up?" I asked once we were both inside with the door shut.

Carter didn't sit. Instead, she braced her palms against her desk, as if she needed the furniture to stop herself from beating me over the head. "I got an interesting call just now. Can you guess what it was about?"

My heart thumped against my rib cage. "Uh, no?"

"It was from a woman named Corrine Corral," Carter announced. "Apparently, you entered her house

97

last night and searched through her things without a warrant. Is that true?"

My thumping heart dropped into my stomach and splashed acid across my organs. "I got a tip from Alan Spitz—"

"You mean the husband of the victim who was in the drunk tank for six hours before he was sober enough to go home?" Carter demanded. "That Alan Spitz?"

"Yes, he came to the station last night," I said, "and told me Jenn and Corrine had made fast friends. It seemed fishy, so I swung by Corrine's last night, hoping to talk to her. Her husband—"

"Oh, I heard all about her husband," Carter said. "You thought you were being slick when you realized she wasn't there, huh? Thought you could go through her things because her husband invited you inside?"

"I asked him if I could take a look around," I insisted. "He said it wasn't a problem. I didn't do anything wrong."

Carter slammed her fist on the desk, and a box of paperclips danced across the rattling wood. "Don't give me that shit, Ryder. You knew what you were doing was a breach of standard operating procedure. Tell me something: did you tell the husband what you were doing at his house? That his wife might be a suspect in a murder investigation?"

I clasped my hands behind my back and looked

away. Carter rolled her shoulders and tilted her neck side to side. Then she took a deep breath.

"Look, Alex," she said in a less agitated voice. "I know you're doing your best to crack this case, but you can't do it like this. Corrine accused you of going through her jewelry business information. *Private* information that you didn't have any right to access. The husband's on her side. He's not going to have your back. He'll say he didn't understand what he was consenting to. If they decide to pursue this, you won't have a case. You'll be on probation until God knows when."

"Corrine Corral is leaving Tampa today," I said. "She's going on a five-day cruise to the Bahamas and the Caribbean. Guess when she booked the trip?"

"Am I supposed to care?"

"A week ago," I replied. "Who books an expensive luxury cruise only a week in advance? Where did she get the money if all she does is sell jewelry? Why does she want to get out of Tampa so quickly?"

Carter opened her mouth to argue.

"Lieutenant, just listen to me for one minute." I held up a finger. "One minute. That's all I ask."

Carter fixed a wrathful glare on me. "One minute. Go."

"I spoke to a source of mine this morning," I said as quickly as my tongue would move. "A victim from the Benson case. She said Sydney Mallone befriended her about a month before Sydney kidnapped and tortured her in her own home."

"You spoke to Dominique Benson?" Carter asked. "You can't do that, Ryder. What the hell—"

"You said I had a minute."

She made a frustrated gesture as if to say, "Carry on."

"Dominique told me that Sydney pretended to be her friend," I hurried on. "She felt like Sydney knew her best because they got so close so quickly. Before Dominique knew it, Sydney had taken both her and her husband hostage in their own house. Plus, we know Sydney had more than one victim. The swimming pool—"

"Was full of acid and decomposing body parts," Carter finished. "Yeah, I worked the case too. Get on with it, Ryder."

"When I talked to Alan Spitz last night, he said that Corrine and her husband had just moved into the neighborhood a few weeks ago," I said. "In that short amount of time, Jenn and Corrine became best friends. Then all of a sudden, Jenn ends up dead and Corrine wants to leave the country? Something doesn't add up."

Carter lowered herself into her chair and massaged her temples. "It's a lead, Ryder. It doesn't mean you con your way into the Corrals' house to look for something that makes her a suspect."

"I was doing my job," I said. "This person murders for fun then she leaves the body behind for us to play with. I can't take the risk of not following up on a lead the second it comes to my attention."

"You can't take the risk of getting kicked off the force either," Carter replied. "But if you keep doing shit like this, you're going to get canned and you won't have the chance to solve the case. Does any of this make sense to you, Ryder?"

"Yes, ma'am."

"Good. Get out of my office."

I didn't move.

"What?" she snapped.

"I'd like permission to bring Corrine Corral in for questioning today. She leaves for her cruise at four o'clock, and if she gets on that ship—"

"No," Carter said.

"Lieutenant, come on," I argued as Carter buried her face in paperwork. "I can't *not* question her. Alan Spitz wouldn't have mentioned her unless it mattered, right?"

Carter signed a few papers with illegible penmanship. "Alan Spitz is a drunk, grieving man who probably resented his wife for spending time with a new friend while he had to take care of their kids. He needs to blame her death on someone. You should know better than to be so sure his tip was valid. Yes, Corrine needs to be questioned, but it can wait until after she returns from her vacation. Until then, follow up on your other leads. You're a good detective. You can't pigeonhole yourself by narrowing this case down to one person. Keep sleuthing."

Carter turned her back on me to file the forms, and I knew the conversation was over. I excused myself from the office and returned to my desk, where the contents of the case stared up at me, as if pleading me to do something with them. I flipped the pictures and notes upside down and leaned back in my chair to cover my eyes for a moment. This wasn't how I expected things to go today.

"Expect nothing," Sandy's voice echoed in my head from a previous session. "Accept everything. When we have expectations for something, we are often disappointed. If you let go of those expectations, you'll either be prepared for the consequences or pleasantly surprised."

"So having no expectations is essentially the same as being a pessimist?" I had asked her.

"Don't twist my words, Alex."

I gathered everything for the case, stuffed it in a few file folders, and relocated to one of the meeting rooms in the back of the station. It was full of rookie officers on break or eating early lunches. They spun around in the chairs and drew all over the white boards like a bunch of schoolchildren.

"Get out," I ordered. "Don't you all have something to learn? Go find your training officers."

The rookies, who looked younger and younger each year, scurried out. I slammed the door and locked it then pulled the rolling cork board from the corner of the room. One by one, I pinned the photos to the cork board along with my notes, information on potential suspects, and whatever else I had on the case so far. Once the board was full and everything was laid out in front of me, I stepped back to examine the case as a whole. Sometimes, it was easier to make connections if all the facts were visible at the same time.

I went through everything. I followed every thread from beginning to end. Lacey Braham, Becca Bailey, and the mysterious blonde woman reported to be at the scene. The maintenance van, the blocked cameras, and the position of the body. Alan Spitz, Joe Corral, and his abominably annoying wife. I called witness after witness, researched other companies called MMS, and combed the police database for recently active female killers. After six hours without a break, I hadn't found a fresh lead. This case was dead as a doornail. Except for Corrine Corral.

I checked my watch. It was 2:45. If I hurried, I could still catch Corrine before the *Emerald Adventure* left on its five-day voyage to the Bahamas. I spun in my chair, mimicking the rookie officers who were probably running speed traps right now. The motion cleared my head and made my stomach turn at the same time. I whirled to a stop and made the only decision that made sense.

. . .

THE PORT of Tampa was hopping with activity. It was a Saturday, and all of the cruise terminals were full with enormous luxury cruise liners. Tourists ran to and from, hauling their suitcases from their cars to the curb. The port employees tagged luggage, valeted cars, and pointed cruise-goers in the right direction. It was the worst kind or organized chaos. Everyone was in a rush for a different reason.

I joined the line of cars heading for the *Emerald Adventure* terminal. At the front of the line, a security officer stopped each driver and directed them to valet, self-parking, or the exit if they were in the wrong place. I rolled my window down as I got closer.

"Boarding the *Adventure*, ma'am?" the security guard asked me.

"Actually, I'm investigating one of the people on board." I flashed my badge. "Is there somewhere I can park away from the madness?"

He shielded his eyes as the sun glinted off my gold shield. "You can pull up to that curb over there. You'll have to show ID to get into the terminal, and I'm not sure if they'll allow you onto the ship without a ticket."

"I'm a detective," I reminded him. "They kind of have to let me on."

Unfortunately, the security guard wasn't entirely wrong. Once I parked, I had to show my badge and my passport to another security officer at a gate outside. Inside, I fought against agitated parents, foreign tourists, and a sea of children to skip the line to the metal detectors. The officers there insisted on frisking me before I went up to the check-in area. There, I argued with the customer service representative for ten minutes before she agreed to let me board the ship. By the time I made it up the gangplank, it was 3:42. I didn't have much time.

I emerged in the main lobby of the ship, somewhere on Deck Four. The grand entrance took my breath away. An intricate crystal chandelier hung over royal emerald carpets, sweeping staircases, glass elevators, and gold filigree accents. A live band played on a small stage beneath the mezzanine. Extravagant double doors led to one of the ship's three dining rooms. People rushed here and there to find their staterooms as soon as possible. A few of them already wore swimsuits and white smears of sunscreen. The excitement was palpable. For everyone on board the *Adventure*, it was vacation time at last.

I approached the guest services desk, surprised to see there was already a line. I skipped to the front and waited for one of the cruise employees to free up. Someone gently tapped my waist, and I looked down to see a small boy—maybe seven or eight years old—gawking at the badge on my belt.

"What's up, little man?" I asked. "Are you okay?"

"I can't find my mom," he said.

"Uh-oh, that's not good, is it?" I ruffled his hair. "Hang on. I'll get someone to help you." I tapped on the guest services desk. "Excuse me?"

"One moment, ma'am," the closest employee said before returning to her customer.

The woman behind me cleared her throat loudly. "There's a line, you know."

"I'm a detective," I told her.

"I don't care who you are," she said. "You can wait in line like everyone else."

The little boy tugged on my hand. "Please! I want to find my mom! Miss, I need your help. Can you come with me?"

"Sorry, kid. I really can't—"

Tears welled up in his blue eyes. "I'm l-l-looost." He drew out the last syllable with a terrible sob, and everyone in line fixed their attention on me and the crying kid.

I checked my watch. 3:48. It was going to be a close call.

"Okay, fine," I said to the kid. "Where was the last place you saw your mom?"

"On the pool deck."

He locked his tiny, grubby hand in mine and hauled me away from the guest services desk. I had no choice but to follow along behind him and hope Corrine Corral showed up along the way. The kid led me through the throng of people boarding the ship, hopped in an elevator, and pressed the button for Deck Ten.

"You sure know your way around," I said. "You been on this cruise before?"

"Twice."

The elevator dumped us out on one of the top decks, where the kiddie pool stretched across the middle of the ship. It was already full of kids who'd boarded the ship earlier that day. My kid dragged me through the reclining chairs, soda machines, and watchful parents.

"What's your mom look like?" I said. "Did she have a place for you to put your things? Like one of these chairs?"

"Uh, I don't know."

"Well, what's your stateroom number?"

"I don't know that either."

We wasted several minutes combing the pool deck for a glimpse of the kid's mother. I pointed out every woman who looked concerned enough to have lost a child, but the kid refuted every face. At last, I pulled aside one of the cruise employees who was tending the soda machines.

"This kid has lost his mom," I told the employee, a young man with broad shoulders and a winning smile. "I need you to take him to security or whatever. I've got a job to do."

The young employee eyed my badge, nodded, and knelt down on the kid's level. "Hey, Buddy! I'm Trent. I can help you find your mom. Do you want to be friends?"

"No!" The kid screamed and hid behind my legs.

I took him gently by the shoulders. "Listen, kiddo.

You have to go with Trent, okay? He'll take care of you. I don't have a lot of time—"

The ship's foghorn blew, and half the kids on deck plugged their ears. The kid in front of me, however, perked up and pointed to the other side of the pool.

"There she is!" he shouted. "Thanks, miss!"

The kid ran off. I clasped Trent on the shoulder before he could go back to his job.

"What does that foghorn mean?" I asked him.

He flashed a cheerful smile. "It means we're leaving port!"

7

I sprinted up the stairs to the topmost deck of the ship and peered over the railing. Sure enough, the gargantuan cruise liner had pulled away from the dock and begun sailing out of the port. Several meters of ocean separated the ship from land and me from my job.

"Oh, no," I muttered. "This is not good."

I caught the first cruise employee that passed by. Her name tag read Sandy. It seemed fitting that the universe would mock me with a reminder of my therapist at a time like this.

"Sorry, Sandy." I let go of her arm, realizing I'd grabbed her like a cop grabs criminals. "I need to speak with the captain of the ship. I'm a detective. I'm only on board because I was trying to find someone who might be related to my case. I'm not supposed to go on a five-day long cruise."

Sandy smiled in the same cheerful way Trent had a few minutes earlier. My guess was they were trained by *Emerald Cruises* to do so.

"My, that's troublesome, isn't it?" she said in a voice that burned brighter than the sun. "I'm not sure we can get you to the captain since he's pretty busy right now!" She spread her arms to indicate the massive ocean in front of us and laughed at her own joke. "But I can take you to security to see what can be done."

"That'd be great," I said. "And you can tone down the customer service shtick. I'm not a ten-year-old or a guest aboard this ship. I need an adult."

Sandy's shoulders slumped. "Oh, thank God. Come with me."

Sandy, relieved of her smiling duties, turned out to be a valuable asset. She led me straight to the security offices on one of the upper decks. Right across the hallway, I spied the door to the bridge. The captain was in there, and he was the only one with the power to turn this ship around.

Sandy rapped her knuckles against the door to the security office. As we waited for an answer, she said, "Sorry, I don't have access. I just deliver towels on the pool deck."

"It's fine."

A bulky man with a crew cut and a thin pale line on his pink head where his sunglasses usually rested came out of the security office. He, too, wore the official cruise outfit, a teal-and-white striped polo and khaki shorts, but he also wore a badge on his belt to denote himself as part of the security team.

"What is it?" he asked gruffly, eyeing me up and down.

"She needs to get off the ship," Sandy said. When the man glared at her, she backed away. "Good luck," she muttered to me before taking her leave.

I squared my shoulders and faced the massive security guy. "I'm sorry to bother you, but I'm Detective Alex Ryder. I boarded the ship with the intention of tracking down a suspect in a murder investigation, but I couldn't locate her in time. I need to return to shore."

The security guy cracked a wry grin. "You're kidding."

"No, sir. I work with the homicide department of the Tampa Police Department, and—"

He guffawed and held his belly. "You're not getting off this ship."

"Okay, what is your name?" I demanded. "I need to speak to your superior because I don't think you understand the severity of this situation. I am working a *homicide* case—"

The man tapped his name tag, which I hadn't noticed before because his pecs were so massive that they overshadowed the font. "I'm Clint. I'm the head of security aboard the *Adventure*, so you're already speaking to a superior. Sorry for the confusion. I don't mean to be an ass, but you gotta be a first-year detective to have gotten yourself into this mess."

"Third year, thank you very much," I declared. "And it wasn't my fault. I had twenty minutes to spare, but this kid lost his mom, and I couldn't get away from him. Forget it. Can you help me or not?"

"I'm more concerned with the fact that we might have a homicidal maniac on board than with getting you back to shore," Clint said. "You want to fill me in on that?"

"She's a suspect," I said. "We don't have any evidence on it yet, and I won't be able to *get* any unless I go back to the station. Seriously, can I speak to the captain or not?"

Clint's responding chuckle echoed deeply at the back of his throat. "Alright, Detective Ryder. I'll take you to see the captain, but don't get your hopes up. This ship doesn't do U-turns."

Clint's full body took up the doorway as he emerged into the hallway, blocking the rest of the security office from my view. He took the lead, scanned his employee badge against an electronic pad, and opened the door to the bridge.

My stomach plummeted. The bridge was nothing but control panels and windows, beyond which was an unimpeded view of the sea. Water stretched out for miles in every direction. Unless the ship had a rear view mirror I didn't know of, there was no sign of land.

A few crew members milled about. They were all

dressed in white officer outfits rather than the teal striped shirts of the pool deck employees. One of them manned a shockingly small steering wheel for such a large vessel. Other monitored the control panels or watched as the ship made its way to the middle of the ocean.

Toward the right side of the bridge, a woman in a similar outfit with a navy sweater leaned over a red-capped microphone and hit the all-call button. A pleasant tone rang through the speakers.

"Good afternoon and welcome to the *Emerald Adventure*," the woman announced. "This is Captain Marianna speaking from the bridge. I hope you are all enjoying your first day at sea. As we continue toward our first port in Nassau, I'll keep you updated on our progress. Until then, eat, drink, and be merry!" Captain Marianna turned off the all-call mic and noticed us waiting by the door. "Afternoon, Clint." She gave me a once-over. "Did we have a VIP tour of the bridge scheduled today? I don't recall."

"No, Captain," Clint said. "This is Detective Ryder. She's stuck on board and has requested a return to shore."

Captain Marianna chortled, observed my lack of laughter, and canned her own. "Oh, you were serious? Uh, sorry, Detective. That's not the way things work around here. I can't make a U-turn."

"That's what I said," Clint commented.

"This is an emergency situation." I gestured to the

badge on my belt in case Captain Marianna hadn't seen it yet. "I'm not supposed to be here. I don't have a stateroom or a ticket or clothes, for that matter. I have to get back to my division."

"You made your way aboard without a ticket," Captain Marianna reminded me. "And we can help you out with the stateroom and the clothes. The cruise isn't completely booked, and we sell plenty of items in our gift shops. But I'm afraid we can't get you back to shore."

I pointed to the small boats riding alongside the *Adventure*. "What about those boats? Can't I get one of them to take me back?"

"Those are our escort vessels," Captain Marianna said. "They help us get past the port. There's no place for them to dock on this ship for you to join them. I'm sorry, but I can't help you. Unless you plan on jumping ship, you're stuck with us."

I considered the distance from the top deck to the water and shuddered. I wasn't that desperate. "Fine. I at least need to interview a suspect in a homicide case. Her name is Corrine Corral. Can you confirm that she's on board?"

The captain approached the sailor at the steering wheel and looked over his shoulder at the navigation maps. "Nice job, Krupe. Switch to autopilot."

"Switching to autopilot."

Krupe let go of the wheel so the *Adventure* could steer herself. My stomach rolled over itself. The thought that computers manned this vessel for most of the time at sea didn't sit well with me. On the upside, there was less room for human error.

Captain Marianna scanned the horizon and clapped her hand on my back. "Let's take a walk, Detective. Clint, why don't you come too?"

With the captain and the head of security at my side, I felt more like a criminal than a detective with a job to do. They led me to a private deck beyond the bridge. It was at the highest, front-most part of the ship. The railing came up to my elbows, and thought there was a decent amount of Plexiglas between me and the drop to the ocean below, I kept my distance from the deck's edge. The captain had no such problems. She strolled right up to the railing, rested her arms on it, and gazed into the distance.

"Corrine Corral," she called over the noise of the wind. "Is she dangerous?"

"She might be," I answered. "If she committed the crime I intend on questioning her for, she absolutely is."

"She might have murdered someone?"

"Yes."

The captain turned so her back was to the water and tipped her chin up toward the sun. "I don't personally keep track of everyone on board, but you have my permission to ask guest services to locate this Corrine Corral for you."

"Seriously?"

"Why are you so surprised?" Captain Marianna asked. "I can't take the chance that this suspect of yours is the actual killer. If we don't look into it and she hurts someone on board, it becomes my responsibility. Every person on this ship is under my protection, and I refuse to have that protection compromised. Clint?"

The head of security stood in a loose version of attention a little ways from us. He had heard everything whilst giving the Captain an illusion of privacy. "Yes, Captain?"

"Take Detective Ryder to guest services please," the captain ordered. "Get her a room and some complimentary gift cards so she can buy herself a few essential items. Once she's settled in, help her track down her suspect."

"That won't be necessary," I jumped in. "I work alone."

Captain Marianna adjusted one of the gold buttons on her shirt. "This is my ship, Detective Ryder. I won't have you running around willy-nilly, lest it result in panic. These people are on vacation. They spent thousands of dollars to get away from the stressors at home. If I can avoid alerting them to your duty aboard this ship, I will do so. You will involve Clint in your investigation, or I will assign a security guard to tail you twenty-four seven."

I glared at Clint. He flashed me the signature *Emerald Adventure* smile.

"Fine. Come on, Clint. Let's get moving. I have work to do."

AT THE GUEST services desk on Deck Four, where I boarded the *Adventure*, Clint did as the captain promised. He secured me a stateroom and asked for an upgrade. According to the guest services representative, I had a concierge suite with a private veranda, the normal price of which I was scared to question. Apparently, the concierge suites were so expensive that they rarely sold out, even during the high season. Clint also secured me several hundred dollars in Emerald Cruises credit. The guest services representative loaded the money onto the keycard for my room, so I only had to carry the keycard and a form of ID.

Clint walked me to my room, and for once I was glad for his company. Without his supervision, I would have lost my way in the long hallways of the *Adventure*.

"The carpets are color-coded according to your position on the ship," he pointed out helpfully. "Blue is forward. Gold is midship. Red is aft. There's a map in every staircase as well. Your room is toward midship. Best place to be if you get motion sickness."

"I don't, but thanks."

"Didn't want to take that chance," Clint said. "Here we are. Deck Seven, stateroom 7028. You lucky duck."

I flashed my keycard against the pad. It flickered green, and the lock disengaged. Clint pushed the door open for me. As I made my way inside, I couldn't help but let a gasp of wonder slip from my lips.

The room was enormous, nothing like the small cabins most of the ship-goers would be staying in for the duration of the next five days. The concierge suite included a living and dining room combination, a private bedroom, and a full bathroom. The toilet and tub, of course, were both ship-sized, but the counter space made up for it. But the best part of the room was the private deck space. I stepped onto the verandah and was met with the freshest breath of salty air. The breeze wound invisible fingers through my hair and gave me the best scalp massage I'd had in years. From here, I couldn't see the other guests' balconies above, below, or to the sides. It was like I had the entire ship to myself.

"Wow," I breathed. "Why haven't I booked myself a cruise before?"

"Nice, isn't it?" Clint said. "But don't you have a job to do?"

The reality of why I was there slapped the grin off my face. I probably wouldn't have a whole lot of time to take advantage of my private verandah, not unless I cleared Corrine Corral as soon as I found her.

"I have to call my lieutenant," I told Clint. "She doesn't know about this fiasco. Can you give me a minute?"

"You're not going to give me the slip, are you?"

"You can wait right outside, if you want."

Clint nodded and let himself out. I pulled my phone from my back pocket. With some arguing, I'd convinced Clint and the guest services representative to give me unlimited Wi-Fi and phone services while I was on board. If they hadn't agreed, it would have cost me an arm and a leg to pay for the ability to contact people on land. I navigated to my favorites page. Dominique was at the top of the list, followed by Lieutenant Carter and Angela.

Carter was going to kill me.

I tapped her name to dial her number and put the phone to my ear. I hoped she wouldn't answer, but my luck for the day was already at an all-time low.

"Where the hell are you, Ryder?" she demanded without a greeting. "I'm staring at your empty damn desk. You better be chasing after a lead!"

"I am," I assured her. "I need you to be calm, Lieutenant."

A beat of silence.

"What have you done?"

A lump rose in my throat. "I followed Corrine Corral aboard the *Emerald Adventure.*"

"You did *what?*" Carter's voice got low and quiet when she was pissed. Somehow, it was scarier than when she yelled. "You followed that woman after I explicitly told you not to? She better have the best damn statement I've ever heard, Ryder. What did she say?"

The lump doubled in size. I swallowed to release

the pressure in my throat. "Actually, Lieutenant, I haven't spoken to her yet."

"Yet? I thought the boat left port at four? It's 5:07."

"That's why I'm calling—"

"Ryder, don't you dare tell me you're still on that ship."

The lump turned into stomach bile and filled my mouth with a bitter taste. "Lieutenant, believe me, it wasn't my intention—"

"*You're still on the ship?*"

I clenched my teeth and held the phone away from my ear.

"Yes or no, Detective Ryder?"

"Yes, Lieutenant."

On the other end of the line, something crashed and shattered, as if Detective Ryder had thrown the ceramic mug that held all her pens across the room. I winced and braced myself, but Carter was done yelling.

"Listen to me, Detective," she warned in a whisper-quiet voice. "Listen very closely. You are suspended from this force—"

"Lieutenant—!"

"Do not interrupt me," she continued. "You disobeyed a direct order from me. You abused your authority by boarding that cruise ship without a ticket. You put yourself in danger *and* you removed yourself from an active case. Your job is *here*, Ryder. Tell me, how the hell do you expect to solve a murder while you're on vacation for five days?"

I pinched the skin above my hip to redirect my stress to a place beside my head. If I lost my temper with Carter, I would most likely lose my badge too. "I believed I was doing the right thing, Lieutenant. I meant to get on and off the ship before it left port, but I was distracted."

"I don't care what happened," Carter said. "It doesn't change the decision you made. There's a safe in your room, I assume?"

I checked the roomy closet and located the safe beneath spare towels and a stack of life vests. "Yes, there is."

"Good. Put your badge, your gun, and any of your other effects that you brought with you in the safe," Carter ordered. "While you are on board that ship, you are no more than a civilian. Enjoy your cruise, Detective Ryder."

The phone clicked. She hung up on me. A slow buzz filled my head as I lowered the phone from my ear. It got louder and louder, like a wasp circling its prey. I waited for the sting, but it never came.

Clint knocked on the door. "Detective! Everything okay in there?"

The buzzing stopped, thanks to Clint's deep, authoritative voice. Maybe it wouldn't be so bad to keep him around.

"Everything's fine," I called. "I'll be out in a minute."

I read the directions for the safe, programmed a code, and put my badge, my gun, my cuffs, and my reload ammunition inside the safe. I almost closed the door and locked it, but at the last second, I took the badge out and slid it into my back pocket. No one else had to know I'd been suspended from my job.

When I emerged from the room, Clint eyed my empty belt. I wasn't stupid enough to think he wouldn't notice my lack of equipment.

"What did your lieutenant say?" he asked.

"She has to file some paperwork in order to give me permission to operate on board," I lied easily. "It might take a few hours, but I don't have privileges until then."

Clint nodded, and my heart rate eased up a little bit. He'd bought it.

"In that case, I'll leave you to get to know the ship," he said. "If the captain wants me to babysit you, I don't have a problem doing it, but I've got some work to do on my own. Can I trust you not to get in trouble without me?"

I lazily saluted him and earned an arched eyebrow in return. "Don't worry, Clint. I can handle myself."

"Uh-huh. Sure."

Once Clint disappeared down the hallway, I headed in the other direction. Despite Clint's carpet trick, everything looked exactly the same. After a few minutes, I finally found a set of stairs and sidestepped a wet, swimsuit-clad family to check the map. The stores were two decks below in the middle of the ship. When I reached them, the entrances were all shut. No one was shopping. The other cruise-goers were too busy enjoying their time on the pool deck.

I spotted a shop employee inside the first store and tapped on the window. She came over and pushed open the door.

"Sorry about that," she said cheerfully. "We aren't open while the ship is in port, and we don't expect many people to shop before dinner on the first day. But by all means, come on in!"

I thanked the woman, and she went about her business preparing the store for other customers. Soon enough, additional employees arrived to help open the businesses, and shoppers began to trickle in.

Every piece of clothing was decorated with Emerald Cruises' logo, a large green gem with the letters "EC" smack in the middle of it. The women's clothes were all sundresses and tourist T-shirts with phrases like *Lost at Sea, Don't Find Me* printed in obnoxious block letters across the front. There was nothing inconspicuous or non-tacky to wear. I finally settled on a few different golf polos with a less intense version of the logo on the chest, a pair each of tan shorts and pants, and—for the hell of it—a black one-piece swimsuit. Then I stocked up on toiletries. A toothbrush was eight dollars, the mini tube of toothpaste was ten. Deodorant was fifteen bucks a pop, but they really screwed you over on sunscreen. One small bottle was twenty dollars.

I carried my haul to the register and dumped it on

the counter. The woman who'd helped me before—Andrea—sifted through the items in search of the price tags.

"Wow," she said. "Did you forget to pack?"

"Something like that," I answered.

She scanned each item, and I watched the price get higher and higher on the register. She folded the last polo shirt, placed it neatly in a bag, and said, "That'll be three hundred and twenty-two dollars and nineteen cents."

I handed over my key card and silently thanked Captain Marianna for the Emerald Cruises credits. Without them, this shopping trip would have cleaned out my bank account.

I returned to my suite, organized the toiletries in the bathroom, and hung the polos in the closet. The locked safe caught my eye. I punched in the code, and the door popped open. Inside, my gun, cuffs, and reload ammo rested in the same place I'd left them. I hung my head and shut the safe again.

I changed into my new swimsuit, smeared twenty-dollar sunscreen across my face and body, and returned to the verandah. I pulled one of the recliner chairs into the sun, set down a towel, and lay down. For the next five days, my only duty was to enjoy myself. There was no point in worrying what Lieutenant Carter would do to me when I returned home because there was nothing I could do about right now. She was right. I'd made a mistake, but why not enjoy the consequences of that mistake before everything went to hell?

I closed my eyes and watched red and orange lights dance beyond my eyelids. The sun seeped into my pores. It was warm and inviting. The ocean spray whispered up from below and kissed my skin. I could do this all day.

Before long, sweat beaded up along my brow and underneath my armpits. The patterned plastic of the chair pressed annoying criss-crosses against my shoulders. A loose thread on the towel tickled the bottom of my right foot. The sun shone hotter, like God was using a magnifying glass to focus the light on me. The ocean spray had turned into a fishy mist across the face. Somehow, I was unbearably hot and annoyingly clammy at the same time. Worse still, I couldn't get my mind off the case.

Carter was right about one thing. I'd unintentionally cut myself off from the investigation on land. However, I had not completed the part of my job aboard this ship. Corrine Corral—a possible killer—roamed free. If she was innocent, all I had to worry about was the ramifications of my poor decision-making skills once I returned to shore. But if Corrine was guilty—if she had the capacity for murder—then every single person aboard the *Emerald Adventure* was at risk. And it was my job to protect them.

8

I washed off the sweat and the sunscreen and the salt in the shower, dressed in one of my new *Emerald Cruises* golf polos, and arranged my hair the best way I could without access to a flat iron. It dried in messy waves around my face. I usually hated it that way, but I looked appropriately windswept for a guest aboard a luxury cruise. When I checked my reflection in the backlit vanity mirror, the person looking back at me didn't resemble Detective Alex Ryder at all. With a little imagination, I could be anyone I wanted, including a sun-drenched vacationer whose highlights were totally real.

"You're not anyone," I told myself sternly in the mirror. "You are Detective Alex Ryder, and you have a job to do, no matter what Carter said."

I couldn't do it. I couldn't spend five days twiddling

my thumbs while Carter assigned some other detective to *my* case. Sure, it had only been two days since we had discovered Jenn Spitz's body, but I knew this case best. No one else was going to put the pieces together like I could.

It was a dumb move, disobeying Carter's orders, but no one aboard the *Adventure* was going to question my authority when I had the captain and the head of security on my side. At the very least, I could investigate Corrine Corral, and that was exactly what I planned to do. The first challenge was locating her. According to my research, the *Adventure* was a temporary home to a maximum of four thousand passengers and over a thousand crew members. I was unlikely to run into Corrine by coincidence.

The second challenge was far more pressing: I had no idea what Corrine looked like. While I was snooping around her house, I was too busy worrying about her husband catching me to do more than glance at the framed photos on the walls. All I remembered was her blonde hair and pointed chin.

I returned to guest services. This time, I waited in the long line to get to the front, doing my best to blend in with the other civilians. At the desk, cruisers complained about all sorts of things. The lights in their room weren't working. They had requested a room with a pull-down bunk bed and received a pull-out sofa instead. This or that employee hadn't accommodated them in the buffet line, on the pool deck, or at the bar. The list went on and on, but I had to give credit to the guest services representatives. They never lost their cool, no matter how frustrated the guest in front of them was.

"I'll look into that for you right now, ma'am."

"I'll have extra towels delivered directly to your door, sir."

"We have an open stateroom with a pull-down bunk bed *and* a pull-out sofa bed. Would you like me to upgrade you to that room, free of charge?"

When I finally got to the front of the line, one of the guest services representatives waved her hand to get my attention. I approached her desk, thankful she wasn't the same person who had helped Clint get me a room earlier. I needed someone who didn't recognize my face if my lie was going to work.

"Hello, ma'am!" The representative, a young brunette with a French accent and a vivid shade of pink lipstick, greeted me with a practiced winning smile. "My name is Adrienne. What can I help you with this afternoon?"

I put on my best expression of exasperation. "I'm so sorry to bother you, but I'm afraid I've lost one of my friends. We had two different boarding times, and we were supposed to meet at the bar on the adult pool deck an hour ago, but I haven't seen her! I'm not sure if we got our wires crossed, but I'm worried about not locating her. She gets nervous on her own, and I don't want to leave her for long."

"What's your friend's name?" Adrienne said.

"Corrine Corral. C-O-R-R-A-L."

"And the number of her stateroom?"

I pressed my palm to my forehead and feigned frustration. "Oh, goodness. I should have written it down. Gosh, what is it?"

Adrienne scrolled through a screen on her computer. "6045?"

"Yes!" I tapped the desk in mock victory. "I don't suppose you can tell me where she is?"

"Unfortunately, we don't put trackers on our guests," Adrienne replied with a hint of polite sarcasm.

"But she definitely made it on board?"

"Yes, we have her identification picture on file," Adrienne said. "The one that is taken before you get on the ship."

I drummed my fingers. I needed to get a good look at that picture. "Is there any way I can get ahold of her?"

"You can call her stateroom from the phone in your room," Adrienne offered. "You can also download the Emerald Cruises app on your smartphone. It will allow you to send a direct message to your friend via the ship's Wi-Fi."

"Perfect. Can you show me how to do that?" I took my phone out and purposely fumbled it. It went flying over the desk and landed behind Adrienne's chair. "Oh, I'm so sorry!"

As Adrienne turned her back on me to fetch my phone, I leaned over the desk for a glimpse at her computer screen. Corrine's ID picture showed a woman with brown eyes and blonde hair pulled into a long ponytail with a fuchsia ribbon. There was the pointed chin I remembered, along with a pointed nose that looked too straight and perfect to be a birthright. She had a smattering of freckles across her cheeks and a thin line of pale skin right across her hairline that gave away her spray tan. She wore a flowery orange dress and a matching necklace with gaudy yellow gems, no doubt a piece from one of her catalogs.

I resumed my place and smiled sweetly as Adrienne turned back around to set my phone on the counter. "Thank you so much."

"Of course," she said. "As for the app, it's pretty straightforward. Once you download it, turn your phone on airplane mode and connect to our Wi-Fi, Adventure@Sea. Log in with your stateroom number. To connect with your friend, you'll need her last name and stateroom number as well. When she accepts your invitation to connect, you're good to chat for the entire cruise! Is there anything else I can help you with?"

Her spiel was so well-practiced that she must have performed it for several other guests before I reached her desk. She folded her hands and waited for me to reply. Just behind her smile, I almost caught a glimpse of her impatience.

"No, that will be all," I assured her. "Thanks again."

"You're so welcome, and thank you for choosing to sail with Emerald Cruises."

I WENT to Corrine's room first, once again getting lost in the maze of hallways below deck before I made it to stateroom 6045. Corrine's room, like mine, was near the middle of the ship, but the door was slightly smaller. My guess was she had a regular-sized cabin, not concierge. I knocked briskly and waited for an answer.

I wanted to get this over with. I wanted Corrine to give me a solid alibi for where she was during Jenn Spitz's death. Then I could call up the station and verify her story, clear her name, and not have to worry about this for the rest of the cruise. Of course, things never quite happened the way I wanted them to.

Corrine didn't answer. I knocked twice more to be sure she wasn't in then gave up when a gaggle of ten-year-olds ran past and showered me with pool water. No one stayed in their stateroom when there was so much to do on board the *Adventure.* I had to do this the old-fashioned way and go looking for Corrine amongst the other four thousand people on the ship.

I rode the elevator all the way to Deck Ten and emerged on the main pool deck. The *Adventure* was a family cruise line, so the biggest swimming pool mostly catered to children and their parents. The water was shallow, the lifeguards were plenty, and a huge high-definition screen showed the latest kids' movies high above the pool. I already knew Corrine and Joe didn't have children, so unless she'd kidnapped a neighbor's kid, I'd be hard-pressed to find Corrine in this section of the ship.

I passed the service counters that served burgers, fries, pizza, and sandwiches all day long and slipped through the white dividers that separated the regular pool deck from the adults-only area. Near the front of the ship was a smaller pool with a built-in bar. The private, eighteen-plus section also sported two heated Jacuzzis with glass floors, a café that served booze as well as coffee, and a pool guard whose main assignment was to shoo any ballsy kids out of the adult area. Each time he escorted another wayward teenager or preteen through the dividers, the adults on the deck nodded and cheered in appreciation.

I did a quick visual sweep of the adult pool, but there was no sign of Corrine. Inside the café, I did the same, then gave in to a cup of iced coffee with a dash of Kahlua at the barista's insistence. The café was styled like a cigar lounge, with a polished dark wood bar top, leather armchairs, and a teal patterned carpet. As I sipped my coffee, it was hard to remember I wasn't actually on vacation.

I headed to the next deck up, which looked over the

pools like one huge mezzanine. At midship, there was a line of kids and adults waiting to get on the twisty slide that led into the pain pool. A double staircase led to the basketball courts and miniature golf course on the topmost deck. There was another bar and a small smoking section, neither of which Corrine was present at. I passed through yet another divider and came across the second adult deck area. This one, hidden away from the rest of the boat, sported a larger pool with a circular fountain in the middle of it. In addition, there were more available loungers here than there had been downstairs. And of course, there was one more bar.

At first glance, Corrine Corral was nowhere to be seen on the top deck either. Every other woman had blonde hair, and while I thought Corrine's orange dress would stick out like a long black hair in a Chicken Alfredo dish, most of the cruisers wore bright, obnoxious colors. My white golf polo, in contrast, was the least conspicuous article of clothing on board. I spun around, scanning the deck again for any woman that resembled Corrine. Finally, I spotted her between two other women. She sat on the edge of the pool with her feet in the water, holding a piña colada and laughing merrily. She had swapped her ugly orange sundress for a violet two-piece bathing suit, a wide-brimmed straw hat, and round sunglasses that covered half her face. No wonder I hadn't spotted her before. She was practically incognito.

I observed the trio from a distance. Corrine seemed to know the other two women already, so I doubted she'd made friends with them in the short time they had all been aboard the *Adventure*. I didn't recognize either of them. The first looked similar to Corrine. She had long blonde hair, though hers was curly, and a pointed chin with plump cheeks. Their third companion was the odd woman out. She had lovely, naturally tan skin and dark ringlets of shiny hair that reflected sunshine like a black mirror. She wore a bright yellow swimsuit that contrasted perfectly with her natural tan. Once or twice, I caught Corrine staring wishfully at the woman's long, dark thighs before she snapped her attention back to the conversation.

The universe was betting against me. As soon as I took a step toward the trio of women, the all-call tune blew across the deck and the cruisers paused to listen to an automated voice announcement.

"Please report to your assigned stations for the lifeboat drill by 5:45. This is a mandatory drill for all guests on board. Please report to your assigned stations for the lifeboat drill by 5:45. This is a mandatory—"

Corrine Corral and her two companions pulled their feet out of the pool and shared an eye roll. No one wanted to interrupt their first day of vacation with a boring lifeboat drill. Corrine's lurid orange dress rested on a chair nearby. She tugged it on over her head and the flowy fabric fell to her feet. Then, believe it or not, she took the gemstone necklace from her pool bag and fastened it around her neck. Her friends immediately fawned over it.

"So gorgeous," the blonde one said, her voice floating across the deck as she covered her swimsuit with a slip dress as well. "That piece is exquisite."

"Thanks, Gretchen," Corrine said.

"You *have* to get me involved," the darker woman added. "Darrell keeps telling me to get a job because I won't stop complaining about how bored I am at the house while he works all day. This is perfect."

Corrine simpered, looking pleased with the amount of adoration her friends displayed. "All in due time, LeeAnn."

LeeAnn pouted. "That's what you always say."

Corrine strapped a watch around her wrist, the band of which sported equally garish fake diamonds. "Come on, ladies. We're going to be late for the drill."

I followed them off the pool deck and into the crowded stairwell. Everyone on board was making their way to their assigned station down on Deck Four for the drill. Cruise employees wearing bright orange life vests and yellow safety sashes directed traffic. People bunched up in the elevators, hoping to beat the hordes on the stairs.

I lost Corrine and her friends in the throng more than twice, but thankfully Corrine's awful orange dress stood out enough for me to always catch sight of her again. When we arrived on Deck Four, a cruise employee stopped me before I could follow Corrine and her friends outside.

"Stateroom number?" the employee asked.

"Uh, 7028."

The employee—Dirk—checked his clipboard. "You're heading the wrong way. Your drill station is on the opposite side of the deck."

"I know," I said, though I didn't. "I was trying to catch up with my friends actually."

"You can catch up with your friends after the drill," Dirk said politely. "Right now, it's important everyone get to their appropriate stations as quickly as possible. That way, we can all get you out of here in time for dinner."

With an open palm, he directed me away from the door Corrine and her friends had slipped through. I craned my neck for one last useless look before giving in to Dirk's directions and following the rest of Deck Seven's occupants to the opposite side of the ship.

THE LIFEBOAT DRILL was boring but blessedly short. For fifteen minutes, we stood in cramped groups as the assembly instructors told us where to find our life jackets, how to put them on, and what specific horns the boat would play if we ended up in an emergency situation. As a cop, I listened to every word, though most of it was common sense. The other cruise-goers weren't as attentive. Everyone wanted to get back to their vacation as soon as possible.

After the drill, it was almost time for the scheduled 6:30 dinner. Everyone on the ship ate in two shifts, early or late dinner. I had no idea which one I was scheduled for, but it didn't matter. I intended on going to whatever one Corrine and her friends were assigned to. I hurried through the crowd and waited inside the stairway closest to Corrine's drill station for a glimpse of her. When she came inside, chatting merrily to her friends, I let a few other cruisers get in between us before heading up the stairs after her.

"I knew we should have done the late seating," Corrine was saying. "It's so much more laid back. All the people with kids go to the first seating so they can put them to bed early."

"I hear first seating gets the better food though," her blonde friend chimed in. "That's good, right?"

"As long as I get to eat, it doesn't matter to me," LeeAnn declared.

Since swimsuits weren't allowed in the dining room, the trio headed back to their rooms on Deck Six to change. It gave me the time I needed to check on a few things in my own room.

First, I checked which dinner I was assigned to: second seating. That meant I didn't get to eat until 8:30 unless I ordered room service. It also meant I couldn't spy on Corrine and her friends in the dining room, simply because there wasn't a seat for me. I wasn't too put out. The dining rooms were huge, and your placement was assigned. It was unlikely I'd get placed close enough to my suspect to overhear any decent conversation.

I grabbed the room service menu, my phone, and the complimentary Emerald Cruises stationary from the in-suite desk. Then I headed out to the verandah. Without the sun so high in the sky, it was a pleasant, balmy evening. I propped the lounge chair into a seated position, got comfortable, and dialed Angela's number.

"This better be good," she answered. Her voice sounded fuzzy over the phone, but since I was miles out to sea, I didn't expect perfect reception. "I'm still mad about earlier."

"I need you to do me a favor."

"Ha! Have you checked the time, Ryder?" she said. "It's after five. I'm off duty. Call one of your other lackeys."

"Look, I'm sorry for earlier," I said. "You hit a nerve, okay? But I need your help. I can't do this without you."

Angela huffed into the phone to make sure I knew she was still annoyed with me despite my half-assed apology. "Where are you anyway? You weren't at your desk at all this afternoon. And what's that whooshing sound?"

"Waves," I answered. "I'm on a cruise ship."

"I'm sorry, what?"

"I followed Corrine Corral, one of my suspects, onto the *Emerald Adventure*," I told her. "And it left the port before I managed to get off. That's why I need your help."

"Carter's going to kill you, man."

"You can't tell Carter I called," I hissed. "I'm in deep enough shit already."

Angela gasped in realization. "Hang on, this is why Brock got reassigned to your case, isn't it? That's why Carter was livid this morning! Wait a second—did you get suspended?"

My jaw clenched. "If I say yes, are you still going to help me out?"

Angela whistled. "Dude, you *are* in deep shit. What are you going to do?"

"I'm going to solve this case," I told her. "I can't let a potential suspect roam around a cruise ship with no supervision. Corrine's here with two other women. I need you to tell me who they are."

"Are you nuts?" Angela whispered. "I can't access the database for you while you're suspended. Do you want me to get in trouble too?"

"I want you to go about this as quietly as possible," I said. "Please, Angela. I'm trying to solve a homicide here."

"You've been suspended," she reminded me. "And your case was reassigned. Let this one go, Alex. Brock and his team will take care of it."

I kicked the small drink table with more force than I meant to. It flew across the verandah and ricocheted off the railing. Thankfully, the glass top didn't break.

"Brock doesn't know a damn thing about this case. He's not going to find any leads that I haven't already found. Corrine Corral is an open thread, and so are her friends if they all knew Jenn Spitz. Please, Angela. This isn't for me. This is for everyone who's been affected by Jenn's death, including her husband and kids."

I almost felt bad for using Jenn's kids to convince Angela to break the law. Ever since Jess got pregnant, Angela had a soft spot for children. Sure enough, she sighed wistfully over the phone.

"Fine," she said. The plastic wheels of her desk chair squeaked. She was still at the station, despite having told me she was off duty. "What do you got?"

"Two women, both mid-thirties," I reported. "First one is named Gretchen. Blonde, brown eyes, and too-much-cardio kind of skinny."

"Got a Gretchen Wagner," Angela reported in a low tone. "No priors, but she's stayed in our care about a domestic incident. I'm guessing that involved her husband because she filed for divorce shortly after we had her here. That's about it though. Who's the other one?"

"LeeAnn." I scribbled Gretchen Wagner's details on my pad of stationary. "Black hair and dark brown eyes. Latina, I'd guess. She's muscley, especially in her thighs and glutes, like she does a lot of deadlifts."

"Got something," Angela said a minute later. "LeeAnn Rhodes. She was arrested once three years ago for breaking into her ex-boyfriend's. Looks like she threatened his new girlfriend. Neither one of them pressed charges though."

"But she's been violent towards women before," I muttered, more to myself than to Angela as I took notes. "That's something. Anything on how they know Corrine? Or how they might be connected to Jenn?"

"Both Gretchen and LeeAnn have addresses in Pelican Point."

"Neighborhood pals."

"Uh-huh. Alex, are you sure you want to do this?"

I flipped the stationary book shut. "We talked about this. Three women who all knew Jenn Spitz fled the Tampa area the day after her murder. Don't you think that's suspicious?"

"Maybe. Or maybe they decided to go on a last-minute vacation together."

"I doubt it," I said. "I'm probably going to need you again, so look out for my calls, okay?"

"Alex, I don't—"

"Thanks, Ang."

I hung up on her and checked the time. It was only seven o'clock. I had another hour and a half to burn before Corrine, Gretchen, and LeeAnn were done with dinner. With nothing but time, I decided to order the most expensive thing on the room service menu, courtesy of Captain Marianna.

SHORTLY BEFORE 8:30, I made my way to the dining

room and waited for Corrine and company to come out. They emerged laughing at raucous volumes, no doubt the result of several shared bottles of wine. But the women weren't done quite yet. I tailed them all the way up to Deck Ten, where the nightly pool party was in full swing.

Corrine, Gretchen, and LeeAnn grabbed cocktails at the bar then made their way onto the dance floor. I climbed the stairs to the mezzanine on Deck Eleven and watched them from above. Like this—drunk and dancing—there was nothing suspicious about any of the women. Gretchen sucked down her frozen daiquiri with unparalleled speed but showed no signs of brain freeze, Corrine performed an awkward, shuffling dance with absolute no shame, and LeeAnn quickly located a single dad to spin her from one end of the dance floor to the other.

The revelry was contagious. Soon enough, I found myself bobbing my head along to the thunderous dance music the DJ played. When my phone rang, I didn't hear it but felt the vibrations against my thigh. I checked the caller ID; it was Dominique. I plugged one ear with my finger and answered, turning away from the pool deck to find a quieter space to talk.

"Hello? Hey, Dominique?"

The service on the ship was terrible. All I heard from the other end of the line was fuzzy static.

"Dominique? Hey, are you there?"

A panicked scream from the lower deck made me

drop my phone. As I fumbled around for it, chaos erupted below. People yelled and pushed each other. The dance floor turned into a mob as everyone tried to get away from the pool. I looked over the railing to see what all the fuss was about. My stomach plummeted as if I'd thrown myself over the side of the ship.

A body floated facedown in the pool. The water was blood-red.

*a*s everyone else fled the scene, I rushed toward it. The panicked crowd thinned, and a lifeguard jumped into the water to pull the body out of the pool. I pushed aside cruise-goers and fought against the flow to reach the pool. As soon as I saw the woman—white, blonde, thirties—I knew she was dead. Her face was pale, drained of blood, though she didn't appear to have a large enough injury anywhere on her body to explain the amount of redness in the water. The lifeguard checked the woman's pulse, then put a plastic mouthpiece between her lips and began performing CPR.

"It's no use." I crouched at the lifeguard's side as he began compressions. "She's dead already. Too much blood loss. I need you to back away, please. This is officially a crime scene."

The lifeguard—Chris—was no older than twenty.

He flicked his damp hair out of his eyes and continued CPR. His pretty blue eyes were wide with fear, and his plump cheeks were pink with effort. If I had to guess, this was one of his first days on the job, and he'd never had to pull a lifeless body out of a pool before.

"You don't know." He blew another breath into the woman's unmoving mouth then went back to compressions. "You don't know she's dead."

I steadied his hands, but he yanked away from me. "She has no pulse, Chris. She's gone. It's not your fault."

"No!" He studied me with furrowed brows, taking in my civilian attire. "Who are you? You should get out of here. It's not safe."

"I'm a homicide detective." I reached for my badge then grimaced when I came up with nothing. I'd left my badge in my stateroom after dinner. "Detective Alex Ryder. That's why I need you to step away from the body, Chris. You could be compromising my evidence."

Chris's compressions slowed. "I don't know what happened. I was watching the pool this entire time. I saw her fall in. By the time I got to her—" His voice cracked as he cut himself off.

I gently placed a hand on Chris's shoulder. When he didn't throw me off, I carefully turned him away from the body. "This wasn't your fault. She lost a lot of blood. You couldn't have saved her. Right now, I need you to go back to your room. It's not safe here."

"What the hell is going on here?" a deep voice

demanded from above us. It was Clint, with a whole team of security guards behind him. When he spotted the body, he said, "Oh, shit. Is she—?"

"Dead. Yeah." I helped Chris to his feet and turned to face Clint. "I tried to warn you that something like this might happen. You need to put this ship on lockdown until we find the killer."

Clint stared at the body and the bloody water. Maybe he hadn't seen a dead body before either. "That's impossible. We can't ask everyone to stay in their rooms until we make port."

"At least for tonight," I ordered. "You have to give me a head start on this investigation, unless you want another guest to end up dead. I'm guessing that would be bad for business."

Clint addressed one of his backup men. "Lou, radio the captain. Update her on the situation and have her make an announcement that everyone needs to report to their rooms immediately and stay there. After that, notify the Coast Guard of our situation."

As Lou walked off to radio the captain, I patted Chris on the back. "You said you saw her fall in the water," I said to him. "Did you happen to see anything else? Were people fighting around her?"

Chris's eyes had glazed over. He was going into shock. "I—I'm not sure. I don't think so. Everyone was dancing around the pool. Then she fell in, and I saw the blood."

"Was she bleeding before she fell in?"

"I don't know. I think so?"

"Sir!" Clint's thunderous bellow made both me and Chris jump. "You need to return to your room right away. The pool is closed."

A guy in his early twenties with a square jaw, a dark crewcut, and neon-pink swim shorts had stayed behind after the rest of the crowd departed. None of us had noticed him until now.

"Sorry," he said. "I thought I might be help. I'm Officer Derek Scott."

"You're a cop?" I asked him.

"I'm a rookie," he admitted. "But all the homicide detectives like when I work their cases because I have a photographic memory."

"Got a badge?" Clint asked gruffly.

Derek shook his head. "I didn't bring it with me on vacation, but I have a ton of pictures on my phone with me and my buddies in uniform. I can also call my training officer and ask him for permission to work this case."

"Where are you from?" I asked him.

"Chicago," he replied. "South side."

"So you work a lot of homicides?"

"More than I'd care to count for someone who just started this job less than a year ago." Derek tapped his head. "This memory thing comes in handy. Believe me, you could use my help."

The all-call tune sounded over the speakers.

"This is Captain Marianna speaking from the

bridge." Despite the situation, the captain kept a calm, easy tone. "Due to an emergency situation on Deck Ten, the *Adventure* is officially on lockdown for the rest of the evening. All events have been cancelled. Please return to your staterooms in a quick and orderly fashion as soon as possible. Do not let anyone you are not familiar with access to your cabin unless they are a confirmed member of the ship's crew. Please do not leave your stateroom. If you have an emergency, dial the appropriate number from your in-suite phone, and our staff will see to it that you are taken care of. I repeat, due to an emergency on Deck Ten…"

"Can I go?" Chris asked. He shook from head to toe. "Please, I can't be here anymore. I can't look at her."

"Yes," I answered. "Go back to your cabin and don't leave. I might have to talk to you tomorrow though, okay? Whether you like it or not, you're a witness to murder."

He swallowed, took one last look at the woman's lifeless body, and nodded. Then he ran from the scene as fast as he could. I knelt beside the body.

Clint's hand came down on my shoulder. "Whoa, whoa, whoa. Not so fast, Miss Detective. You don't know that this has anything to do with your case. They could be completely unrelated incidents."

"They could be," I agreed. "It would be stupid of me to rule that possibility out. However, I'm most likely the only homicide detective on board, so how about you let me do my job?"

"I'd feel more comfortable waiting for the Coast Guard and the FBI," Clint said. "We don't know who has jurisdiction in these waters."

"A woman is dead," I reminded him shortly. "You and your security team failed to protect her. The least you can do is let me examine the scene and possibly determine cause of death. When you call this woman's family to let them know she died under your watch, what would you rather tell them? That you failed to investigate the situation because you weren't sure whose jurisdiction it was or that you tried everything you possibly could to figure out who murdered a member of their family?"

"You don't *know* that she was murdered," Clint growled. "It could have been an accident."

"Are you willing to take that chance?" I challenged him. "Because if you're wrong, it means you have a murderer on board with free rein to do whatever he or she wants."

Clint was spared from having to answer as the captain rushed down the stairs and onto the pool deck to join us. She examined the scene. Though her face screwed up in empathy when she spotted the body, she kept herself together.

"What happened?" she demanded. "What do we know?"

"I could tell you," I offered, "but your lackey here won't let me examine the body."

Clint crossed his arms and glared at me. "I'm trying

to keep some form of procedure alive aboard this ship. What do you want me to do, Captain?"

"Notify the Coast Guard."

"Done."

"And the FBI."

Clint sent another one of his security guards to attend to that. Captain Marianna stepped in front of the large man to address the remaining members of the security team herself.

"I want each of you stationed at equal intervals on every deck," she announced. "Make sure all the guests return to their staterooms. I need at least five of you watching the cameras in the security office. If you see anyone behaving suspiciously, report it to me right away. Go!"

The security team, except for Clint, dispersed.

"What do you want me to do, Captain?" Clint asked.

Captain Marianna scanned the deck for trouble then addressed me. "This is your wheelhouse, isn't it?"

"Yes, ma'am."

"You believe this woman was murdered?"

"I can't say without examining her," I reported. "But that much blood doesn't usually appear out of nowhere."

The captain nodded. "You have my permission to do whatever you need to do. Under one condition. I need the body out of here before morning. If people find out someone died on the *Adventure*, it will cause an uproar. We need to get through the next five days."

"Understood," I said.

"When the Coast Guard gets here, you'll defer to them," she ordered.

"Yes, ma'am."

Captain Marianna beckoned Clint toward her. "Two things, Clint. First of all, supervise your team. Make sure they're not falling asleep on the job. If we have a killer on board, we need to stay alert. Second of all, listen to Detective Ryder. Think of her as your boss now. If she needs something, give it to her."

"But, Captain—"

"If we had listened to Detective Ryder earlier and returned this ship to shore, we wouldn't be in this situation," Captain Marianna interrupted. "We made a mistake, and it cost someone their life. I would like to prevent that from happening again, wouldn't you?"

Clint dropped his stern gaze. "Yes, ma'am."

Derek, the rookie cop, raised his hand. "Should I go? I don't want to be in the way."

"Yes," Clint said.

"No," I objected. "I need him."

"Who are you?" Captain Marianna asked, eyeing Derek's bare chest and neon shorts.

He bowed his head. "Officer Derek Scott, ma'am. Excuse my attire. I'm on vacation with my girlfriend, but I thought I could help out here."

"I can use him," I told the captain. "I'd like him to stay."

"Very well," she replied. "Get to work. I have to go put out some fires. Clint, keep me updated."

"Yes, Captain."

As Captain Marianna took her leave, I finally got a closer look at the body without Clint interrupting me. I beckoned the rookie over. His flip flops slapped across the deck as he hurried toward me.

"What do you see?" I asked him.

His inquisitive eyes narrowed as he scanned the woman from head to toe. Up close, I could see the woman was younger than I originally thought, maybe twenty-two or twenty-three. She was blonde and pretty, with light blue eyes and a creamy complexion. Jenn Spitz's face flashed in my memory. She, too, was blonde and pretty, as was Dominique and the other victims from the case I'd screwed up eight years ago.

"No wound," Derek muttered. "I don't see a wound anywhere. How can that be? How else would she have lost so much blood? Do you think it's internal?"

"No. You're not looking hard enough." I took a pen out of my pocket and used it to lift the woman's skirt above her knees, just high enough to get a glimpse at her thighs. "Now what do you see?"

He leaned forward and squinted. "Is that a puncture wound?"

On the inside of the woman's right thigh was a small gash about an inch wide. Blood seeped weakly from the wound, following no rhythm or pulse. The woman's legs were stained pink, though most of the blood had washed off in the pool.

"Femoral artery," I told Derek. "It's the main arterial supply to the leg and thigh. She bled out in minutes. No one noticed until she fell into the pool."

"Someone stabbed her?" Derek asked. "How?"

I studied the wound. "With a knife, I'd guess. A switchblade, maybe?"

"No, I meant how did someone stab her without being noticed by anyone else?" Derek asked. "There were at least two hundred people on deck for the pool party, and no one realized she was bleeding to death?"

"In this line of work, you'll find that most people are completely oblivious to anything that doesn't concern them," I said. "Get your phone out. We need to take pictures of the crime scene."

He hurriedly pulled his phone from his back pocket. "Where should I start?"

"You take the left side of the deck," I told him. "I'll take the right and the body. You know how to do this, right?"

"I've seen CSI do it a couple of times."

"Be thorough," I advised. "Look at everything from every angle."

Derek nodded and started at the other end of the deck to do as I asked. Clint watched as I began taking pictures of the body with my own phone.

"What do you want me to do?" he asked.

"Just watch and learn, Clint."

. . .

BECAUSE SO MANY people had been on the pool deck at the time of the murder, there was no clean evidence on the scene. The massive puddle of blood from where the woman was stabbed had been smeared in every direction thanks to the panicked stampede of the other cruise-goers. Bloody footprints coated the deck in every direction, leading up to Deck Eleven, the elevators, the stairs, and everywhere else. There was no way to tell which set of footprints might have belonged to the killer.

The woman had no ID on her, and Clint couldn't identify her without the number of her stateroom. He would have to scroll through all four thousand pictures of the onboard guests in security's computer system to find her, which he deemed "a colossal waste of time." Still, he radioed one of his men to start looking for the woman's name in this manner anyway.

As the night wore on, we expected to hear from the woman's family or friends, but no on reported her missing. She could have been sailing alone, but Clint doubted it. In his experience, the only people who sailed alone were elderly, retired people who had already been widowed. I considered arguing that I had decided to sail alone before I remembered I hadn't boarded the *Adventure* with the intention to vacation by myself.

After Derek and I photographed every inch of the scene, it was time to relocate the body. Clint cleared a room for us on Deck One, all the way at the bottom of the ship where most of the crew members slept. The cabin contained a single bed and wardrobe with a TV. Before we arrived, one of Clint's guards draped the bed with a piece of heavy plastic tarp they'd found in storage somewhere. We used a second piece of tarp to wrap and transport the body.

It was horrible work. In my time as a detective, I'd never participated in this part of the process, but since I didn't want any of the security guards potentially damaging the body, it was up to me and Derek to move the woman onto the tarp. Though we wore disposable gloves borrowed from the kitchen, I could feel her cold flesh beneath my fingers. My stomach roiled until she was safely wrapped in the tarp, at which point I allowed the security guards to carry her down to the assigned room.

The custodial staff was tasked with cleaning the blood off the deck and out of the pool. All of its members had taken a mandatory class on how to safely clean up bodily fluids, so they were technically certified for the job. I doubted they ever expected to apply that knowledge to the scene of a murder, but they were stalwart and professional nonetheless.

Derek and I settled into our makeshift morgue. I turned the cabin's air conditioning to the highest setting, hoping to preserve the body for as long as possible. In a couple of hours, the woman's muscles would stiffen with rigor mortis and the stench of bacteria and decay would begin to manifest.

"We can't keep her in here, right?" Derek asked, the same worries going through his head. "It's not sanitary."

"No, it's not," I agreed. "I'm sure the Coast Guard will decide what to do with her. Until then, we have to get as much information from her as we can."

"I thought we already did that?"

A knock on the cabin door interrupted Derek's question. I looked through the peephole to find Clint's enormous chest on the opposite side.

"What is it?" I asked when I opened the door. "We're working."

Clint was so tall that he had to duck to fit inside the cabin. With all three of us, plus the body, there wasn't room to swing a mouse. Clint eyed the body with distaste.

"I'm supposed to be supervising," he reminded me. He squeezed himself into the spare chair next to the wardrobe. "By the way, the Coast Guard got back to us. They'll be here within the hour."

"Super," I said. Once the Coast Guard arrived, this case would no longer be under my control. I had less than an hour to get what I needed. "Sure you want to stay, Clint? It's gonna get gross in a minute. No offense, but you don't look like you have the strongest stomach."

With a dramatic flick, I unraveled the tarp and exposed the woman's pale, shriveled body. Clint's face turned white. He stood up.

"I'll wait outside," he announced.

Once Clint was gone, Derek pulled on a fresh pair of nitrile gloves. Thankfully, the rookie had found a shirt in the time since we inspected the scene on the pool deck.

"So what's your story?" He began to rearrange the body as it would be for an autopsy. "Is it a wild coincidence that a homicide detective ends up on a cruise where a homicide happens on the first night out of port?"

"It's no coincidence." I watched as he carefully laid out the woman's arms. "You've done this before, huh?"

"My dad's an embalmer," Derek said. "I worked summers with him. Needless to say, I didn't want to go into the family business."

"So you became a cop?"

"Yup. It fit my skill set. I want to be a homicide detective like you though." He glanced up at me. "So? It's not a coincidence, huh?"

I observed Derek. He was a rookie with limited experience, but he had also put a romantic night with his girlfriend on hold to inspect a dead body instead. He weathered the chilly cabin temperature in his damp, pink swim shorts and a white T-shirt. That meant he was resilient and determined to do the work despite his discomfort. Plus, if he really did have a photographic memory, he would be an invaluable asset to my investigation on board. That settled it. I trusted him.

"I've been investigating a series of murders in the Tampa area." I crossed my arms over my chest to keep the chill away. "They started eight years ago. The victims were all pretty blonde women in their twenties and thirties. When I got on board today, it was with the intention to question one of the suspects for a homicide that occurred two days ago. The last thing I expected was for another murder to happen on board this ship."

"But it has," Derek said. "That means your suspect is the murderer, right?"

"I wish it was that easy," I told him. "But jumping to conclusions can get you into trouble with a case like this. Besides, there are too many differences between this murder and the previous ones. I can't automatically assume they were performed by the same person."

"What kind of differences?"

I needed to pace. I did my best thinking when I could get my blood flowing, but the cabin was too tiny to allow for pacing. I settled for tapping my heel against the floor. The repetitive sound grounded me and my thoughts.

"First off, the last murder was premeditated," I told Derek. "The killer posed the body and left it for us to find. Second, the previous victims were subjected to torture before they were killed. The perp wrapped wire around their fingers to cut off the blood supply."

Derek wrinkled his nose. "Effectively amputation, right?"

"Yes." I gestured to the wound on the woman's leg. "This is quick, effective work. The victim didn't see it coming. She wasn't tortured, and her death wasn't drawn out. However, the killer *is* known for her knife skills."

"So it *could* be your killer," Derek said. "Or it couldn't be."

"You see the problem."

Clint pounded on the door. "Hey, Ryder! Come out here."

I rolled my eyes, removed my gloves with a sharp snap, and tossed them in the wastebasket. "Keep an eye on her, Derek."

"Yes, ma'am."

I joined Clint in the hallway. "What can I do for you, big guy?"

"Got a radio call from one of my boys upstairs," Clint reported. "He says some guy was wandering around the hallways, looking for a security guard."

I tapped my foot impatiently. "So?"

"*So*," Clint said, "the guy said he knows your dead friend in there. He might be able to ID the body. I had my guard take him to the office. You want to talk to this dude or what?"

"Yes," I said, shocked that Clint had something helpful to contribute. "Let's go."

UP IN THE SECURITY OFFICE, Clint's guard had detained

the man in question in a small meeting room. When Clint let me in, the man looked up at me with a hopeless expression. He was a tall, skinny individual with bony elbows and knees. His elven features—pointed chin, high cheekbones, and flaxen hair—were diminished by exhaustion. He looked positively spent.

"It's her, isn't it?" he asked in a hoarse voice. "It's Christine?"

"Sir, I'm Detective Alex Ryder." I sat across from him and folded my hands. "Can I ask your name?"

"Owen," he replied. "Owen O'Donnell. Please tell me it's not her. Please tell me I didn't see what I think I saw."

"What do you think you saw?" I asked him quietly.

"We were dancing, and everyone panicked," Owen said. "There was blood everywhere, and someone fell into the pool, but I didn't think it was Christine. I thought she was in the crowd ahead of me, but then she never came back to the room when the lockdown was announced—" He cradled his head in his hands. "Oh, man. I hope it's not her."

I flipped to a fresh page in my stationary book. "What can you tell me about Christine, Owen? Was she your girlfriend?"

"No," he answered. "We came with a group. A therapy group."

"A therapy group?"

"For adults who need support overcoming and living with mental health issues." Owen misread my

160

expression and added in an icy tone, "Don't worry. We're supervised."

"Oh, that's not why—"

"One of the guys, Max, has borderline personality disorder," Owen went on. "He's impulsive, emotional, and nuts. I don't like to say that about anybody. We're all going through our own shit, but Max is different. One second, you're his best friend. The next, you're his worst enemy. I know it's his disease, but it makes it hard to trust him."

"Are you saying Max might have hurt Christine?"

"He has a massive crush on her," Owen reported. "She told him she didn't feel the same way, but he's persistent. If someone killed her, Max would be at the top of my list of suspects."

Before I could ask any other questions, Derek burst through the door of the meeting room with Clint close behind him.

"I don't know how it happened," Derek gasped. "I went to the bathroom for, like, two minutes."

"Slow down," I said. "What happened?"

"The body," Derek said, panting. "It's gone."

10

*C*lint, Derek, and I sprinted from the security office to the elevator. The ride all the way down to Deck One felt longer than it did before. Derek kept apologizing with every combination of words possible, but nothing mattered until I got back to the cabin and saw the empty tarp on the twin bed. Sure enough, the dead woman was gone. Before the Coast Guard came to collect it. Before the FBI showed up to investigate. Before we even got the chance to properly ID the body.

"Search the floor," Clint bellowed, and his team of security guards jumped to it. "Knock on every cabin door. Check the storage rooms. I want this entire deck cleared!"

I inspected the cabin for clues. When I came up empty, I slammed my fist into the wardrobe. One of my knuckles popped out of place. I pushed it into position with a defeated sigh. If Sandy had seen me lose my temper like that, she would have scolded me big time.

"I'm sorry," Derek said, yet again. "How could this have happened?"

"I told you to stay with the body."

"I had to pee," he protested. "I was gone for two minutes, tops. It's not like she could have walked out of here on her own!"

"You never leave the body of a murder victim unattended," I told him. "Especially when the murderer might still be in the vicinity. It's a rookie mistake."

"Okay, I get it." Derek ran his hands through what little hair he had. "What are we going to tell the Coast Guard?"

I sat in the spare chair by the wardrobe and rubbed my eyes. It was late, I was tired, and Derek wasn't the only one making mistakes. I should have never left a rookie with the body. Then again, I wasn't used to doing everything myself. I never appreciated CSI as much as I did in this moment.

"Let's see if Clint comes up with anything first."

Derek smacked his forehead with his palm. "God, I'm such an idiot!"

"Hey," I said. "Sit down. Relax. Shit like this happens. The first time I worked a homicide case, I let the killer get away. You're going to make mistakes."

"I don't," Derek insisted, jabbing his thumbs into his chest. "I'm the guy who doesn't make mistakes. That's why I volunteered to help you. Because it was the right thing to do."

"I commend your righteousness," I told him, "but it's time to put the torch down. If the body's actually gone, it takes this case to a whole new level."

Clint's massive form filled the open door. "We've got nothing so far. Kid, are you sure you didn't see anything? Did you hear anything?"

"I thought I heard the door slam," Derek said, "but I figured it was one of you guys. I'm sorry—"

"Enough apologies." I stretched and stifled a yawn. "Clint, did you check security footage? There are cameras down here too, right?"

Clint twirled an Emerald Cruises pen between his sausage fingers. "One of my guys watched the tapes. He said the camera went out right before the body disappeared. No one in the hallway."

"What about the adjacent hallways? In the elevators?" I asked. "Top decks? We're on a ship in the middle of the ocean. There are only so many ways one can disappear a body. Chucking it into the water is the easiest option."

"I have people stationed on every deck," Clint reported. "If someone dumped a body, we would have seen them. We got nothing. This perp's a ghost."

"Or well-practiced," I muttered.

"What are we supposed to do?" Derek asked. "How do we conduct an investigation without a body?"

I plucked the twirling pen out of Clint's hands.

"That was making me nauseous. I got what I needed from the body except for an identification. Clint, can you ask that Owen guy what this Christine's last name is? Then look her up in the system and see if her photo matches the body."

Clint reached for his radio. "Hey, Russo. You still got that blond guy up in the office?"

The radio buzzed, and Russo's voice came back. "Yes, sir."

"Ask him for his friend's last name, then look up her up in the security database."

"Yes, sir," Russo responded. "Oh, and sir? The Coast Guard's here."

IT WAS a good thing the guests on the *Adventure* were confined to their rooms for the rest of the night, because the Coast Guard didn't know the definition of inconspicuous. As we made our way to the top deck to meet them, the roar of helicopter blades met my ears. The bright orange vehicle hovered above the ship and cast a strong wind across the deck. The pool water— already cleaned and filtered of blood by some cruise ship maintenance miracle—rippled and whirled. The *Adventure* didn't have a helipad, but Deck Twelve had an open space large enough to accommodate the Coast Guard should an emergency occur. The copter didn't land. Instead, the crew manning it dropped a rope ladder to the deck, and two guys in orange jumpsuits descended from above.

Derek pulled me aside before I could follow Clint up to meet the Coast Guard officers. "Detective, do you need me for this? My girlfriend's probably wondering where I am, and I really don't want to explain to the Coast Guard that I lost a dead body."

"They're going to want to know what happened." I took in Derek's red face of shame and gave in. "Fine. I'll tell them what happened. Go and salvage the rest of your night, Officer. You deserve it."

"You think so?"

I clapped him on the back. "Don't make me change my mind. Come find me tomorrow. I need a partner for this case, and I could use that brain of yours."

Derek grinned. "Will do."

As Derek returned to his girlfriend, I hustled up the stairs to join Clint and the Coast Guard officers. The two that had landed on deck both sported muscles larger than tree trunks, but one was taller than Clint and the other was shorter than me. They wore matching expressions of severity.

"Ah, here she is," Clint said, gesturing me toward them. "Gentlemen, this is Detective Alex Ryder. We're lucky to have her on board. Detective, this is Officer Cooper" —the taller man with a tuft of fluffy red hair peeking out of his orange hood— "and Officer Sullivan" —the shorter guy who appeared to have no hair at all.

"Nice to meet you, Detective," Cooper said. "We understand there's been a murder on board. We're here to sweep the ship and remove the body from your custody."

I glared at Clint. "You didn't tell them?"

"No, I thought I'd give you the pleasure," Clint said with a gleam in his eye. "Since your rookie's the one who's at fault here."

"What's going on?" Sullivan asked. "Can we see the body or not?"

"We ran into some trouble," I told the officers. "We moved the body below deck for safety purposes, and I left my rookie unsupervised while I went to interview a potential witness. The body's gone."

Officer Cooper rolled his eyes, and Sullivan was bold enough to laugh.

"Oh, man," Sullivan said, holding his belly as he wiped his eyes. "That's a good one. I get it, Detective. You think this is your case because it happened right under your nose, and maybe if we were on land, that would be true. In the water, things are different. We're the bosses around here."

"That's great, Officer," I said, "but I'm not pulling your leg. Someone stole the body and either hid it or dumped it. Clint's team already performed a search, but you're more than welcome to conduct your own."

Sullivan wiped the grin off his face and radioed up to the chopper. "Body might have been dumped overboard. Send down the rest of the crew so we can search the ship. Then get a floodlight on the channel behind us."

Three ropes flew out of the helicopter, and a team of officers landed on the deck. Then someone pulled the ropes and ladder up as the helicopter pulled a sleek U-turn. An enormous floodlight illuminated a circle of the dark water below as the chopper searched for the body. Somehow, I doubted they would find anything.

Sullivan hollered instructions at the rest of the crew. "Sweep the ship! Body was last seen on Deck One! Check everything accessible." Cooper and the other officers rushed to obey as Sullivan turned to Clint. "What about the staterooms? Have you done a roll call yet?"

"We're working on it," Clint said. "Have you heard from the FBI?"

"The FBI won't address this," Sullivan answered. "Once you're out of American waters, they no longer have jurisdiction."

"You're kidding," I said. "Someone on this ship is endangering every person on board, and the FBI said they don't want to get involved?"

Sullivan tugged his orange hood off and wiped sweat from his forehead. "You're three-quarters of the way to Nassau. If you want help, the best thing to do is alert the Bahamian authorities."

"The Bahamian authorities don't have a third of the resources that the Bureau does," Clint argued. "They won't help at all."

Sullivan shrugged. "That's the best I can offer you. If we can't find a body, we can't help you. We're not detectives, Mr. Clint. That's your job."

"It's hers, actually," Clint muttered with an elbow to my ribs.

I stepped aside to dodge Clint's jab. "Don't worry. This was my case long before it came aboard this ship. The Captain already approved my investigation."

"What about your lieutenant?" Clint asked. "Did she get that paperwork filed? Do you have privileges?"

The lump in my throat returned in full. I coughed to clear it. "Yeah, everything's all set."

"Great," Sullivan said. "Once my team's done, we'll get out of your hair. I'll say one thing though. When this boat gets back to Tampa, Emerald Cruises might want to take a long look at the way they handle emergency situations." He took in Clint's sneer and shook his head. "This never would have happened on a Disney Cruise."

As Sullivan turned to follow his team, Clint hollered after him, "Do I look like freakin' Mickey Mouse to you?"

"Can it," I told Clint. "Antagonizing him isn't going to help. *I* need your help, Clint. If we don't work together and catch this perp, it could mean more dead bodies."

Clint huffed and crossed his arms, still staring after Sullivan. "I'm all ears, Ryder. What you got for me?"

His easy acceptance of my authority threw me off

for a second, but I stepped into command mode as soon as I realized he wasn't messing with me. "First off, radio your guy and ask if they found this Christine girl in the system. We need an ID on the body if we're going to make any progress."

As the Coast Guard did their thing, Clint and I did ours. We returned to the security offices. Owen had been excused for the moment. That worked for me. I needed to sort a few things out before we started talking to witnesses.

"Christine Sherry." Russo—an ex-Marine with a severe crew cut and bulging biceps that threatened to burst the seams of his teal-and-white striped shirt— reported to us as soon as we reached the offices. He handed Clint a tablet with Christine's picture and information on the screen. "Does her picture match the body?"

"That's her," Clint said.

I yanked on Clint's elbow to bring the tablet down to my height and looked over his shoulder. Sure enough, the woman in the identification photo when she boarded the *Adventure* yesterday afternoon was unmistakably the same woman who had fallen into the pool earlier. A pang of guilt squeezed my heart as I examined her bright eyes and eager smile. Yesterday, Christine Sherry had gotten on this ship to escape from her problems and enjoy life unhindered for a mere five days. Today, she was dead, and it was probably my fault.

"That's her," I echoed Clint. "Did you tell that Owen guy?"

"No," Russo answered. "I sent him back to his stateroom once we located her in the system. I thought it best to keep this quiet for as long as possible. The Captain said she didn't want people panicking."

"Good thinking," Clint said.

"It doesn't matter," I told them both. "Everyone at the pool party tonight knows something went down. The entire ship is on lockdown. By tomorrow morning, the rumors will have spread far and wide."

Clint clicked the button to black out the tablet's screen, as if he could no longer bear to look at Christine Sherry's happy face. "We can deal with rumors. There are ways to head them off."

"If you say so." I gestured to the room next door to our office, the one labeled *Surveillance.* "Can we get in there? I'd like to review the tapes from the pool party. Maybe we can identify the killer."

"It's a long shot," Clint said. "The first night of the pool party draws a huge crowd. Probably won't be able to see anything."

"Or we might get lucky," I replied. "Do you want to catch this perp or what?"

Clint pursed his lips and scanned his badge to get into the surveillance room. The interior boasted an impressive amount of television screens, each of which showed a different section of the ship. Every few seconds, the screens switched to a new angle. Three guards watched the monitors. They lazed in their chairs, propped their feet on on the desk, and drank coffee to keep themselves awake throughout the night. They didn't notice when we came in, and though they kept their eyes on the screens, they also chatted easily with one another.

"Fifty bucks says the Coast Guard finds the body ten miles behind us," the first guard said. "Anyone?"

"No way," said the second. "The killer would have had to go up at least three decks to dump the body. We would have seen them on the monitors."

The third guard glanced over his shoulder and noticed me and Clint standing there. He whipped his head back toward the monitors. "Shut up, guys. We're supposed to be working."

The other two guards caught on. They took their feet off the desk and scooted their chairs closer to the monitors for better viewing.

"Kiss-ass," the first one muttered to the third.

"At least he's not a regular ass." Clint knocked the first guard's shoulder in what was meant to be a playful way, but the guard gritted his teeth and rubbed the sore spot when Clint wasn't looking. "Get out of here, noobs. We have real work to do."

"But, sir," the third guard said. "Who's going to watch the monitors while we're gone?"

Clint shook the rolling chair out from under the

third guard's butt. "We've got it handled. Check in with the Captain. Ask her if there's anything she needs. If not, rotate through patrols with everyone else. I'll radio you when I need you back on the monitors."

The three guards left, stretching out their limbs as they went. Russo, Clint, and I took their seats. I got the third guard's. It was uncomfortably warm. Clint, like his men, kicked his feet up and rested his hands behind his head to watch the monitors.

"Russo," he said. "Bring up what we need."

Russo left most of the screens live. While he fiddled with the lower monitors to find the footage from the pool party, I scanned the hallways of the *Adventure.* Surprisingly, none of the guests had made attempts to escape their rooms. Every once in a while, one of them stepped out into the hallway to ask a security guard what was happening, but they were quickly directed back inside. I checked my watch. It wasn't quite midnight. On a normal night at sea, these people would be drinking, dancing, and enjoying the rest of their evening. I wondered how long the lines were going to be tomorrow morning at guest services to file complaints for tonight. Perhaps Emerald Cruises would give the cruisers a partial refund for the night the killer robbed them of.

"There!" Clint said as he pointed to the monitor Russo was manipulating. "I just saw her go into the pool. Back it up, Russo."

The three of us leaned in as Russo rewound the

footage and pushed play again. I squinted at the screen and tried to make sense of the mass of writhing bodies at the pool party. It was odd to watch people jump and dance without a soundtrack. They pumped their fists, spilled drinks over one another, and ground their hips against each other. Thank goodness the pool deck was off limits to kids after a certain time. Without warning, Christine's body fell from between two gyrating men in the crowd and splashed into the pool.

"Again." My eyes watered as I got even closer to the monitor. "I didn't see what happened."

Russo rewound and played it once more. This time, I tried to find Christine in the crowd before she fell, but with everyone moving around so much, it proved more difficult than I'd thought. The grainy footage was black and white, and the flashing dance lights didn't help either. It was hard to distinguish one person's facial features from the next. There were more than a few women Christine's age dancing, so it took me a minute to pinpoint her. At last, I spotted her face as she did a twirl and kept my eye on her for the remainder of the footage. She danced in and out of the people around her, occasionally disappearing behind taller guests. At no point did she seem to react to being stabbed, nor did she exhibit signs of blood loss. Her head bobbed along to the music until she fell into the pool.

"Again," I repeated.

"What exactly are you looking for?" Clint asked. "I told you we wouldn't be able to see anything."

"Again, Russo," I ordered. "Please."

Russo shrugged and did as asked. Clint heaved a sigh, leaned his chin on his fist, and watched the monitor with tired eyes. I studied Christine by the second and analyzed every frame of her movement.

"There!" I tapped the space bar to freeze the video. "Did you see that? She goes limp, but it's hard to tell because everyone thinks she's still dancing." I checked the time stamp on the video. "It's a minute before she falls into the pool. The killer has to be nearby. Rewind it again, Russo."

Clint knocked Russo's hand from the controls. "Wait!"

"Clint, this is the job," I said, frustrated that he kept interfering. "Sometimes, it means watching the same three minutes of security footage over and over again. Either get on board or get out because you're not helping."

"Shut up, Ryder," he growled. "I saw something." He pointed to another guest in the crowd. "This woman was dancing close to Christine. Thirty seconds later, she's halfway off the dance floor. Moving pretty quick too."

I peered at the frozen footage. "You can't see her face."

Clint took over Russo's job and rewound the footage. His index finger followed the other woman

175

next to Christine. "Watch. She's right next to her. Then —look!—Christine kind of jerks away from the woman, and she runs off."

On screen, the mystery woman cut through the crowd as easily as a silk ribbon and sprinted out of the camera's view. A few minutes later, Christine fell into the pool.

"It's something," I admitted. "Russo, do you have footage on where the woman ran off to?"

Russo scrolled through the files from that time stamp and opened a view from another camera. "Here we go. Deck Ten, inside hall midship. Looks like she ran into the bathroom, ma'am."

We watched as the woman sprinted across the hallway with her hand clasped over her mouth. Her body convulsed as she made it to the ladies' room.

"Crap," I muttered. "She's seasick, not a killer."

"Or maybe she got sick because she saw who stabbed Christine," Clint suggested. "You can't rule it out."

I leaned away from the monitors and massaged my watering eyes. "You're right. She was closest to Christine, and she fled the scene. We should question her as soon as possible. Russo, are you able to identify her?"

"If you give me a minute, ma'am."

Russo, it seemed, was a bit of a whiz with surveillance. He rewound the hallway footage and captured a still of the mystery woman right as she turned toward the camera. For a split-second, she looked right into the lens. Russo took a screenshot, cropped the picture, and dropped it into a facial recognition search program. The program scanned through every passenger's identification photo. Russo sat back as the pictures flashed by. After a minute, the program landed on a single photo, and the screen flashed three times to let Russo know the computer had found a match.

"Here we go." Russo clicked on the photo to bring up the woman's file. "Daniella Barrar. She's thirty-two. From Miami."

"Is she traveling with anyone?" I asked.

Russo sucked on his teeth as he clicked on Daniella's details. "Nope. Her file isn't connected to anyone else's. Looks like she's all alone."

I elbowed Clint. "What do you think? Retired or widowed?"

"Neither," Clint grunted. "It's weird."

I pushed my chair away from the desk. "Let's check it out."

"You're going now?" Russo said. "It's almost midnight."

"It's better to get interviews from witnesses as soon as possible," I told him. "Memory recall ruins hundreds of cases every year. Got a room number for me?"

Russo checked Daniella's file. "7031."

"Great," I said. "Right across the hall from me."

. . .

CLINT and I went down to Deck Seven together, but when we approached the door to stateroom 7031 and knocked, no one answered. We tried again. Still nothing. The Do Not Disturb sign swung from the doorknob.

"Miss Barrar?" I called through the door. "This is Detective Alex Ryder with the Tampa Bay Police Department. I'd like to talk to you about what you might have seen at the pool party on Deck Ten earlier?"

No answer.

"Do you have a universal key?" I asked Clint. "Or a battering ram?"

"Got a key."

As he pulled it from his belt and reached forward to scan it against Daniella's door pad, one of the security guards on the floor turned the corner and ran toward us.

"Boss, don't!" he said, knocking the key from Clint's hand. "You can't do that."

Clint glared at the young security guard. "You better have a damn good reason for laying hands on me, Tosh."

Tosh, whose security uniform looked several sizes too big for him, blushed and ducked to retrieve Clint's key card from the floor. "Sorry, sir, but you can't go in there."

"Why the hell not?" Clint bellowed.

"Because she's sick," Tosh whispered, as if to remind Clint that the guests behind the other cabin doors might be asleep. "She was exhibiting signs of the stomach flu. Nausea, vomiting, diarrhea—"

"I know what the symptoms of a stomach flu are, Tosh. What's your damn point?"

"Sir, protocol aboard the *Emerald Adventure* states that any guest exhibiting symptoms of a contagious issue like the stomach flu must be quarantined to their room until the symptoms have passed and a medical professional has cleared the guest to interact safely with others aboard the ship," Tosh reported in a robotic voice like he had memorized the manual for health safety word for word. "If you go in there, you risk exposing yourself to whatever she has. Then you could spread it to the rest of the ship. With all due respect, sir, I can't let you access that stateroom."

11

The insides of my eyelids glowed red and orange as the morning sun streamed into my stateroom from the verandah and laid across my face. I rolled over and hid beneath a pillow. I did not want to get up. Getting up meant facing the day. Getting up meant going back to a reality where I had been suspended from my job and was working without permission to solve a homicide case I was no longer assigned to. Getting up meant dealing with my problems. Then again, sleeping in wasn't the best solution either. Night terrors have haunted me for hours. My limbs shook as I yanked the sheets off my chest and took note of my rapid breathing. It had been another restless night.

"I don't give a damn about the ship's protocols," I remembered shouting at Tosh. "If she saw something at the scene, we have to talk to her."

I hammered on Daniella Barrar's door. From the other side, a handle squeaked and the terrible sound of someone heaving into a toilet met my ears. I withdrew from the cabin's entry and wiped my hands on the seat of my pants.

"He's right," Clint had grunted. "The ship has rules for a reason. We can't risk spreading a stomach flu around the ship."

"Fine." I fished a travel bottle of hand sanitizer out of my pocket and slathered it on. "But as soon as she's well, I want to speak with her."

We had called it a night after our failure to speak with Daniella. By the time I returned to my stateroom, it was two o'clock in the morning and the ship had sailed into utter darkness. No one told you just how black the sea was at night. I'd sat out on the verandah for an hour or so, wrapped in a blanket, and stared across the monochromatic horizon. A dark void—one the stars couldn't lighten despite their ferocity—stared back. When I couldn't handle it anymore, I'd gone inside to face the void of sleep.

I tossed the thick duvet off with a heavy sigh. My brain spun too fast for me to go back to sleep. I couldn't avoid the day any longer, so I crawled out of bed and stumbled into the bathroom. As I washed my hands, I examined myself in the mirror.

It didn't look good. I looked more like someone a cop might chase down rather than a cop myself. The bags under my eyes had deepened and left purple half-moons sunken into my cheeks. I'd slept on my hair funny, so it was frizzy and terrible on one side and slightly less frizzy and terrible on the other side. Worst of all, I'd injured myself again while riding out my night terrors. My forearms were covered in thin scratches, like a poltergeist had had its way with me while I slept.

I washed the scratches with soap and water. It would be impossible to hide them. I didn't have any long-sleeved shirts, and an extra layer would only guarantee heat stroke. I'd have to deal with it.

Once out of the bathroom, I glanced through the verandah doors and let out a little gasp. The *Adventure* had come to port in the cruise terminal at Nassau. The island and all its colors stretched out before me. The water was a stunning shade of perfect blue. The buildings were all yellow, pink, and orange pastels. Across the way, I spotted the unmistakable outline of the Atlantis resort. Once, as a teenager on the streets, I'd found a postcard in someone's garbage from Atlantis. Since then, one of my dreams was to be successful enough to stay there. Now, it seemed like the universe was mocking me yet again.

I got dressed and went to breakfast. The buffet-style dining room was practically dead, and the lines were non-existent, so I strolled up and loaded my plate with fresh, hot food. As I settled at a table on the outside deck to take advantage of Nassau's beautiful view and the warm breeze, I checked the time. It was half-past ten, and the majority of the cruise-goers had already gotten off the ship to explore the island. I'd slept in too much for investigative purposes. My head started spiraling again, but I shut it up with a huge bite of a Belgian waffle. I focused on the fluffy fried batter and tart blackberry glaze, clearing my mind of anything else. I couldn't go into this day with a cloud of anxiety and stress hanging over my head. I dialed Dominique's number. She was my go-to in a crisis, and I hadn't had time to call her yesterday evening.

"Must be some case, huh?" she answered. "You skipped our nightly call twice."

"I know, I'm sorry," I said, my mouth full of waffle. "You'll never believe what happened to me yesterday."

"Why does it sound like you're calling me from the moon?"

"Because I'm in the Bahamas, and the cell service here sucks."

"You're in the Bahamas?"

"That's what I'm trying to tell you." Between bites, I filled Dominique in on everything that had happened since the last time we spoke. "…so we couldn't speak to one of the main witnesses because of this dumb rule. Then again, I'm not keen on catching the stomach virus while I'm trapped on a cruise ship for the next four days, so maybe that was for the best. Anyway, that's all I got so far. I'm sorry I forgot to call you last night, but this shit show has been running my life lately."

Dominique gave a quiet sigh. "I cannot believe the messes you get yourself into."

"Life of a homicide detective."

"You need to be careful," she said. "How many people aboard the ship know you're investigating this?"

I stabbed a wayward blackberry and popped it in my mouth. "I'm not sure. The captain, Clint, and most of his security staff. A few of the guests maybe. Why?"

"Because the killer is on that ship," she answered. "If he or she finds out that you're not there for vacation, you're going to be in trouble. I don't want you to die, Alex."

A chill that had nothing to do with the sea breeze swept across my scalp and traveled down to my toes. "You worry too much. I'll be fine. This isn't my first rodeo."

"No, but it is the first time you've been trapped with your perp in a confined space," Dominique pointed out. "Don't be so blasé about this. Promise me you won't do anything stupid."

"When do I ever do anything stupid?"

"All the time," she shot back. "Come on, Alex. Don't you think you're getting in over your head? Your boss put you on probation for a reason. You're not supposed to be sticking your nose into this case anymore."

I stirred a packet of stevia into my black coffee and took a sip. "What am I supposed to do? Let it go? Let the killer do whatever she wants?"

"Turn it over to security," Dominique urged.

"Please, Alex. Do it for me. I don't want you to get hurt. You've always wanted to go to Atlantis, right? This is your chance. Forget about the case for a day and go enjoy yourself."

I gazed across the island at the orangey-pink resort. "You've got a point."

"I do," she insisted. "Please."

A glimmer of movement caught my eye through the window of the dining room, and I turned to see Clint at the waffle-making station. "Dominique, I gotta go. I promise to call when I can."

"Alex, don't be stupid—!"

I hung up and left the rest of my breakfast on the tray to rush inside. Clint leaned lazily on the counter as he instructed the kitchen worker who manned the waffle maker.

"Not too much chocolate sauce," he was saying. "Just enough for the taste."

"Hey, Clint?"

He groaned and let his elbow flop off the counter. "Damn it, Ryder. I was hoping to have a quiet morning. What do you want? Your investigation is on hold until everyone gets back on the ship, isn't it?"

"My investigations never go on hold," I replied. "I need to look at the security tapes from the pool party."

"Again?"

"It'll help me compile a list of witnesses and potential suspects."

Clint collected his waffle from the counter. "Fine.

Go up to the office and ask Russo to get you the tape. You can watch it in another room. Don't bother my guys. They've got work to do. You got that, Ryder?"

I gave him a double thumbs-up and strolled off.

"I'm going to enjoy my waffle!" he called after me. "I better not hear anything from you for at least an hour!"

Most of the security crew had gotten lucky and left the ship to enjoy the Bahamas with everyone else. The guys who had drawn the short straw stayed behind to monitor the guests who had decided Nassau wasn't for them. Russo didn't seem to mind that he was missing out on a perfect vacation spot. He provided me with a laptop, a quiet place to sit with a nice view of the ocean, and the tapes from last night.

"Let me know if you need anything else," he told me before returning to the surveillance room.

"If only Clint were so accommodating," I muttered to myself.

I took out my notebook—or stationary set—and pushed play on the first video. Last night, we'd been so focused on Christine's fall and Daniella Barrar's involvement that we hadn't picked out any other details. Hundreds of people attended the pool party. All I had to do was figure out which one of them stabbed Christine in the thigh. Easy peasy.

It took several additional viewings of the incident from different angles to identify all the people who had been close enough to harm Christine. I wasn't surprised to find Corrine Corral, LeeAnn Rhodes, and Gretchen Wagner on the dance floor. All of them held drinks in their hands as they danced adjacent to Christine. Any one of them could have stabbed her, but the video was too compromised by the other dancers to get a clear shot of the actual crime.

In additional to the Pelican Point women, Daniella Barrar, and Owen—the fair-haired man who claimed to know Christine—there was one other person who danced closed enough to get a shot in. I froze the footage and zoomed in for a look at his face. He was tall, muscular, and good-looking. He had curly hair, a strong jaw, and a nose with a bump in it, as if he had broken it once or twice. I took a screenshot, collected my notes, and carried the laptop into the surveillance booth.

"Need some help?" Russo asked when he saw me.

"Can you do another facial recognition search?" I set the laptop on his desk and pointed to the screenshot. "I need to figure out who this guy is. He was dancing with Christine for most of the evening."

"Let's see what I can do." He pulled up the photo on his own computer and ran the search. In less than a minute, the program found a match. "Looks like his name is Max Woods. He's thirty-eight. Passport says he was born in Seattle, but he's got a Florida address on his driver's license. He came aboard with a group of people."

"Did that group include a guy named Owen?"

Russo pulled up a picture of the group that had been taken in front of a paradise-y backdrop yesterday when everyone had boarded the ship. Max towered over everyone else in the back middle, sporting a huge grin as he hugged the people around him. Off to the side, Owen smiled half-heartedly at the camera, his arm looped through the woman's beside him.

"Owen O'Donnell," Russo confirmed. He pointed to the woman beside Owen. "And that's Christine. Not sure why the system says she boarded alone."

I'd been so focused on Max and Owen that I hadn't noticed Christine standing there. My heart sank as I examined the photo. Christine looked happy. This group of people was her family.

"Can you send this picture to me?" I asked Russo.

"Sure thing, Detective. You got a lead?"

"I've got a few." I wrote Max's name in my note-book, along with his details. "Hey, where does everyone go when they get off the ship here? I need to track some people down."

Russo cleared the facial recognition search from his screen and returned his attention to surveillance. "Depends on the guest. Most people with families either stay on board or go to the closest beach. That's Junkanoo, about a fifteen-minute walk west. But if you're looking for these guys, they probably went to Cabbage Beach near Atlantis. That's the most popular spot. Take a cab there. It's too far to walk."

· · ·

WITH RUSSO'S ADVICE, I disembarked and grabbed a cab from the port. Nassau was not so pretty on ground level. The grime and crime were more visible when you were driving through it. Locals sold overpriced tourist crap, like straw hats, neon shirts with inappropriate phrases on them, and shot glasses with Nassau, Bahamas decals that would probably wash off in the dishwasher anyway. Once the cab crossed the bridge to Paradise Island, it was less sketchy. The resorts took up most of the view. As we passed Atlantis, I longed to stop and explore the vacation spot of my dreams. Alas, I had a job to do, so I said nothing to the cab driver and we continued on.

Cabbage Beach was a secret find on the north side of Paradise Island with an unimpeded view of the ocean. As I tipped the driver, I spotted several guests of the *Adventure* right away. They laid out in the white sand, frolicked in the crystalline water, and frequented the nearest bar for frozen margaritas and piña coladas. I bought a day pass for Atlantis—it was the only way to take advantage of the resort's amenities—rented a chair, and slathered sunscreen across my face and body. I placed my chair in a high traffic area and scanned the beach. From here, I could keep an eye on almost everyone. I had a view of the beach, the bar, and the pathway between them. If any of my suspects were here, I'd spot them on their walk past me.

It wasn't long before I noticed Owen O'Donnell amongst a group of his friends. They shared a large canopy a little ways down the beach. Without his shirt, Owen looked skinny and pale. He had not rubbed his sunscreen in all the way, so his back and chest were decorated with white streaks. His group seemed in good spirits despite that one of their own had been murdered the night before. Then again, no one knew anything official about Christine. Maybe they all thought she'd stayed aboard the *Adventure.*

Another member of the group tossed a football at Owen. He fumbled the catch, and the football bounced away, knocking a full cup of beer across one of their bikini-clad friends. Owen laughed, apologized, and handed the woman a towel to mop up the spill. He looked like he was enjoying himself, but when everyone else turned away, a mournful expression replaced his delightful grin. My stomach flipped. The poor guy didn't deserve this.

I studied the group picture Russo had sent me. Max Woods was the only one not accounted for out of Owen's friends. I would have noticed him instantly due to his impressive height. His absence set off my bullshit radar. Where was he off to all on his own? I surveyed the beach, checking for Max's curly mop of hair. He was nowhere to be found.

"What are you up to, Max?" I doodled a caricature of Max next to his name alone with several bubbly question marks. Not a second later, I glanced up at the bar and found the tall, handsome man speaking to the bartender. "Oh, that's what."

I set my things down, covered them with my towel, and made my way to the bar. I sidled in next to Max and flagged down the bartender for the purpose of blending. Max easily had eighteen inches on me, and he was annoyingly attractive up close. His dark blue eyes shone out of his tan skin, and he smelled sweetly of coconut lotion.

"What'll you have?" the bartender asked me.

"Water, please."

"You're kidding."

Max leaned on his elbows to bring himself closer to my level. "Get her a water," he told the annoyed bartender. "Maybe she's sober."

"At least order a Coke," the bartender muttered as he filled my order.

I offered Max my hand. "Thanks for that. I'm Alex."

"Max." He smiled at me as he returned the handshake. He had a nice smile. And a nice handshake. His palms were warm and callused, like he did a lot of weightlifting. His boulder-like shoulders attested to that as well. "Don't worry about it."

"I'm not sober though," I said. "Just dehydrated."

The bartender returned with my water and four frozen drinks. He set them in front of Max, who picked them up and easily balanced two plastic cups in each massive hand.

"Drink all of that," Max advised, nodding at my water. "Avoid the headache, or worse, the passing out."

I hurried after him as he headed back toward his group. "Thanks for the advice. Do you travel often?"

"Not much nowadays, but I used to do some wave-chasing when I was younger." Every one of his strides was three of mine. When he stopped short, I almost ran right into him. "Why don't you just ask me whatever you want to ask, Officer?"

I planted my hands on my hips. "It's Detective. How'd you know I was a cop?"

Max chuckled. "It's pretty obvious. First of all, you're the only one wearing actual clothes out here. Second, you walk like you're got a gun on your hip even though you don't. Third, you didn't buy a drink even though you're not sober. You're clearly on the job."

"Detective Alex Ryder," I introduced myself. "You have some decent deductive skills yourself."

Max didn't fall for the compliment. "What's this about, Detective?"

"I'd like to talk to you about the events that happened last night," I told him. "Regarding Christine Sherry."

His charming smile fell. "What happened to Christine? She was in her cabin this morning."

"Did you see her?"

"No." The frozen drinks in Max's grasp were beginning to melt. "Owen said she'd had too much to drink last night and wanted to rest today. Why?"

I'd seen people play stupid before. Either Max was really good at it or he had no idea what had happened to Christine. "Max, I'm sorry. Christine is dead."

He stumbled backward, and a glob of strawberry-flavored ice washed over his hands. "No. She can't be. H-how?"

"That's what I'm trying to figure out," I said. "You were dancing with her at the pool party last night. Would you be able to answer some questions for me?"

Max shook his head. "I'm sorry. I have to get back to my group."

"Max, wait—"

"Some other time, Detective."

Max walked off, with less of a bounce in his step than before. When he returned to his group, he pasted on a smile and passed out the drinks. He didn't tell them about Christine. If he had, the group's attitude would have changed in an instant. They remained blissfully unaware, cheering as Max chugged a beer. After he wiped his mouth, Max's eyes landed on me. Subtly, he pointed to his group and shook his head. He didn't want me to tell them either.

I returned to my chair and took notes. Max Woods did not act like a man who suffered from a personality disorder. He was well-spoken and sure of himself. In the wake of the bad news, he had maintained his composure for the good of his group. As I watched them from afar, he appeared to lead the conversation. Everyone looked to Max with admiring eyes. The one exception was Owen, whose gaze kept wandering out to sea instead.

ABOUT AN HOUR LATER, I had a stroke of luck. The Pelican Point women—Corrine, Gretchen, and LeeAnn —emerged from the resort area and onto the beach. An attendant set up three lounge chairs for them a mere ten feet from where I was stationed. The women tipped the attendant and settled in with their drinks. As soon as they began speaking, their voices wafted across the beach to my ears.

"We have to talk about Jenn at some point," LeeAnn said as she sprayed tanning oil across her long legs. "We might as well get it out of the way before it ruins the rest of our cruise. Who do you think did it?"

"Do we have to talk about this?" Corrine asked. "It's so… distasteful."

"I agree," Gretchen added quickly. "I don't want to talk about Jenn. I don't even want to think about her."

LeeAnn passed the tanning oil to Corrine, who shook her head. "Aren't you ladies worried? Did you know that most planned homicides are committed by friends or family of the victim? Who did Jenn have bad blood with?"

Gretchen took a huge sip of her drink, swallowed it

too quickly, and coughed. Corrine smacked her on the back until she caught her breath.

"Everyone liked Jenn," Gretchen gasped, eyes streaming.

"Everyone except her husband," Corrine added nonchalantly. "Jenn was always talking about how much she thought he hated her. Maybe he did it."

"Alan would never!" Gretchen said. "I mean—I don't think he would do something like that. Marriage is messy, but that doesn't mean you kill your wife."

"What about a business partner?" LeeAnn nudged Corrine. "Didn't you get Jenn into the jewelry-selling business? What if she outsold one of your other ladies?"

Corrine plucked the umbrella out of her drink and tucked it behind her ears. "Jenn just started working for me before she died. She wouldn't have had time to make enough sales to cause drama like that. Besides, we might be competitive, but we're not killers. None of my girls would kill someone." She wagged her fingers. "They might break a nail."

A phone rang. Corrine and LeeAnn groaned as Gretchen dug through her purse.

"I'll be right back," Gretchen said, clutching the phone to her chest.

"Again?" Corrine asked. "Tell your husband to fuck off! We're on vacation."

Gretchen whispered half-hearted apologies as she backed away from her friends, tripping over the uneven sand. I kept an eye on her as she answered the phone and an immediate smile decorated her face.

I leaned toward Corrine and LeeAnn. "Excuse me, ladies? I'm so sorry to bother you, but I was wondering if I could borrow some sunscreen. I left mine on the ship. Do you mind?"

LeeAnn tossed me her bottle of tanning oil. SPF 5. "Have at it."

"Thanks." I spread the tanning oil on my thighs. "Where are you ladies from?"

"Florida," LeeAnn answered. "How about yourself?"

"Santa Fe," I lied easily. "I couldn't help but overhear your conversation. Did you say one of your friends was killed?"

Corrine lifted her sunglasses and studied my profile. "Wait a minute. I know you! You're that cop that broke into my house, interrogated my husband, and went through my things without a warrant! LeeAnn, don't tell her a thing."

"I'm a detective," I corrected her. "By the way, I didn't do any of those things. Your husband invited me inside *and* he gave me permission to search the house."

"My husband is an idiot," Corrine spat. "Don't mistake me for one. I spoke to your superior. She assured me you were thrown off this case. Did you *follow* me onto this ship?"

"Ma'am, I don't have to answer to you."

Corrine gathered her drink, her beach bag, and her chair and dragged her belongings to a space farther away from me. "Come on, LeeAnn. This woman is nuts. I didn't pay this much money for a cruise so I could be interrogated by a child."

LeeAnn stacked the other two chairs and carried them to Corrine's new spot. I gritted my teeth and tossed the tanning oil into the sand. So much for getting any information undercover. Apparently, I had to play hardball. A shadow crossed over me. It was LeeAnn, back to fetch the tanning oil

"You should probably back off," she advised me. "Corrine's favorite thing to do is sue people. Unless you want to ruin your career, I'd stop investigating her."

"I'm trying to do my job, Miss Rhodes."

LeeAnn smirked. "Yeah? So am I. Like I said, back off."

"*D*etective? Alex? *Alex!*"

I woke with a start to find Derek, the rookie cop, leaning over me with a concerned look on his face. My skin felt warm and crispy. My mouth was as dry as the sand beneath my feet. Sweat coated my entire body. When I looked around, I realized everyone on the beach was staring at me.

"What happened?" I asked Derek. "Did I fall asleep?"

"Yeah," he said, looking relieved that I had come to. "You were thrashing around and screaming. It looked like you were having some kind of fit. Are you okay?"

Panic pooled in the pit of my stomach. I had had a night terror in the middle of the day, in front of who knew how many witnesses. I pulled my lower lip between my teeth and bit down. The sharp pain forced me to focus and take note of everything around me.

"I'm fine," I told Derek. I started packing up my things.

"Are you sure?" he asked. "Because it didn't look like you were okay. Are you epileptic? Does this happen to you on a regular basis? Do you want me to get you some water? Detective, you shouldn't rush off. Let me—"

"Derek!" I shouted, yanking my towel out of his annoyingly helpful grasp. "I don't need you to take care of me. You blew me off today, remember? You said you'd help me out."

"I'm sorry," he said. "My girlfriend wanted to go to the beach."

Over Derek's shoulder, a pretty blonde woman in a pink bikini waited for him to finish his conversation with me. When I caught her eye, she made a gesture as if to say, *Well? Give me my boyfriend back.*

I shoved my towel into my beach bag. "Don't worry about it. Go have fun. You didn't come on this cruise to work."

"I don't mind helping out."

"Seriously, Derek. Your girlfriend's going to blow a gasket if you don't get back to frolicking soon."

Derek glanced at his girlfriend, who waved him toward the blue water. "Okay. If you're sure."

"I'm sure."

As he jogged off, I finished packing my things. It wasn't until I was halfway to the bar that I realized what was missing. I sprinted through the sand to catch up to Derek.

"Ugh, what now?" his girlfriend asked, kicking salt water across my shins. "You know he doesn't actually work for you, right?"

"My notes," I gasped. "Derek, did you see my notes when you came to wake me up? I wrote them in the ship's complimentary stationary."

Derek shielded his eyes from the sun as he scanned the beach. "No, Detective. I'm sorry, but I haven't seen them. Did you leave them on the ship accidentally?"

"No," I murmured and backed away from the happy couple. "No, I definitely had them here."

"Can I help you find them? Ow!" Derek flinched as his girlfriend smacked his bare abdomen. "What was that for, babe?"

"We're on vacation," she hissed.

"It's fine," I said. "Enjoy yourselves. I have to go."

Derek called after me, but his voice got lost in the breeze as I made my way up the beach. I wasn't naive enough to think my notes had blown away in the wind. The stationary book was heavy enough to weigh itself down in the sand. Someone had taken it, someone who wanted to know exactly where I was in my investigation.

As I hailed another cab to get back to the ship, my head spun in a way I knew wasn't good. The world blurred around me. Colors bled into each other like a melted painting. Conversations muddled together and became incomprehensible. My skin burned white hot. My face felt like it was on fire. My tongue felt heavy in my mouth. I fell into the cab.

"No," the cabbie said after one look at me. "I don't give rides to drunks. I hate vomit."

"I'm not going to vomit," I gasped. "Just get me back to the cruise terminal."

He glared at me through the rearview mirror. "Double charge if you puke in my car."

"Whatever. Deal."

He hit the gas and tore through the streets, as if hoping to make it to the port before I had the chance to vomit across his vehicle's upholstery. If I was actually drunk, his driving would have put me over the edge. But a panic attack was another thing entirely. I curled up in a ball on the back seat and clutched my knees to my chest. I squeezed my eyes shut and focused on my breathing. It came in short, purposeless gasps. It had been a few years since I'd hyperventilated like this, and I only knew one way to stop it. I dialed Sandy.

"Hello?" she answered.

"It's Alex," I rasped. "Please. I need help."

She went into emergency response mode. "Where are you? Are you safe?"

"Yes?"

"Do you have your medication?"

"No," I replied. "It's not with me."

"We're going to count breaths then, okay? You can do this, Alex. You can get through this."

"Okay."

"Are you with me?"

"Yes."

"Inhale," Sandy ordered.

I took a deep breath.

"One, two, three, four. Hold it!" she commanded.

I held my breath at the top of the count, making sure my diaphragm was participating in the exercise.

"Exhale," Sandy said. "One, two, three, four. Again."

We went through several rounds until my pulse evened out, my breath calmed, and my head stopped feeling like it was going to explode. A minute later, the cab jolted to a stop outside the cruise terminal.

"Get out," the cabbie commanded. "And leave a good tip!"

I smacked a couple of bills into his palm. "I didn't puke."

"So proud."

He drove off. I stumbled toward the *Adventure*.

"You still with me, Alex?" Sandy asked.

"Yes, I'm here."

"Do you want to tell me what triggered your attack?"

The *Adventure* looked miles away. I needed to rest. I sat on the edge of the dock and dangled my feet over the pretty blue water. "It's a long story, Sandy."

"I've got the time," she replied. "I don't have a patient for another hour."

I rested my head in my hands and stared into the

water, wishing I could dive into its depths and never resurface. "I'm an idiot. I did something stupid. I did a lot of stupid things."

"That's negative self-talk," Sandy pointed out. "Reframe your thinking and tell me what happened. Start at the beginning."

"Remember that case I told you about?" I filled Sandy in on everything that had happened since the last time I'd seen her in her office. She stayed quiet and let me blab on and on until the story was complete. "… but I fell asleep on the beach and had a night terror in front of everyone. They probably all think I'm crazy. That's not the worst of it though. Someone stole my notes."

Sandy waited a moment to make sure I was finished. "Let's back up," she said. "First, you need to acknowledge that your actions have been out of line. What you do directly affects the things that happen around you. You were suspended from this case, and you pursued it anyway."

"I get it," I said shortly. "I know I messed up, but how do I fix it?"

"That's for you to decide, not me," Sandy answered. "Though I do have a suggestion you're probably not going to like."

"I'll take anything I can get at this point."

"Call your lieutenant," Sandy advised. "Come clean to her about the mistakes you've made."

"I can't do that!"

"I said you wouldn't like it," she reminded me. "But I urge you to consider your mental health. You're going backward, Alex. You're entertaining harmful thoughts and behaviors. Sure, you may think you're doing your job, but you're purposely putting yourself in harm's way to solve this case even though it's no longer your responsibility. That says something about you."

"Yeah, that I want to catch this killer," I insisted. "Someone died on that cruise ship, and you expect me to what? Drop everything and let the security team handle it? They have no idea what they're doing!"

"They're trained to deal with these types of situations," Sandy countered. "As much as you may not want to believe it, they can handle this without you. Stop chasing ghosts, Alex. You're only hurting yourself, and you may be flushing your career down the toilet too. Is that what you want?"

I rubbed my fingers against the rough concrete beneath me, needing something real to feel under my touch. "No, I don't want that."

"I didn't think so," Sandy said. "Take my advice. Call the station. Come clean to the lieutenant. Yes, you'll be reprimanded. Yes, your probation might be extended. But in the end, it's important to take responsibility for the mistakes you've made. You'll feel better, and you'll learn something for next time."

The thought of telling Carter what had happened in the last two days scared me more than coming face to face with the killer. Still, I said, "Okay."

"Okay?"

"*Okay.*"

Sandy sighed into the phone. "Good luck, Alex. Get home safe. Oh, and I expect to see you in my office next Friday at two o'clock. I think it's best if we resume our regular appointments."

"Great."

I WAS one of the first people to return to the *Adventure*. Other than the families with small children who tired easily, everyone else was milking as much time on the beach as they possibly could. It was the perfect time to take advantage of the empty adult pool, the sauna, or the spa. While everyone was on shore, the ship was at its most peaceful. But I didn't feel like being in a public space, even if I was one of the few there. I returned to my suite, filled the tub with cold water, and submerged myself until my toes shriveled up.

When I got out, I wrapped myself in the complimentary fluffy white robe, grabbed a bottle of aloe vera, and curled up on the freshly-made bed. As I smeared cool, soothing gel across my pink skin, I dialed the station and put it on speakerphone. It rang and rang. With every passing second, my heartbeat quickened.

"Hello?" someone answered.

My entire body relaxed at the sound of the familiar voice. "Angela."

"Alex?" she said. "What the hell are you doing calling the regular station phone? What if Carter had picked up?"

"I was actually calling to come clean," I told her, "but thanks for stopping me from doing that."

"I didn't—"

"You answered," I interrupted. "That's a sign. How's everything going over there? Has Brock and his team made any headway on the case?"

Angela chuckled humorlessly. "Are you kidding me? Brock couldn't find his asshole without a map."

"Nothing new, then?"

"Not even a whisper of a lead," Angela replied. "Every time I see Carter, her head looks more and more likely to explode."

I peeled my robe off and rubbed aloe across my chest. "It's only been a day. How bad can it be?"

"Honestly, I'm surprised she hasn't reinstated you yet," Angela said. "Brock's driving her nuts. Anyway, how's it going with you?"

"Another body showed up."

Angela gasped, then I heard a quiet pop, as if she'd covered her mouth with her palm. "You're kidding me."

"Nope," I said. "Last night. Someone jabbed a woman in the femoral artery at the pool party then dumped her body before the Coast Guard could collect it."

"Holy shit," Angela muttered. "You think it's the same person? One of the Pelican Point women?"

I blew cool air across my chest to dry the aloe. "I don't know. This kill was different. Quick. No torture. The woman wasn't affiliated with our Pelican Point ladies, but she was young, blonde, and pretty. I can't rule them out."

"So all three are suspects now?" Angela asked. "Have you talked to them yet?"

"I tried today, but I screwed up," I said. "Corrine knows who I am. She won't give me anything."

"Suspicious," Angela said. "If she's innocent, she would have told you so."

"That's what I thought too. Something's going on there."

"What about the others?"

"Also weird," I replied. "Gretchen Wagner is glued to her phone. It sounds like she keeps ducking away from the rest of the group to take calls from her husband."

"Are you sure it's her husband?" Angela asked skeptically.

"Nope." I capped the aloe vera bottle and set it aside. "But I don't know who else it would be. LeeAnn gave weird vibes too. She warned me to stop investigating Corrine. That's a little pointed, don't you think?"

Angle hummed as if her brain was buffering. "I think you should stay with them. It's like you said. You can't assume this new murder is unrelated, and the Pelican Point women are definitely hiding something."

"I agree," I said. "But I have other suspects to deal with too. Do you have a Max Woods in the system?"

She gave a little huff. "Look, Alex. I want you to solve this case. I really do. But I'm not sure I can keep feeding you information. If Carter finds out, I'm dead in the water too. No pun intended."

"No, I get it." A twinge of annoyance pricked my skin, and it wasn't because of the sunburn. "You've got a baby on the way."

"You can't possibly blame this on Jess."

"That's not what I'm trying to do."

"Alex, I'm doing the best I can."

"I know," I insisted. "So am I. Forget I asked. I don't want to make you feel uncomfortable. Can you at least let me know if Brock finds anything? I need all the help I can get. By the way, my notes were stolen."

A crash echoed from the other end of the line.

"Angela?"

There was some static, then Angela said, "Sorry, I dropped the phone. Did you just say you lost your notes?"

"No, I said someone stole them," I repeated. "When I fell asleep on the beach."

She breathed in then blew quick, short breaths out.

"Are you doing birthing exercises?"

"It's calming," she shot back. "Are you telling me that the killer has your notes? That he or she walked right past you out in the open while you were on the beach?"

I tugged the robe tightly around my body and gave myself a hug. "Something like that."

"This is bad, Alex. Really bad."

"You think I don't know that?" I asked. "I'm doing the best I can, but I don't have any resources. I don't know where to go or what to do next."

"What would you do if this was happening at home?" Angela said. "If you ran into a dead end here at the station, what steps would you take to find a new angle?"

I brushed my wet hair out of my eyes. "I guess I would start from the beginning. Go over the information from the crime scene, interview all of my witnesses and potential suspects again, and then move from there."

"Then do it."

CLINT, as usual, was hanging out in the security office when I went to go look for him. He sat behind the desk in the surveillance room and studied the cameras with quiet concentration. The other guys chatted amiably and watched the screens as well, though they were less infatuated with the ship's inner workings than Clint was. When he caught sight of my reflection in the monitors, he gave an overdramatic groan.

"What now?" he growled.

"I need you to switch my dinner slot to early seating," I requested. "Most of my suspects go to the early dinner, and if I'm going to figure this case out, I need to be close to them at all times."

"Go to guest services."

"The early seating is full," I said. "Guest services won't switch my seat because they'd have to boot another table out."

"Then you're out of luck, I guess."

I planted my hands on the back of Clint's chair and spun the massive man around to face me. "You can ask guest services to change my seat. Say it's a matter of security."

Clint hardly had to lift his head to look me in the eye. "Is this going to make that much of a difference?"

"I'm at a dead end," I admitted. "Usually, I have a partner or a team to bounce ideas off of. Here, all I've got is you and a rookie cop whose girlfriend rightly wants to enjoy her vacation with him. Are we partners or not, Clint? I don't like playing these hot and cold games. Besides, I saw how closely you were watching the monitors. You want to catch the killer too. It's probably eating you alive that this happened right under your nose. How does this affect your reputation anyway? Does Emerald Cruises have a board to review circumstances like this? Because I'm pretty sure they'll declare you inept."

Clint glared at me as I concluded my speech. I hadn't said any of it to piss him off, but I needed him to find enough truth in my words to come completely to my side. To put his full faith in me. That was the only way we were going to crack this case.

He grabbed the receiver sitting on the desk and dialed a number. "Hey, Suze. It's Clint from Security. I need you to do me a favor. Can you switch a passenger's dinner assignment to the 6:30 seating please?" He twirled the phone cord between his meaty fingers. "Yes, I know it's full. I need you to boot someone so my guest has a place to sit. I wouldn't ask unless it was important. It's a matter of security."

"Ask her to put me near Corrine Corral's table," I hissed.

Clint waved at me to hush. "If possible, I need you to seat her next to Corrine Corral—"

"Not next to!" I protested. "She can't see me. She won't say anything if she knows I'm sitting right next to her."

Clint clenched his teeth. "I'm sorry, Suze. *Not* next to Corrine Corral. About two tables away. Yes, I know it's a very specific, last-minute request. I'll make up for it, I promise." To my utmost shock, Clint's cheeks flushed pink. He spun the chair around so I couldn't see his face and lowered his voice. "I can tell you all about it tonight."

The other security guys looked pointedly at one another then at me. I flashed them both a wide grin. So this was Clint's weak spot. He was hooking up with one of the guest services representatives.

"Thanks, Suze. I owe you one." He hung up, spun

back around, and spotted my shit-eating grin. "Wipe that smirk off your face. I got you what you wanted, didn't I? At personal cost!"

"Oh, Clint." I clapped my hand to my heart. "You big softie."

"Get out of my office."

DINNER WAS a business casual kind of affair, so I picked out the nicest golf polo out of the two I hadn't worn yet and pulled on a fresh pair of tan pants. When I checked to make sure I was presentable, I looked more like I was ready for a day on the green rather than dinner on a cruise ship. Hopefully, I didn't stand out enough for Corrine to notice me.

I checked the scratches on my arm. Now that my entire body was the same shade of light pink—thanks to my impromptu nap on the beach—the scratches were less noticeable. The shallow pink lines blended in with everything else. I dabbed on additional aloe vera to keep them from scarring. Then I collected the new stationary notebook I'd asked room service for and headed downstairs for dinner.

The assigned dining room that night was called Royal Dining, and it was appropriately designed to suit its name. Glittery gold paint coated hand-carved accents on every wall. Portraits of unnamed kings and queens lorded over the diners. The chairs were gold with purple velvet seats. The only things that didn't fit in were the tourists dressed in Hawaiian shirts, maxi dresses, sneakers, and wedges.

I'd underestimated the anarchy of dinner. Everyone showed up at once, so there was a huge line to get into the dining room. Once I made it inside, a host ushered me to my assigned table, where my head server and assistant servers bombarded me with questions about how I liked my meal.

"Water? Wine? Food allergies?"

"Water's fine," I reported to Glenn, the man who placed my napkin in my lap. "No food allergies."

I sat at my table alone with three empty seats. Two tables over, a host seated Corrine and LeeAnn. Gretchen was late. Corrine sat with her back to me, and I let myself relax. LeeAnn, I hoped, was less likely to notice me through the families that separated us. However, as the servers got down to business, I realized the problem with my plan. I couldn't hear a word of conversation from Corrine's table. The dining room was too loud.

"Ma'am?" Glenn waved a menu in my face. He'd been trying to get my attention for a good thirty seconds. "May I recommended the pecan-crusted trout and asparagus soup? They are both delicious."

"Sure, whatever." I set the menu aside. "Sounds great, Glenn. Hey, can you do me a favor?"

"Of course, miss. What is it?"

I jerked my head toward Corrine and LeeAnn. "Could you send a bottle of wine over to that table?"

"Certainly. What's the occasion?"

"It's the blonde woman's birthday," I lied. "She's my friend, and I want to surprise her with something special. Don't tell her it's from me though."

Glenn raised an eyebrow. "Right away, ma'am."

I kept an eye on Corrine's table, waiting until Glenn returned from the kitchen with the bottle of wine in hand. As he beelined for Corrine, I got up and slowly walked toward them, zeroing in on Corrine's purse hanging off the back of her chair.

Glenn offered the wine. Corrine and LeeAnn shared a pleased look of surprise. They weren't looking at me. I got closer. Close enough to grab the purse. I reached out. My fingers grazed the fake leather.

I didn't take it. The purse dropped to the floor as I made a quick U-turn and returned to my table. Another server picked up Corrine's purse and offered it to her. She thanked him profusely. She hadn't noticed it had fallen.

I plunked into my seat. If Sandy had seen me do that—stealing a suspect's property in the hopes of unearthing evidence—she would have set me straight. Forget Sandy. If Carter knew I'd done something like that, she would fire me for sure. Sandy was right. I was going too far.

As I watched Corrine's table, Gretchen finally turned up. Both Corrine and LeeAnn gave her crap for it, but they eventually made Gretchen sit down and try the wine I'd sent over. Gretchen set her phone on the table where she could see the caller ID if someone wanted to contact her.

I waved Glenn down on his way back from Corrine's table.

"They were very grateful for the bottle," he said, beaming.

"Great," I said. "Get me a bourbon."

13

*F*or the remainder of the meal, I checked my actions. I studied the group of women from afar but made no moves to disrupt or interfere with their meal. Instead, I focused the rest of my energy on enjoying my own meal. The pecan-crusted trout was delicious, but the asparagus soup tasted like boiled vegetables and parsley. Fortunately, Glenn was more than happy to replace it with the loaded baked potato soup instead.

By the time Glenn returned with the dessert menu, I was quite full and a little tipsy from the bourbon. Though Corrine and her cohorts occupied a small corner of my mind, the rest of me imagined what it would be like to experience this level of luxury with my own friends. When the bourbon really kicked in, I pretended that Dominique sat across from me. We laughed, drank, shared food, and reminisced on our day at the beach on Nassau. Gone from my head were thoughts of murder, missing notes, and snobby suspects.

Then a woman from another table stood up. Like so many of the women I'd encountered lately, alive or dead, she was blonde, attractive, and in her early thirties. I wouldn't have noticed her if Corrine's head hadn't snapped up to track the woman as she excused herself from her table. I watched as Corrine's eyes followed the woman's path out of the dining room.

"Don't do it," I muttered to Corrine. "Don't make me get up."

Corrine wiped her mouth, set her napkin aside, and made an apologetic hand gesture toward Gretchen and LeeAnn as she stood up. I hung my head, waited for Corrine to pass me, then slipped out of my seat and followed her.

Thankfully, the dining hall was too loud and busy for Corrine to notice me. The woman in front of Corrine didn't notice she was being followed either. I gave both of them a wide berth as the first woman led us out of the dining room and into the hallway beyond.

A wave of people emerged from the adjacent movie theater, and I lost sight of Corrine in the crowd. I pushed my way through and craned my neck to get a glimpse of her again. I looked too far ahead. It turned out she was right in front of me. I accidentally stepped on the heel of her shoe and pulled the strap off.

She stumbled and whirled around to look for the

culprit, but I ducked behind a family of five. Corrine fixed her shoe strap then quickened her pace to catch up with the woman she was following.

"Sorry about that," I said to the family I'd cut off. "Had a little too much wine."

I cut around them and caught up with Corrine. The first woman paused near the closest bathroom, caught sight of the massive line that wound from the door, and kept moving. As Corrine followed her—and I followed Corrine—the crowd thinned. I put more and more space between me and Corrine, hoping she wouldn't hear the sound of my footsteps against the plush carpet.

At long last, the woman arrived at another, less busy bathroom. I peeked out from behind a corner as she went in. When Corrine followed her inside, I ran across the corridor and pushed the door open an inch to spy on what was going on inside.

"I have something I think you'll like," Corrine was saying to the blonde woman.

I tensed as Corrine reached into her pocket. Her fingers enclosed around something long and cylindrical, like the hilt of a knife. My muscles tightened as I got ready to spring into the bathroom.

Corrine drew out a rolled-up catalog. My body went slack as she unfurled it and handed it to the blonde woman. It was one of the magazines for Corrine's jewelry company.

"I couldn't help but notice that beautiful piece

around your neck," Corrine said, admiring the blonde woman's emerald and diamond necklace. "I had to show you some of the things in my collection."

"Oh!" The woman took the magazine. "These are breathtaking."

"Aren't they?"

A hand wrapped itself around my wrist. I let the bathroom door snap shut and tried to pull free, but the person the hand was attached to wasn't having it. The bourbon swishing around in my head didn't help either. Before I knew it, I was pinned up against the wall with my hands behind my back.

"I told you to let it go," an aggravated voice whispered in my ear.

"LeeAnn?"

She released me. I pulled my cheek off the wall and rubbed my sore wrists. LeeAnn's cheeks were flushed, either from chasing me through the hallways or from something else.

"Do you know what you're doing?" I did my best to sound authoritative, but the bourbon kept my tongue loose and my words slow. "You're interfering with a homicide investigation. I could have you arrested."

"Oh, yeah?"

"Yeah."

LeeAnn stepped closer and forced me against the wall again with sheer intimidation tactics. She was taller and more muscular up close. She certainly wasn't built like the average housewife in Pelican Point.

"See, I don't think you could arrest me," she whispered. "Because I don't think you have privileges aboard this ship. If you made an arrest, you would have to inform your superior, who you're clearly disobeying. What's your story, Detective Ryder? Why are you this desperate to get close to Corrine?"

I turned my head and tried to avoid eye contact. "You don't know what you're talking about, and you're threatening a member of the police."

"I know exactly what I'm doing," LeeAnn said. "I warned you earlier today. Corrine isn't the person you're looking for. You got that? Focus your investigation somewhere else. Better yet, give up. You're not making the best impression, Ryder. Ask yourself this. When the *Adventure* docks in Tampa, what are you going to do? Where are you going to go?" She thumped her knuckles against the wall, close enough to my head to make me flinch. "Get out of here. If Corrine sees you followed her *again*, I'll make sure you regret it."

My pulse raced as I ducked under LeeAnn's defined bicep. The floor spun beneath my feet as I stumbled off. Was it the alcohol or was it another panic attack? Either way, I couldn't break down in front of a potential suspect, especially one with this much insight into my personal and professional problems. Without looking back to see if LeeAnn was watching, I jogged off.

． ． ．

An hour later, I ended up at one of the bars. I ordered a tall glass of water and stared into the bottom of the cup. Though I couldn't feel the ship's vibrations as it cut through the ocean, the water in front of me could. It rippled with the movement of the ship, mirroring the waves beneath us. I plunked a straw in and swirled it around.

"What are you drinking?" a deep voice asked. It belonged to a nice-looking man in his early forties. He was an inch or two taller than me, with a soft face and salt-and-pepper hair. Like me, he wore a golf shirt.

"Water," I answered.

"That's no good." He took the seat next to mine without asking if it was occupied and flagged down the bartender. "Let's get you something stronger. On me. What do you say?"

"No, thanks."

"Oh, come on," he said. "These ships are some of the best places to meet new people, right? You're on your own. I'm on my own. Get the picture?"

The bartender made his way over. "What'll be, folks?"

"Two vodka sodas," the man ordered. As the bartender filled the order, the man scooted his stool closer to mine. "I'm Charles. What's your name?"

"Not interested."

"That's a lovely name."

I edged away from him. His minty toothpaste

couldn't cover up his smelly breath. "Seriously, dude. Back off. I'm not in the mood."

Charles chuckled and lifted his hands in a gesture of innocence, but he didn't make any attempt to put space between us. "You're a hard one to make friends with. I'm just trying to be nice. You know, the seventies music trivia event starts up in five minutes. What do you say you and I take out the competition?"

"I wouldn't be much help." With a pointed look at his graying hair, I added, "Can't say I'm old enough to know much seventies music."

It was a complete lie. Growing up, I'd loved the seventies. I would kill at seventies music trivia, but this persistent asshat didn't need to know that. The subtle insult didn't go over his head. His upper lip curled up as the bartender returned with the drinks.

"I bought you a drink," Charles said.

"I didn't ask for one."

"You should be grateful I came over here at all," he spat. "You look like hell, did you know that? No other guy would ask to be friends with you."

"What a dream," I said.

He snorted hot air from his nose like an angry bull. Then he checked his attitude, pushed his hair back, and pasted on a smile. "Why don't we start over? Hi, I'm Charles. I'd really like to spend a nice evening with you. Nothing naughty. Just simple conversation."

"Hi, I'm still not interested. Get out of my face."

"Come on, honey." He moved in closer and slipped

his hand around my waist. "I promise you won't regret it. I'm a catch."

As soon as I felt his fingers squeeze my hip, I spun around and thrust the heel of my hand into his upper arm, near his bicep. Right away, his entire arm went limp. He grunted in pain.

"You stupid bitch," he growled under his breath. No one had noticed our exchange in the busy bar, and I had a feeling Charles wanted to keep it that way. "You could have said you didn't want to talk."

"I did," I reminded him. "Several times. By the way" —I pulled out my badge and angled it so the bar lights reflected into his eyes— "my name is Detective Alex Ryder. I'm close friends with the head of security on this ship. I think it's best if I alert him. Let him know that a guy named Charles is harassing women at the bar."

I reached for my phone. Charles tried to steady my hand but thought better of it. He winced as he cradled the arm I'd punched.

"There's no need to call security," he assured me. "I'm heading back to my stateroom anyway."

I put my phone away. "You better be telling the truth. I'll know if you end up at seventies music trivia instead. And if I see you talking to any other women aboard this ship, I'll make sure you're banned from booking a cruise with Emerald for the rest of your life."

Charles abandoned his drink and the barstool as he

raised his hands. This time, the gesture was genuine. "I'm out of your hair. I swear."

Charles disappeared, and I returned to the business of staring into my cup of water. A few moments later, Derek hopped onto Charles's vacant chair.

"I gotta say, that was impressive," he said, chuckling to himself. "I thought you were going to strangle that guy."

"Don't think I didn't consider it," I replied. "How was Nassau?"

"Fine. Are you going to drink that?"

I pushed the untouched vodka soda toward him.

"Honestly, I don't think I was made for this kind of vacation." Derek took a sip of the drink and shuddered. "Oh, God. That tastes like college."

"What do you mean you're not made for vacation?"

"No, *this* type," he said and spread his arms to indicate the rest of the ship. "I'm not cut out for relaxing day in and day out. Lying on the beach or by the pool for hours. Lying in the spa. Lying on the verandah. It's like *all* we've done for three days is lie down. I wanted to book some of the excursions, but Lindsey doesn't like them. We could go zip-lining or jet-skiing, but no, all she wants to do is tan." He shook his head, drained the rest of the drink, and shook the ice. "I don't get it."

"Where's Lindsey now?" I asked.

"Getting a massage," he answered. "I told her I was going to the gym to blow off steam."

"And you ended up at the bar?"

Derek waved at the bartender and pointed to his glass. "Actually, I was looking for you. What happened on the beach earlier was pretty intense. I wanted to make sure you were okay."

My face flushed as I remembered waking up on the beach in a complete panic. "I appreciate it, but I'm fine."

"Something else is going on with you, isn't it?"

I didn't answer. The bartender dropped off Derek's drink. He plucked the mint leaf garnish off the top and stuck it between his teeth.

"This is my second year as a rookie," he said. "I had to repeat my training program because of an incident."

I sat up a little straighter. "What kind of incident?"

"My training officer and I answered a call in a bad neighborhood." He swirled his drink but didn't taste it. "You probably already know that the south side of Chicago is infamous for drugs, gangs, and gunshots. Half the time, we don't engage, but someone had called in a GSW. For a child." His voice locked up, and he cleared his throat. "By the time we got there, the kid was mostly dead. She was four, maybe five? When I saw her, I knew she wouldn't make it to the hospital."

"What happened?" I asked gently.

"My training officer told me to leave her," Derek answered. "He said there was nothing we could do for her, and we needed to clear the area. I couldn't do it. She was still alive. I tried to stay with her, tried to convince her to keep fighting until we could get an ambulance. Next thing I knew, a group of gang members surrounded us out of nowhere. We both got shot. My training officer didn't survive. Neither did the little girl."

I nudged Derek's leg with mine. "I'm sorry that happened to you."

"Yeah, me too," he said. "After I recovered, I thought about quitting the force. Maybe I wasn't cut out for it if I couldn't make the right decisions in moments like that."

"What made you change your mind?"

He smiled sadly. "My training officer's mom heard that I quit. She came to my house to tell me I couldn't. She said I wasn't allowed because her son had worked too hard to make me a good cop for me to quit. She wanted me to go back to work."

"So you did?"

"I couldn't not," Derek said. "She had a point. I owed my training officer a debt. I had to honor his memory, go back to the force, and become the best cop possible. That's why I can't lay out in the sun all day while you're chasing a murderer. If you want help, I'm here for you."

I took in his earnest expression, the faint lines at the corners of his eyes that would deepen and lengthen as his career stretched on. He had the perfect cut out for a cop. All he had to do was fill in the middle with years of experience and that can-do positive attitude.

"You're a good kid." I patted his hand. "But I can't ask you to get involved with this case anymore."

His face scrunched up. "Why not?"

"Because I don't have the authority to bring you into this," I admitted. "I don't want you to get in trouble and jeopardize your career because I made a stupid mistake. I'm not your training officer. You don't owe me anything."

Derek scooted his stool closer to mine, but unlike with Charles, I didn't feel threatened or crowded. "Whatever happened to you that you're not telling me, I get it. I'm not offering to help because I feel like I owe you. I'm offering because it's the right thing to do. Whether you like it or not, I'm helping you find that killer."

A rush of gratitude flowed through me, but before I could thank Derek, the sound of glass breaking echoed through the bar. Everyone cheered and lifted their drinks. Across the room, one of the servers swept up the broken glass. No one noticed the actual cause for the disruption: a man and a woman struggling with each other in the corner. By the look of offense on her face, it had been her drink that fell, and *he* was at fault. As the woman headed to the bar to get another drink, the man grabbed her wrist to stop her. I caught a glimpse of his face.

It was Max Woods.

"I'll be right back," I told Derek.

I slipped off my stool and wound through the crowd. As I watched, the woman yanked out of Max's grasp. He let her go, but not without a verbal warning.

"Diane, come on," he called over the noise of the

crowd as she sauntered off. "You don't want to do this! Damn it—"

As Diane put more people between them, Max swore under his breath. I almost reached him, but a dancing couple stepped between us. By the time I made my way around them, Max was halfway to the exit of the bar.

"Who was that?" Derek asked. He'd followed me across the room. "One of your suspects?"

"Yeah," I said. "According to a source, he has borderline personality disorder. Apparently, he had a huge crush on our victim. I haven't gotten close enough to question him yet."

Derek stood on his toes to look over the crowded bar. "You could talk to that woman. She's ordering a drink."

Sure enough, Max's adversary had found an empty stool. She looked familiar, but I couldn't place her face. As I made my way over to her, Derek kept up.

"Hi," I said to the woman as she received a dirty martini from the bartender. "I'm Detective Alex Ryder. I've been working on a missing persons case, and your friend that broke your glass might have something to do with it. Do you mind answering a few questions about him?"

"He's *not* my friend." She stirred her martini with the decorative plastic sword, olive and all, but didn't take a sip. "He was way out of line. What do you want to know?"

I took out my pen and stationary set. "What's your name?"

"Diane Star."

"Thanks, Diane. Are you acquainted with that man? Max Woods?"

"Somewhat," she said. "We met on the first day of the cruise. He was cute enough, so we flirted for a little while, but I didn't want to get tied to one guy for five days. He didn't get the hint. He's been stalking me ever since we first talked and won't leave me alone."

I jotted this down in my notebook. "Did Max tell you anything about himself? Where he's from or who he's with?"

Diane waved her plastic sword around. "If I eat this olive, does it count as drinking the martini? Since it was in the glass?"

I regarded the airborne olive. "I'm not sure. Can you focus, please? Do you mind answering the question?"

"He's from Oregon," Diane said. "Likes to hike and surf. I don't know who he's here with, but I feel bad for them. Do you think his wife knows what he's doing?"

"Did he say he was married?"

"No, but he has a tan line where his wedding ring should be."

I wrote all of this down too. "Did he seem *off* to you in any way? Did you get the feeling that he was dangerous?"

Diane pushed her untouched drink away. "No, I

suppose not. His only crime is being annoying. Can I go now?"

"Sure," I said, disappointed. "You're not going to finish your drink?"

She pouted at the martini. "No, I don't think so."

"One more question." I closed my notebook with a snap. "Do you have any idea where Max would have gone?"

"The upper deck probably," Diane called over her shoulder. "He's a sucker for stargazing."

As Diane disappeared into the crowd, I pushed Derek into her empty seat. "You stay here," I ordered him. "I'm going to check the deck."

I TOOK the stairs two at a time. My quads burned as I reached the top deck. Max wasn't the only one who wanted to stargaze. The deck was crowded with couples enjoying the clear night and low light pollution. Since no one had gotten the chance to do so last night with the lockdown, double the amount of people populated the top deck. I scanned the top of the crowd, hoping Max's height would separate him from everyone else.

I spotted his head of curly hair in the middle of the deck and dove into the throng to go after him. He moved quickly for someone so lanky. People parted automatically for him, but the path Max carved closed off as I followed him. The crowd did not pay so much attention to me. I fought my way through with elbows and subtle shoves, keeping an eye on Max's lush hair the entire time.

My phone vibrated in the back pocket of my pants. I glanced down to get it out and answer it.

"Hello?"

"Hey! It's Dominique. I figured why wait for *you* to call *me* tonight, right?"

I'd lost Max. No matter which way I turned, I couldn't spot him anywhere. "You have terrible timing, Dom. Did you know that?"

"What do you mean?"

I gave up on chasing Max. It was too busy on the top deck to confront him properly anyway. This whole day had been a mess. All I wanted to do was go to bed. I found the closest elevator, got in, and pressed the button for Deck Seven. Thankfully, no one else was in the elevator. I sagged against the wall.

"Never mind," I said to Dominique. "Tell me something happy. How are your parents? Does your mom still do pottery making?"

Dominique's peal of laughter lifted a weight from my heart. "Yes, she does, though I don't think she's getting any better at it. She tried to make me a set of plates for the airstream."

"Oh, no. What happened?"

"Let's just say it didn't go well."

I chuckled. "And your dad?"

"He's good too," she said. "He plays softball with a

bunch of other old guys. He wants me to visit them to watch his tournament. What do you think? Should I come home?"

"To Florida?" I reached my room, flashed my keycard, and went inside. I put the phone on speaker and peeled off my shirt. "You should totally come home, but if you don't visit me, I'm going to be pissed."

She laughed. "I'm always with you, Alex. That's how I can tell something's bothering you. What is it?"

I kicked my pants into the corner of the room and fell onto the bed. The cool sheets felt blissful against my sunburned skin. "I'm thinking about quitting my job."

"What? No, you can't!"

"Why not?" I punched a pillow into shape and hugged it to my chest. "After I get home and come clean about all of this, Carter's going to fire me anyway. I might as well beat her to the punch."

"You can't quit," Dominique said. "I get it. You're upset with the way this case is evolving, but you can't give up."

"I can," I replied. "I just did. It's settled. I'm calling Carter tomorrow to confess."

"Sleep on it," Dominique implored. "You can do this, Alex. Come on. For me?"

"For you, huh? I'll think about it."

14

The following morning, I had room service deliver breakfast. While I sat out on the verandah and gazed at Emerald Cruises' private island, our last port before we returned to Florida, my phone remained inside. I didn't want to look at it or be reminded of what I said I'd do this morning. For a few minutes, I wanted to enjoy the peace of the blue skies, clear water, and towering palm trees blowing in the wind. The breeze tickled my scalp, and I closed my eyes to let it kiss across my skin. If I had a different career, I could actually use my vacation time to go on a cruise of my choosing. Maybe giving myself up to Carter wouldn't be such a terrible waste after all.

I remained on the verandah for as long as my brain allowed me to. After an hour or so, my thoughts turned on me. The relaxed mindset faded away as I engaged a different set of questions. If I gave up now, who would catch the *Adventure*'s killer? Who would free Dominique from the pain and anguish of the last eight years? Who would step up at the station to become the next decent homicide detective in our division? Then there was Carter herself. She was the closest thing I had to a mother figure, and though our relationship was more career-based than family, the last thing I wanted to do was disappoint her.

It didn't matter what I wanted to do. Either way, I was obligated to call Carter and report myself for insubordination. Then it would be her decision as to what to do with me. I went inside to find my phone. It was on the last legs of its battery. I'd intentionally forgotten to plug it in last night, hoping to postpone this moment. With heavy shoulders, I attached the charger and dialed Carter's number from my favorites list. I held my breath as the line rang.

"Ryder, this better be good," Carter answered without a hello. "We're up to our ears in it over here, and I don't have time to deal with you."

"I have to tell you something, Lieutenant."

Carter's office chair squeaked. "Lieutenant? You don't call me Lieutenant unless you want something or you're in hot water. Which one is it this time?"

"Both," I told her. "I need you to take me off suspension, and I need you to give me full privileges aboard the *Adventure*."

"What happened?" Carter asked.

"There was a situation on board," I explained in the

calmest tone I could muster. "A woman was killed on our first night at sea. Carter, she was murdered, and the FBI claimed it wasn't their jurisdiction. The ship's security team is at a loss. There's a killer on board, and no one's investigating it."

She was quiet for a beat. "Except you."

"What was that, Lieutenant? The line's kind of fuzzy. I'm afraid the service on the ship isn't that great—"

"You heard me," Carter said. "I know you, Alex. You can't resist a case like this. It's the reason you're in this mess to begin with. What have you found out so far?"

"That's it?" I stuttered. "No lecture on interfering with an investigation when I'm technically suspended from the force?"

"Ryder, you don't know when to shut up, do you?"

"Uh. No, ma'am. I guess not."

Carter sighed. "Listen, I can't rescind your suspension. I already reported your behavior. It's beyond my control."

I slumped against the fluffy bed pillows. "I understand, ma'am."

"*But,*" she went on, "as far as I'm concerned, I have no knowledge of what has transpired aboard that ship since the last time we spoke. For all I know, you've been the picture of obedience. Is that not the truth?"

I opened my mouth but didn't reply right away, unsure of what Carter was trying to tell me. She was a stickler for the rules and regulations. She thought standard operating procedure was on par with the Bible. Yet, she seemed to be implying that I should lie straight to her face—well, over the phone.

"Detective Ryder, are you still with me?"

"Yes, I'm here."

"What's the verdict then?" she asked in the same strict yet nonchalant tone as before. "Have you breached a code of ethics? Have you operated beyond your own moral standards? Think carefully before you answer, Detective."

I swallowed my nerves and squared my shoulders. "No, Lieutenant Carter. I have not."

"Great," Carter replied. "That saves me a ton of paperwork. I expect to see you in the office when you return from your little jaunt, Detective—aha!"

I jumped at the exclamation. "Lieutenant?"

"Angela Pennacchi. She's been helping you, hasn't she? That's why she's been so squirrely around me lately."

"Ma'am, I have no idea what you're talking about."

Carter laughed outright. "That's what *I'm* talking about. Oh, what have I gotten myself into? Good luck, Detective."

"Thank you, Lieutenant."

With another chuckle, Carter hung up on me. I stared at the home screen on my phone, completely blown away. Of all the ways that conversation could have gone, this was the least expected. If I read between the lines, it sounded like I had Carter's go ahead to continue my investigation.

A loud knock interrupted my thoughts.

"Detective? It's me, Derek. Are you in there?"

"Hang on a minute!"

I cast aside my white robe, quickly got dressed, and opened the door to find Derek in lime green swim shorts, a white T-shirt, and sunglasses on top of his head. I smirked at his ensemble.

"Got something for me, Officer?" I asked.

"Don't laugh at me. I was on my way to the beach with my girlfriend." He tugged on the hem of his shorts in an attempt to cover more of his muscular thighs. "You should have seen how pissed off she was when I told her I had to find you. I'm pretty sure she's going to break up with me when we get home."

"She won't," I promised. "You're doing the right thing. She'll see the good in that. What did you rush up here for?"

"Max Woods," Derek said. "The guy from the bar last night? Your suspect with borderline personality disorder? I found him. He didn't get off the ship today. He's in the fitness center."

My pulse skyrocketed. "Right now?"

"Yeah."

I grabbed my badge, my notebook, and my room key then pushed past Derek and into the hallway. "Go have fun with your girlfriend. I got this."

Derek stayed in step with me. "Are you sure? I did

some research on BPD. People with it can act irrationally and become violent. I think it would be good for you to have some backup."

At the elevators, I pushed the down button and shoved Derek in. "I've got it on my own. You'll thank me for this later when your girlfriend forgives you. My advice? Take her to a waterfall. Women love romantic waterfalls. There's gotta be a waterfall somewhere on this island, right?"

He tried to reply, but the elevator doors closed on him and cut off his response. I shook my head, smiled, and pushed the up button. Another elevator came to collect me, and I rode up a few floors. The fitness center and spa were on the same floor as the adult pool deck. When I walked in, the employee at the reception desk caught me in her customer service gaze.

"Welcome to the Emerald Spa and Fitness Center," she said. "Would you happen to be interested in one of our hot rock massages or a mud bath?"

"No, thanks. Just looking for the fitness center."

"Oh, are you looking to take one of our group classes?" She fanned out a collection of pamphlets. "We have yoga, spinning, a free fitness evaluation—"

I breezed past the reception desk and grabbed two pamphlets at random. "Excellent. These will come in handy. Thanks so much."

"If you have any questions, my name is Natalie!" she called after me.

The fitness center was, thankfully, easy to locate

without Natalie's help. The gym featured glass walls, so that the people passing by could admire the rows of treadmills, weight machines, and spin bikes inside. The opposite wall was also glass, giving gym goers a beautiful view of the private island. There weren't many people in the gym today. Most everyone had disembarked to enjoy the beach. However, a few fitness junkies took advantage of the quiet space, including Max Woods. He lifted free weights in the far corner of the center, wearing exercise shorts and a white cut-off muscle shirt that covered very little of his torso.

As I approached him, he began a set of bicep curls. He was soaked with a layer of sweat, but to my great relief, he smelled only of spicy deodorant and a slight musk. Still, I kept a relatively safe distance.

"You again," he huffed. "Are you here to tell me another one of my friends has died?"

"No," I said. "But I would like to speak to you about Christine."

He finished his set and switched arms, watching the muscle contract as he pulled the weight up toward his chest. "Is this going to help figure out who killed her?"

"That's what I'm hoping."

He set the weight down without finishing his set and mopped the sweat from his forehead with a white towel. "Let's go somewhere private."

Since I had no plans to be alone with a potential murderer, I led Max to the outdoor deck attached to the gym where people could relax and cool off between sets. There was no one out there, and the breeze would sweep our conversation out to sea. Max went to the water filter and filled two cups. He chugged one and offered the other to me.

"I'm good, thanks."

"It's important to stay hydrated. Take it."

"No, thank you," I said again, more strongly.

"Suit yourself." Max sipped from the second cup and took a seat in one of the chairs that faced the ocean. "So what do you want to know?"

I sat across from Max and propped my notes against my knee so he couldn't see what I was writing. "Where were you when Christine fell into the pool?"

"Dancing right next to her," he replied, "which is why I don't understand how this could have happened."

"You didn't see her fall into the pool?"

"No." He wiped his arms with the towel. "To be honest, I'd had a drink or two. I thought it would be okay to let my guard down, but I clearly made the wrong decision."

"You're telling me you were right next to Christine, but you didn't notice when she was harmed?" I clarified. "When she stopped dancing and started losing enough blood to bleed out?"

The lines in the corners of Max's eyes came together. "She bled out? What happened to her? You didn't tell me."

I studied Max's mournful expression and wondered whether or not it was genuine. "She was stabbed in the thigh. By the time anyone realized she was harmed, it was too late."

His blue eyes watered, and he glanced down to keep me from seeing it. "This is all my fault. This was such a huge mistake."

"What are you trying to say, Max?"

He flipped his hair out of his face and wiped his eyes with his towel. "I arranged this trip. I thought it would be good for the group. I thought they could handle it, but recovery doesn't stop, you know? There are too many triggers on a cruise. Too much drama. We're all confined in one space. If I hadn't encouraged Christine to come with us, she wouldn't be dead right now. God, I was only trying to do right by her."

I recalled my short interview with Owen on the night of the incident. "You're a part of a support group, correct? Can I ask what Christine was seeking support for?"

"I shouldn't say," he answered. "She might have passed, but it would have been her decision to share the nature of her troubles with you. Not mine."

"She can no longer make that decision," I reminded him gently, "and I need to get to the bottom of this."

Max pulled the towel between his fingers as if the rough, fluffy texture was a source of comfort. "She had depression. Big time. She's struggled since she was a teenager. Attempted suicide twice and made it out. But she made tremendous progress with the group. Sometimes, all you need is a few people who get what you're going through."

"She was suicidal?"

"*Was*," Max emphasized. "The last time she tried was when she was fifteen, and she never used a knife. It was sleeping pills the first time and antidepressants the second. What are you writing?"

I looked up from my notes. "I can't rule out the possibility that she did this to herself."

Max reached over and took my pen.

"Hey!"

"Just listen." He tapped the top of the pen to pull the ink cartridge back inside the shaft. "Christine would not have done this. You didn't see her on the dance floor before it happened. She was happy. I'd never seen her so happy. It was like she finally realized she had the ability to *be* happy. That's a huge step when you're recovering from depression. She wouldn't have thrown it all away."

He offered me the pen back. I accepted it.

"What about you?" I asked.

Max ran the towel through his damp hair. "What about me?"

"Why are you in the group?" I said. "What kind of troubles are you dealing with?"

"None."

"Oh, come on."

He took another sip of water and shrugged. "Okay, fine. Everyone has issues, but I don't discuss mine with the group. That's not my job. They know the basics. They know I'm not perfect or keeping secrets from them, and that's all that matters."

I leaned forward to study Max at a closer range. "Isn't the point of a support group to share and discuss your experiences with the other members? Otherwise, how are you supposed to make any improvements?"

Max's forehead wrinkled. "Hang on a minute. You think I'm a *member* of the group?"

"Aren't you?"

"No," he answered. "I'm in charge of it. Where exactly are you getting your information?"

I flipped back in my notes before I remembered that the original set—with Owen's details—had been stolen at the beach yesterday. "One of your group members contacted us the night of the incident to report Christine missing and help us identify the body. He said you had a crush on Christine, and that you might be dangerous because of your borderline personality disorder."

Max blinked at me. "You're kidding. No, don't answer that. I know you're not kidding. Damn it, Owen!" He slammed his fist on the railing, shook out his knuckles, and took a deep breath. "Detective, I'm sorry for making all of this so difficult on you. If I had known the extent of this on the first night, I would have done my best to clear things up as soon as possible."

"Clear *what* up exactly?"

Max reached into his gym bag and took out his wallet. "Here's my ID and the certification for my job. I'm a certified group therapist. I don't suffer from borderline personality disorder, though I do work with two individuals that do. Owen is one of them. He also happens to be a pathological liar. I assume he's who you spoke to that night?"

I checked Max's ID and credentials. "Kind of a skinny blond guy?"

"That's him." He put away his details. "I can't believe he knew about this before I did. That explains his behavior yesterday. What else did he tell you?"

"That you had unrequited crush on Christine."

"That's *him*," Max insisted. "It's one of the things we've discussed in our private sessions more than once. Owen was infatuated with Christine, and BPD makes it difficult to separate emotions from reality. Christine was too kind to push Owen away, but he mistook her kindness for affection. Each time she politely turned him down, he spiraled. Skipped private sessions and didn't show up for group work. Twice, I went to his house to make sure he was alive."

"Would this disorder make him want to hurt Christine out of revenge?"

"I'd like to say no," he answered, "but I'm not sure. BPD is complicated. It's usually born out of childhood abuse and abandonment issues. People like Owen lie and manipulate others, including the people they love, because they're terrified of being alone. I don't think

Owen's capable of murder, but if something happened between him and Christine at the pool party, and he reacted instinctively…" He trailed off and gazed out at the ocean. The color of the water near the horizon matched his thoughtful eyes. "I'm not sure, Detective. I'm not sure at all."

I updated my notes, taking down all of Max's statement. "What about that woman from the bar last night? Why were you harassing her?"

"Diane?" Max scoffed in disbelief. "Did she say I was harassing her? I was trying to get her away from the bar. She's an alcoholic."

Diane's unorthodox question about her martini olives floated to the front of my brain. "You were trying to stop her from drinking. That's why you knocked the glass out of her hand."

"That was an accident," Max said. "We were fighting over it, and I lost my grip. I left the bar to call her sponsor. By the time I got back, she was gone. Once again, my mistake. I shouldn't have brought her somewhere everyone was drinking."

"Sounds like you have a lot to think about."

"I thought my group was healthy enough to take a trip like this," he admitted. "I took precautions to keep my sober people away from temptation. The drinks I bought yesterday were all virgin cocktails."

I made the mistake of resting my hand on Max's veiny forearm to comfort him and tried not to grit my teeth as I made contact with his sticky skin. "Sometimes, we have to pull back and look at things from a broader perspective. Believe me, I've made a lot of mistakes lately too."

"I'm sure that's not true," he muttered.

"It is," I assured him. "But talking to you isn't one of them. Please, I have to know. Is there anyone in your group besides Owen that might be considered danger-ous? Anyone who had a connection to Christine or a reason to hurt her?"

"No," he answered. "Owen's the only one."

"Do you know where he is?"

"I gave them free time for the first half of the day," Max said. "We're meeting on the island for lunch then having an afternoon session on the beach."

"So he might already be on the island?"

Max hung his towel around his shoulders. "Yeah, but he's not much of an outdoorsy guy. I'd check the shops and indoor activity stations first."

"Thanks, Max."

"Detective? Who's going to notify Christine's family?"

"Generally, we take care of that."

He bowed his head. "If you don't mind, I'd like to be the one that tells them. They know me. They know how hard she was working to get better. I think it'll be less of a blow coming from me."

"Okay, Max. That shouldn't be a problem."

. . .

On my way out of the fitness center, I stopped by my room to change into something suitable for the island. I'd learned my lesson that a polo and long shorts were too hot for the beach yesterday. As I pulled on the black one piece and a pair of gym shorts, my phone rang. It was buried under a pile of dirty clothes and towels. I unearthed it and answered.

"Hello?"

"Did you tell Carter I was helping you?"

"Hi, Angela."

"Don't 'hi, Angela' me." Her voice was low and tight. "Carter dropped your file off on my desk this morning, gave me a look, and then walked away without a word. What the hell is that about?"

"What do you mean, she gave you a look?"

"You know, a look. The *look.* The Carter look."

"I'm not following."

Angela groaned. "Do you remember when we were all training together, and Jess screwed up that fake case we had to track? She contaminated the fingerprints or whatever?"

"Uh-huh. So?"

"Carter glared at Jess like she was going to murder her, BBQ the body, and serve Jess on hoagie rolls for the whole division to eat. *That's* the look."

"That seems excessive, Ang."

"You know what?" Angela said. "Don't come home. Because when you do, I'm going to kill you. Then

Carter's going to have another homicide on her hands, and I won't have the energy to pretend it wasn't me."

I chuckled and went into the bathroom to find the sunscreen and my beach bag. "Angela, you need to relax. Carter's cool with it."

"Cool with what? Your taboo investigation? Because that can't possibly be true."

"Well, she didn't exactly say she was cool with it," I admitted. "But she pretty much told me to keep doing what I'm doing. By the way, I didn't tell her you were helping me. She figured that out on her own. It's not my fault you can't keep a straight face."

"Is that why she gave me the file?"

"To help me? Yeah, probably."

"I'm flipping through it," she muttered. "God, this shit is crazy. You've been tracking this chick for eight years?"

"Ever since my first day on the job."

"No wonder you're nuts. This would make anyone lose their mind."

"Thanks a lot. Are you going to help me or not?"

Her computer keyboard clacked. "You got something new?"

"Give me everything you got on Owen O'Donnell. He should be local."

While Angela searched the database for Owen's information, I studied my body. The scratches from yesterday had scabbed over and were starting to heal already. The sunburn, on the other hand, was just beginning to bubble. In a couple of days, I was going to look like a peeled grape. I squeezed a dollop of sunscreen into my palms, rubbed it together, and coated myself in the white creamy paste.

"Got him," Angela said. "Owen O'Donnell. Thirty-one. He's been arrested twice."

"Details?"

"He started a bar brawl," she reported. "That was four years ago, so I'm not sure how relevant it is."

"Is the other arrest more recent?"

"Sure is," she said. "Last year, his mother called 911 and reported that he was trying to stop her from leaving the house. Her wrists were covered in bruises. Cops found O'Donnell locked in the basement. Apparently, he lived there for a few years."

"Do you have the mother's information on file?" I asked. "Can you bring her in and ask her if she knows anything about Owen's current state of mind?"

"No can do. She's dead."

"What? How? When?"

"Who, what, where?" Angela mocked. "Slow your roll, Alex. I'm working on it." More keyboard clicking. "Here we go. Mary O'Donnell. She was sixty-seven when she died of stage four metastatic melanoma earlier this year. She was diagnosed right before Owen was arrested."

"She was terminal," I muttered. "Max said people with borderline personality disorder struggle with abandonment issues. Is there any more information on Owen's arrest?"

"Who's *Max*?" Angela asked in sing-song.

"One of my witnesses," I replied firmly. "Can you answer the question?"

"I'm checking the arresting officer's notes," she said. "Apparently, Mary had just told Owen about her diagnosis when he threatened to keep her in the house. The doctors gave her six months to live."

"He couldn't take it," I said. "He knew his mother was leaving him."

"You think he killed his own mother?"

"No, I think he was trying to keep her safe," I answered. "But it doesn't mean he's in the clear. I gotta talk to him. Thanks, Angela. You're the best."

"Don't you forget it."

15

*W*ith beach bag in hand, I made my way down to Deck One to get off the boat. I hadn't been so low on the ship since the day Christine was murdered. As I passed the cabin we housed her body in before it was stolen, a chill washed over me. When the body disappeared, I'd stopped myself from thinking about it in an emotional sense. I didn't consider what we would tell the family or how they would put her to rest. I shut off that side of my brain and let the basics of investigation go to work instead. At that point, which person in my life was I trying to work for: Carter or Sandy?

"Good morning, Detective." Russo had pulled the short straw to work security at the gangplank. From what I'd gathered, patting down damp tourists and making sure they sanitized their hands before returning to the ship was not one of the more pleasant duties listed on the job description. "Any luck on your case so far?"

I swiped my keycard and handed Russo my ID. "Nothing concrete. Anything weird pop up on your surveillance cameras?"

"All quiet on the frontlines," he replied. "Are you sure it was a murder? Perhaps it was an accident."

"I'm pretty sure it wasn't an accident," I said. "No one stabs someone unintentionally. I think our killer's laying low. It's hard to get away with multiple homicides in such a small space. We'll catch up with them eventually."

Russo took off his hat and used it to fan himself. "For the sake of everyone on board, I hope that's true."

"Have you seen Clint lately?" I asked. "He hasn't reported to me in a while."

"Last I heard, the Captain had him working on a special project," he answered. "Top secret. He won't say a word about it."

I rolled my eyes. "That's super helpful. Thanks, Russo."

"Sure thing, Detective. Be careful out there."

THE SUN WAS SO bright that my sunglasses might as well have been for show. I stopped at one of the gift shops on the way toward the center of the island and bought a huge straw hat as well as a long-sleeved cover up with UV protective material. For all the time I'd spent in Florida, I'd never been this exposed to the sun before. I was always wearing a cop uniform or business casual detective wear. It occurred to me that I hadn't been to the beach once in eight years for pure pleasure. The only times I made it out to the shore were on assignments. No wonder I was suffering hardcore from sunburn.

I blanched as the gift shop attendant swiped my credit card. No doubt, my financial institute would flag the purchase as "suspicious" since I hadn't put a travel notice on my account. But when I walked outside, now protected from the sun's rays, I didn't regret it.

It was a long walk from the port to the accessible part of the beach. All of the shuttles were gone, and they wouldn't start up again until it was time for the cruisers to head back to the ship. I jogged along the pathway at a steady pace and reviewed the details of my conversation with Max in my head. Halfway there, one of the employees handed me a map of the island. I opened it up and studied it while I walked. According to Max, Owen wasn't likely to be at the family or adult beaches, but that didn't rule out many options. The small island sported plenty of shops, snack stands, event tents, and bars. Finding Owen might take all day.

The closer I got to the middle of the island, the busier it became. Kids ran here and there, often followed by a harried parent. People dragged inflatable rafts and tubes to and from the ocean. Others rented snorkeling gear or waited in line to sign up for one of the excursion options. I was pleased to see Derek and his girlfriend in the line for jet ski rentals. He caught my eye and waved me over.

"Well?" he prompted when I walked up to him. "Did you find Max Woods?"

"I did." I avoided his girlfriend's glare. "It wasn't him. Owen lied. He's the one with BPD."

Derek let out a low whistle. "Dang, what are you going to do?"

"I have to talk to Owen first," I said. "See if I can get a straight answer out of him."

"I can help," Derek offered.

His girlfriend stepped in front of him. "No, you certainly cannot." She faced me. "I'm sorry, Detective, but Derek is off duty. I didn't book this cruise so he could work a case the entire time. I worry about him enough at home. I don't need to worry about him on vacation too."

"I'm sorry," I said genuinely. "I don't mean to keep monopolizing him. Derek, it's fine. Enjoy the jet skis. If you happen to see Owen, let me know."

His girlfriend lifted a surprised eyebrow. "That was easy."

I smiled at her. "If I could take this day off, I would. You two have fun, but do me a huge favor? Be careful."

"Thanks," his girlfriend said. "We will."

As she rejoined the line for the jet skis, I pulled Derek out of her earshot. "I'm not kidding, Derek. Keep an eye on her."

Derek regarded his girlfriend with worried eyes. "She matches the killer's type, doesn't she?"

"She sure does," I said. "Between you helping me with this case and making sure nothing happens to her, I'd rather you keep her safe. Got it?"

He nodded firmly. "I won't leave her side."

"That's all she wants anyway."

I watched as he jogged to the line and put his arm around his girlfriend. She smiled and kissed his cheek. He smiled back, but when she looked away, he scanned the area with narrowed eyes, always on the watch for danger.

A little farther along, I spotted a bike rental place. The bike path led around the island to the adult side of the beach. Most of the guests without kids didn't stick around the busier parts of the island. I took a guess and figured the rest of Max's support group was probably on the quiet side. I approached the bike rental stand. Fifteen dollars for an hour.

"One, please," I said to the Bahamian woman working behind the counter. I handed over the appropriate bills. "What if I'm not back in an hour?"

"Don't worry about it, honey." Her thick accent washed over me like a refreshing pineapple slushie. "You're on island time now. The blue bikes work for your height. Have a nice time."

I thanked her, chose a light blue bike from the bamboo racks, and swung my leg over the seat. It took me a moment to remember how to ride it. I used my feet to shuffle forward. The front wheel wobbled as I gathered some speed and set my sandals on the pedals. Then my balance evened out, and I instinctively settled in to enjoy the ride.

The path to the adult beach was bordered by thick wild brush on both sides. The fat green leaves of tropical plants created a shadowy maze. Some people strayed off the main path to explore the other routes available. To my right, a rusty water tower climbed out of the foliage. Guests took the stairs to the top to admire the view of the island from above. I also spotted signs for a butterfly garden and historical statues. Part of me longed to ride by both of them. The bike ride was so enjoyable that I wanted to prolong my arrival at the adult beach. I reminded myself that I had a job to do, but that didn't stop me from turning onto the trail toward the butterfly garden. A quick ride-by wouldn't hurt.

The path grew narrow, and the leaves reached out to brush my arms. Twice, a strange bug landed on my arms. I brushed the first one away but left the second one to explore the fabric of my sleeve before it took its own leave. Not many people favored this route, and when I arrived at the garden, I understood why. The garden was overgrown. Tropical flowers grew in every direction, including in the way of the path, and butterflies were not the only insects to examine. It was less relaxing to swat mosquitoes, flies, and bees away from my face, so I turned my bike around and headed back the way I'd come.

A shadow darkened the pathway, and I glanced up to see that a storm cloud had rolled in. It hadn't been there when I'd left the ship, and the daily weather report hadn't mentioned rain either. A brisk wind made its way through the foliage and threatened to knock me off my bike. I pedaled faster and hoped my sandals wouldn't get caught in the wheel spokes.

Right as I emerged from the path to the butterfly garden, someone stepped out in front of me. I yanked the handlebars to swerve around the person, and the entire bike flipped over the front wheel. I flew through the air, hit the pavement, and skidded a good three feet. An involuntary groan found its way out of my mouth. Everything hurt.

"Oh, God! I'm so sorry!"

Smooth hands helped me to sit up. I took account of my injuries. My wrist ached from where I'd braced myself on the way down, and my entire right thigh was covered in stinging road rash. The skin was red, raw, and bleeding, but something else drew my attention. The hands that had helped me up sported bright pink nail polish, and the attached wrist displayed an ugly bracelet with orange jewels.

"Corrine?" I asked hoarsely. "Is that you?"

Corrine's face came into view as she lifted me from the ground and circled around me. She showed her palms in a gesture of innocence. "I swear I didn't do that on purpose, Detective. I saw you heading toward the butterfly garden, and I was hoping to catch you on your way out. I didn't expect you to exit so quickly."

With a poorly disguised wince, I brushed gravel and sand from the messy skin on my thigh. "It's my fault. I got a little claustrophobic in there. I shouldn't have been going so fast."

Corrine picked up my bike and straightened out the wheel. "I think there's a first aid tent on the adult beach. Can I help you get there?"

I studied Corrine's repentant expression. "Am I missing something here? Why would you want to help me? Last time we spoke, you were pretty upset with me."

"I still am," she said, mustering half-assed severity. "You completely invaded my privacy, and you took advantage of my husband's idiocy. It's not his fault he doesn't have any common sense."

I let out a laugh then clutched my stomach. "Oh, man. That hurts. I'm not above accepting help. Can you wheel the bike?"

Watching Corrine steer the bike in her flowing orange cover-up was an odd event indeed. She did it with obvious discomfort. I was several inches taller than her, so the bike was slightly too large for her to handle. Still, she pushed it the rest of the way to the adult beach and lifted it into the bike rack all on her own. Then she dusted her hands and checked to make sure her nails hadn't been damaged.

I spotted the first aid tent. "I can make it from here. Thanks."

"I'll walk you." She hurried to my side and cupped my elbow. "Just in case."

Corrine stayed with me as a member of the first aid team checked my wrist. Thankfully, it wasn't broken, only bruised, so they gave me a pack of ice to tend to it. Corrine continued her watch as the first aid member rinsed the huge wound on my leg, covered it with antiseptic, and bandaged it. By the time he was finished, my entire thigh was wrapped in gauze.

"That's quite a look," Corrine commented as she helped me to my feet. "Though I have a feeling you're no stranger to injuries in your line of work." She avoided the half-healed scratches on my arms as she escorted me to the bar and sat me at one of the umbrella-covered tables. "Want a drink?"

The frozen margarita mix spun in its machine, a lustful temptation, but I shook my head. "No, thank you. I'm on the job."

"Suit yourself." Corrine joined the line, bought a margarita and a soft pretzel, then returned to the table with her wares. She set a cup of water in front of me. "Drink that. You look like a cooked lobster."

"How flattering." As I sipped the water, I studied Corrine. She nursed her margarita, leaving lipstick stains on the white paper straw. Her gaze darted this way and that. "Where are your friends?"

"LeeAnn's on the beach," she replied. "And Gretchen went to the bathroom again."

"Does she have bladder issues?"

"Not that I know of. Why?"

I ripped of a piece of Corrine's pretzel, which she hadn't touched, and ate it. "She disappears a lot. In my line of work, that means she's hiding something."

The straw dropped from Corrine's lips. "You think so too?"

I leaned forward across the table and lowered my voice. "You were looking for me for a reason, weren't you? Do you want to talk?"

She avoided my steady gaze and stirred her drink.

"I'm a detective, Mrs. Corral," I said, reverting to the voice I reserved for witness interviews. "I can notice a change in behavior from a mile away. I can tell something's bothering you. You didn't knock me off my bike for fun."

"That was an accident."

"Sure it was," I joked. "Come on. Tell me. You'll feel a hundred times better once you get it off your chest."

Corrine placed a hand over her heart as if feeling the weight there. "I'm not admitting anything."

"I didn't think you were."

She tossed the straw into the garbage and chugged her margarita straight from the plastic cup, unaffected by brain freeze. With one more look around the bar area, she leaned closer to me and whispered, "I think Gretchen's hiding something too."

I slipped my hand into my pocket and pressed the record button on my phone. "What do you think she's hiding?"

"I'm not sure, but it might have something to do with Jenn Spitz," she replied. "Gretchen and Jenn weren't the best of friends. Sure, we all hung out every once in a while, but Gretchen didn't click with Jenn the way I did."

"Was Gretchen jealous of that?"

"That's what I thought at first too," Corrine said. "But when I asked Gretchen about it, she told me that wasn't the case. Still, it seemed like Gretchen always resented Jenn for something."

"Let's rewind," I said. "Do you think Gretchen had something to do with Jenn's death?"

She swirled the contents of her cup around. "I pray to God she didn't. I don't see Gretchen as a violent person, but the circumstances are strange."

"What circumstances?"

"You've seen it yourself," Corrine answered. "Gretchen's been acting like a psycho ever since Jenn's death. She paid an outrageous amount to get cell service aboard the ship, and I know for a fact she doesn't have that kind of money to blow."

"How do you know that?"

"I bought her ticket for this cruise because she claimed she couldn't afford it."

I pressed my lips together. I had a million questions for Corrine, but not all of them had to do with

Gretchen Wagner. A lot of them were about Corrine herself, but I didn't want to scare her off when she was finally giving me something to work with. Then again, I couldn't not take the risk.

"Can I ask why you booked this trip so suddenly?" I ventured. "I've never planned a cruise, but most people book cruises months ahead of time. That wasn't the case here, was it?"

Corrine raised an eyebrow, and I wondered if I'd gone too far. "It was a last-minute celebration, not a chance to run away if that's what you're asking. I made a major sale with my jewelry business, and I decided to treat my friends to a getaway. I bought two staterooms and four tickets, one each for me, Corrine, LeeAnn, and Jenn."

The information straightened my spine. "Jenn was supposed to come with you?"

"Yes, before she went and got herself murdered."

"Why?"

"Because she was my friend." Corrine's tone implied stupidity on my part. "And because she had had a hand in the jewelry sale. We'd just started working together, but Jenn was a natural."

"Gretchen and LeeAnn aren't though? You are working a pyramid scheme, aren't you? The whole point is to get as many people involved as possible."

Corrine wrinkled her nose. "I understand what you must think of my business, Detective Ryder, but I'm not like those bitties who sell essential oils and anti-aging products. I'm one of the most successful sales-women in my company, so I don't bring people on board all willy-nilly. I can't compromise my reputation like that."

"So Jenn was the only one you thought could handle it?"

"Yes, and I was right," she replied. "Why are we talking about this? I thought we were supposed to be talking about Gretchen."

"Fine. Go ahead. What else?"

The sun shifted, and Corrine adjusted her cover-up to reveal more of her thigh to the sky. "Like I said, she's been taking mysterious phone calls, disappearing on the hour, *and* she lied to us about where she was the morning of Jenn's death."

I latched on to that last detail like a spider to a gnat. "How do you know?"

"Because I was up early that morning," she said, "and I noticed Gretchen's car parked outside the Spitzs' house. It seemed odd, but I didn't think much of it. A few hours later, Alan called me with the news of Jenn's death. Then *I* called LeeAnn and Gretchen to make sure they were okay. Before I could ask Gretchen why she was at the Spitzs' house, she told me she had been at home all morning. I didn't press the matter."

I gave up on playing coy and fished my notebook out of my beach bag. I uncapped the pen with my teeth and started writing. "Can you think of any reason Gretchen would have wanted to murder Jenn?"

"Like I said, they weren't close." Corrine read upside down as I scribbled. "The only thing I can think of is that Gretchen was jealous of how quickly Jenn and I connected."

"What about the woman in the pool?" I questioned. "Christine Sherry? Did any of you know her personally?"

"I'd never seen that woman before in my life," Corrine answered. "I have no idea who could have killed her. I wouldn't peg that one on Gretchen though."

I tapped the pen against the page, thinking through everything. "What about LeeAnn?"

"What about her?"

"She threatened me," I told her. "After I followed you at dinner."

"You *followed* me?"

"I'm trying to solve a homicide here," I reminded her. "Anyway, LeeAnn warned me not to investigate you anymore. It's a ballsy move to threaten a detective. If I wanted, I could have her arrested when we return to Tampa."

Corrine finished off the rest of her margarita. "No, no. Please don't do that. LeeAnn may be abrasive, but she's a good woman. She's protective. That's all."

"How long have you known her?"

"She was one of the first people I met when I moved to Pelican Point," she replied. "She helped us move the refrigerator, and we've been friends ever since."

"You never got the feeling that she was aggressive or violent?"

The tequila began to sink in. Corrine's unusually perfect posture started to waver. "No, LeeAnn isn't like that. She's the most loyal friend I've ever had. What did you just write?"

I scooted the pad of stationary away from Corrine, but I wasn't quick enough. She slapped it away from me and squinted at my cramped handwriting.

"'LR covering for CC?'" She slid the notebook back to me with enough gusto to hurt. "LeeAnn is not covering for me! I didn't do anything wrong!"

Several pairs of eyes shifted in our direction. This conversation no longer felt private. As Corrine caved in to the tequila, she became less and less reliable.

"I have to explore every option," I told her in a quiet voice, hoping to bring things back to a undetectable level. "I'll do my best to clear your name, but I can't take your word for it. I need proof. You said you were out early that morning. Were you with someone? Someone who can vouch for your alibi?"

Corrine let out a small belch. "I'm not telling you anything else. This was a mistake. I don't know why I thought I could trust you."

"Corrine, wait—"

She swung her leg over the bench with some difficulty, stood up, and returned to the bar for another drink. While she wasn't looking, the bartender went light on the tequila. Corrine dropped a few dollars in the tip jar, grasped her fresh margarita with both hands, and stumbled off toward the beach. Once she was far enough ahead, I packed my things and limped after her.

LeeAnn, lounging in the sun, spotted Corrine and got up to help her. She kept a firm hand on Corrine's back as she helped settle Corrine on one of their reserved lounge chairs. As they chatted, Corrine pointed back to the bar. I dove into one of the swinging hammocks, nearly flipping myself over, right as LeeAnn peered in the direction of Corrine's accusatory finger. I peeked out of my hiding place and watched as LeeAnn scanned the bar for a glimpse of me. Thankfully, she came up short and returned her attention to Corrine and her fresh margarita.

"I think you've had enough," LeeAnn said, her voice floating on the ocean breeze. She confiscated Corrine's drink and set it aside. "Let Gretchen finish that one. If she ever comes out of the bathroom."

The bathrooms were right across from the bar. Gretchen should have done her business and returned by now, but there was no sign of her on the beach. I made sure LeeAnn wasn't looking then rolled out of the hammock and went into the bathroom.

"Gretchen?" I called, knocking on each stall door. "Hey, are you in here?"

Gretchen didn't answer, nor did I spot her sparkly beach sandals beneath any of the stall doors. As I made my way out, my phone rang.

"Hello?" I answered in a harried tone.

"Hey, it's me," said Dominique. "Did you do it?"

"Did I do what?"

She huffed impatiently. "Did you quit your job?"

"What? No, I didn't."

"Yes!"

I envisioned Dominique's triumphant fist pump as she cheered. "Don't get too excited. Carter didn't fire me, but my actions are still under review. Besides, I'm running around in circles on this case. I feel like a dog chasing its tail."

"You can do it," Dominique assured me. "I have faith in you. Talk it out with me. What are your next steps?"

"I've got two potential suspects," I told her. "Gretchen Wagner and this Owen guy, but it's proving difficult to pin either one of them down. They both keep disappearing."

"Maybe they're in it together?"

"Or I'm chasing two different killers," I said. "What are the chances that all the similarities between these murders are coincidences?"

Dominique clicked her tongue. "I'm not the detective here, Alex. All I can say is go with your gut."

I pulled my rented bike off the rack and started wheeling it toward the other side of the island. "My gut hasn't been the most reliable lately."

"Then go with what I'm telling you," Dominique offered.

I chuckled. "Did you suddenly nail a degree in crim-inology or something?"

"No." She vocalized the single word to a guitar medley. "But I know one thing. Your killer likes to show off. She wants to get your attention. Why don't you let her know that she has it?"

16

*A*fter I returned the bike, I limped along the regular beach to get back to the ship. Kids frolicked in the water, kept safe by neon-colored arm floaties and rafts. Their parents took turns supervising and snoozing on the beach. Almost everyone was sunburned or tanned. It was the last day of full activities on the shore. Tomorrow, the ship would spend the entire day at sea to return to the Port of Tampa. Though everyone was exhausted, the feeling of desperation hung in the air. It was vital to squeeze every ounce of relaxation out of the private island. Otherwise, the trip wasn't worth it.

A cold, wet hand grabbed mine. I jerked away then looked down to see a small tan child fresh from the sea and wearing a purple swimsuit patterned with goldfish at my side. She poked the bandage on my thigh.

"What happened to your leg?" she asked unabashedly. "Did you fall?"

"Yeah, off my bike." I kept walking, hoping to shake her off. I liked kids well enough, but not when I was in the middle of an investigation. "Always wear a helmet."

She toddled after me. "A helmet isn't going to help your leg."

"Where are your parents?" I asked. "Aren't they going to be worried about you?"

The little girl—maybe seven or eight years old—shrugged. "They went to the other beach."

"And left you alone?"

"No, I'm supposed to be with the group over there." She pointed to a little hut farther down the beach, where a gaggle of other kids her age were busy with arts and crafts projects. "But I got hot and wanted to go in the water."

I scooted her toward the hut. "You should get back. I'm sure someone there is looking for you."

She grabbed my hand. "Only if you come with me. You look lonely."

"I'm not lonely."

"Do you want a slushie? It's free for kids. I can get you one."

"No, thank you. Please let go. I have to work."

The little girl poked her tongue into her cheek. "Isn't everyone supposed to be on vacation right now? Mama told me that means she doesn't have to work."

"It's different for me."

"Are you lying?"

"No, I—"

She tightened her grasp on my hand. "Lying's bad. I'm not letting go. You have to come with me. If you don't, I'll scream."

I glared at her. "You're used to getting what you want, aren't you?"

"You'll thank me when you taste the slushie."

She dragged me along. When I resisted, the skin of my thigh burned, so I gave up and followed her across the beach and into the hut. As my eyes adjusted to the shady interior, the kid ran over to the slushie machine.

"Grape or strawberry?" she asked me.

"Strawberry."

The hut was full of about thirty kids split into groups of five. Each group was monitored by a cruise ship employee and a few parents that had wanted to stick around. The smaller kids kept to simple, safe tasks like coloring and building blocks. The older kids glued macaroni together and painted papier mâché masks in whatever colors they wanted.

"Hi!" Tammy, one of the employed babysitters, waved at me from her station. "Are you here to volunteer? We can always use more helping hands!" She wiggled her fingers at me, displaying a piece of macaroni fastened to each one.

"Uh, no," I stuttered. "I'm just passing through."

The last thing I needed was to get stuck gluing pasta

together. The kid returned to me with the half-melted cup of slushie. It was purple.

"I know you said you wanted strawberry, but it's not as good as the grape," she declared. She stuck out her sticky fingers for me to shake. "I'm Tala, by the way."

I shook her index finger, which looked least saturated with melted sugar. "Alex."

"Isn't that a boy's name?"

"Not always."

"Whatever." She hauled me toward the group of kids painting masks. "Sit down. I'll tell you what colors to use."

I resisted her grip. "Seriously, Tala. I've gotta go. I'm trying to track someone down—" I stopped dead when I spotted a familiar face amongst the other seven-year-olds. "Owen?"

He grinned and held up a half-painted mask. "What do you think, Detective? It's good, isn't it?"

He had decorated the mask in shades of black and gray. The way the brush strokes moved from the center of the mask outward made it look like the wearer was traveling through a hellish dark world.

"It's, uh, inspiring." I sat cross-legged beyond the circle of kids. Tala gave me a look of both surprise and delight as she handed me a clean white mask and a palette of colors. "What are you doing here, Owen? I thought you'd be on the adult beach with your friends."

He frowned, perhaps in concentration, as he drew a

thin white line with a detail brush across his mask. "I wasn't in the mood to hang out with them. This was easier."

I picked a pale beige for my base color, boring and safe, and slathered it on. "I've been wanting to talk to you. You lied to me before."

"I never lie."

"That's not what Max told me."

Owen's lip curled. "You spoke to Max? I told you. He has a disease. You'll never get the truth out of him."

"Cut the shit," I said.

Tala gasped, and the other kids followed suit. "Ooh, Alex! You said a bad word!"

"What's going on over there?" Tammy called as the kids tittered around me. "Is everything okay?"

I clapped my palm over Tala's mouth before she could reply. "Everything's fine. Thanks for checking in, Tammy." I addressed the kids in a lower voice. "Sorry, everyone. It won't happen again."

To prove I would behave, I rinsed my brush and swapped the beige paint for a shade of dark red and began outlining some details. Owen set his brush down and began blowing on his finished mask to dry it. He edged closer to me.

"Fine," he admitted. "I lied about Max. He doesn't have BPD."

"But you do," I said. "That must be a difficult diagnosis to contend with."

"Did Max tell you that?"

"No, my partner did," I replied. "She told me a lot of things about you."

Owen's sneer deepened. "You don't know anything about me."

"I know that you've gone through a lot." I swirled the red paint around the eye holes of the mask. "I know you've already been arrested twice. I know you've lost your mother, and you probably never knew your dad. I can relate to you on the parental matters, and I understand how those kinds of events can affect you."

"You do, huh? I doubt it."

"My mom dumped me in an alley," I confided to him. "I never met my father. So, yeah. I get it. The difference is that I don't let my past control my future."

Big, fat lie.

Owen seemed to take the bait though. His sneer dissipated, and the tension in his neck released a tiny bit. He tucked a grungy strand of blond hair behind his ear. I leaned in closer to create the illusion of privacy. All the while, I kept my focus on my paintbrush.

"What's the truth?" I asked in a low whisper. "What really happened that night at the pool party? Why did you tell me Max was the instigator in all of this?"

"I didn't do anything."

"I didn't say you did," I assured him.

He chewed on his lip, considering whether or not he wanted to talk to me. "I wanted to screw with Max, okay? Christine practically worshipped the guy. She never stopped talking about how he saved her life and how grateful she was that he invited her on this cruise. We're not allowed to have intimate relationships within the group, but Christine made it sound like she wasn't going to need us for much longer. Then she could be with Max and have a normal relationship. What is normal anyway? Was she trying to say that I'm *not* normal?"

"Focus, Owen," I said, sensing his spiral of negative thoughts. "You tried to frame Max for murder. That's no small revenge plot."

"He didn't deserve her," Owen growled. "It's his fault she died. He was the one who invited her on this cruise, even after I said she wasn't ready for it. I only came to watch out for Christine, but Max assigned us to different rooms and wouldn't leave us alone. He should be in jail for her death. *It's his fault.*"

Owen's hand shook with anger, and the kids were starting to overhear our conversation as he grew unable to control the volume of his voice. With my half-painted mask in hand, I guided Owen up from the floor and took him outside.

"I need you to let go of Max," I said. "Forget about him for a minute and tell me what happened on the pool deck. You were right by Christine before she was stabbed. You had to have seen or heard something."

Owen crossed his arms and stared across the ocean. The breeze whipped the hem of his shirt up, and I caught sight of several self-inflicted scars across his abdomen.

"If you don't give me something, I have to list you as a suspect," I told him. "I don't want to do that. I don't want to be the type of cop who automatically assumes the guy with a mental illness is the only one sick enough to commit a crime like this. Please don't make me that cop. Come on, Owen."

He scuffed his toes in the sand, drew a quick frowny face, then wiped it away. "You promise not to arrest me?"

"Do you promise to tell me the truth?"

"Yes."

"Then I won't arrest you," I agreed.

Owen sighed and dropped his arms from where they were crossed over his chest. "Right before she died, she was talking to some blonde chick. They looked alike. Pretty, petite, and perfect. I would have mistaken them for sisters if I didn't already know that Christine was an only child."

"Were they arguing?" I asked. "Did Christine seem hurt or distressed?"

"No," Owen answered. "They were laughing. I'd never been able to make Christine smile like that, and then some blonde woman comes around and gets her laughing in five minutes. I couldn't watch, so I looked away. When I looked back, Christine was in the pool."

"And that's the truth?"

Owen fished his pocket, drew out a stack of folded papers, and handed them to me. "That's the truth. I'm done lying. At least to you. Christine deserves better than a botched investigation."

I unfurled the papers. "You stole my notes."

"I have poor decision-making skills," he admitted. "If it makes you feel better, I didn't read them."

"I'm supposed to believe that?"

"It's true," he said. "I'm sorry."

I refolded the papers and shook them at him. "I *could* have you arrested now. You understand that, right?"

He smiled sadly. "As long as you find out what happened to Christine, I'd be okay with it. By the way, that's some mask. Got something on your mind, Detective?"

I lifted the mask to check my work. Absentmindedly, I'd painted a crown of red around the forehead. The wet paint dripped down the mask, much like fresh blood running down the face of a pale victim.

BACK ON THE SHIP, I reviewed the new information for my case. Unbeknownst to Owen, I'd recorded our conversation. I played it back multiple times, listening for an inflection in his voice or another hint that he might be lying again. Training told me not to trust a word that came out of his mouth. Instinct whispered something different. I believed Owen when he said he didn't kill Christine, but a belief wasn't enough to clear someone's name.

I listened to my discussion with Corrine and reviewed my notes next. No matter how convincing she sounded, something about her didn't sit right with me. Her sudden change in demeanor—from agitated and defensive to frightened and meek—reeked of suspicion. If she'd always known that Gretchen had lied about her alibi, why hadn't she reported it before? Why would she agree to take Gretchen on a private cruise if she suspected her friend had something to do with Jenn's death? Something didn't add up. I needed to find Gretchen Wagner.

With limited options, I returned to Corrine. By four o'clock, everyone was required to return to the ship, so at fifteen after, I knocked on the door of Corrine's stateroom. Hopefully, she'd be there to shower and clean up after the beach.

LeeAnn answered the door. She looked me up and down. "You've got to be kidding me. Didn't I tell you to get lost?"

"Telling a detective to get lost is kinda like asking a cockroach not to munch on Cheetos crumbs." I peered around her broad shoulders. "Is Corrine here?"

LeeAnn shifted to block my view of the room. "She's in the shower."

Behind her, the shower squeaked as someone shut the water off.

"Who's at the door, LeeAnn?" Corrine called from the bathroom.

I titled my head at LeeAnn. "Sounds like she's done now."

LeeAnn gritted her teeth. "It's the annoying detective, Corrine."

"Let her in!"

With a smirk, I stepped past LeeAnn. Their stateroom was smaller than mine, with one queen-sized bed, a pull-down cot, and a window to the sea instead of a full verandah. Corrine, wrapped in a towel, emerged from the stateroom.

"What is it?" she asked. "Did you find something new?"

"Actually, I was hoping you knew where Gretchen was," I said. "I need to speak with her, but she hasn't turned up."

Corrine massaged her wet hair with another towel. The platinum blonde locks fell around her shoulders. "She ditched us at the beach and came back to the ship early. Said she wasn't feeling well. Did you check her room?"

"Where's her room?"

"Right next to ours."

LeeAnn pounded on the door connecting the two suites. When no one answered, she popped it open. "Gretchen, you in here?"

No response came.

"Do you mind?" I asked Corrine, gesturing to Gretchen's room.

Corrine lifted her shoulders. "Whatever. I paid for it anyway."

LeeAnn glared at me as I stepped past her once again and made my way into Gretchen's stateroom. The lights were out, the shades drawn, and the bed made. Gretchen hadn't been here since the cleaning guys had come through sometime that morning. I checked the drawers. Gretchen's clothes were folded with obsessive precision. Not a thing was out of place.

On top of the desk, I found what I needed. A tiny card was propped up against the lamp. It was a reservation for the spa on the upper deck for 4:30.

"Gotcha," I muttered.

MUCH TO MY CHAGRIN, the spa employees wouldn't let me in without a day pass, so I shelled out a hundred and fifty bucks, changed into a white robe and sandals, and made my way in. It was a slow day. A few people lingered in the sauna or occupied the massage rooms, but the spa was mostly empty. I snuck through the different areas and pretended to be interested in the mud baths or stone massages. All the while, I searched for Gretchen.

I happened upon her in the Quiet Room, a small steam room reserved for silence and relaxation. She was the only one present. She sat upon a stone bench in the far corner, her head resting against the wall behind her. The soles of her feet were pink, like perhaps she'd been in the warm room for a few minutes too long. She kept her eyes closed as I entered. If she heard me come in, she made no indication of it.

"Gretchen Wagner?"

She flinched out of her reverie and peeled her eyes open. She put a finger to her lips and pointed to the sign above her. *Please no talking or noise-making in the Quiet Room.*

"There's no one else in here," I said. "I need to speak with you about Jenn Spitz."

Gretchen's lower lip trembled. "I have nothing to say about Jenn."

"Really?" I sat beside her. The stone warmed the back of my thighs to an uncomfortable degree. "Because your friend Corrine told me differently."

The worry lines around her eyes became more pronounced. "Why would you ask Corrine about me and Jenn?"

"She came to me actually," I said. "Apparently, you didn't get along well with Jenn. Is that true?

"I wouldn't say that exactly."

"Then what would you say?"

Corrine shifted in her seat. "I didn't know her as well. I'd never hung out with her until Corrine came into town. I knew Corrine first, but when she and Jenn met, Corrine barely had time for me."

"So you were jealous of Jenn for stealing Corrine?"

"No," she insisted. "I don't understand why you're asking me all these questions. I didn't do anything wrong, and I already gave the local police my statement on the day Jenn died."

The tape on my bandages began to peel off because of the moisture. I flattened them down to keep my raw skin covered. "What did you tell the police that day?"

"I told them the truth," Gretchen insisted. "I was at home during the time of Jenn's murder. I was asleep."

"Do you have proof? Can someone vouch for your alibi?"

"My boyfriend," she declared. "He was sleeping right next to me."

"He was asleep between the hours of 5:30 and 7:30 that morning?"

"Yes," Gretchen said confidently. "He was there the entire time."

I crossed my ankles to keep one butt cheek off the uncomfortably warm stone bench. "Then tell me this, Gretchen. If your boyfriend was asleep, how would he be able to vouch for your alibi?"

The color drained from Gretchen's cheeks, despite the steam room's warmth. "I don't—I have no idea what you're trying to do here, Detective, but I can assure you—"

"Where were you on the morning of Jenn Spitz's death?" I demanded.

"I was at home. I-I was sleeping. I s-swear—"

"You and I both know that's not true, Gretchen." I slid across the bench and closed in on her. "I'll give you one more chance, but before you answer, think about this. With the information and the evidence I have on you, you're my number one suspect for this case. Tell me the wrong thing, and I'll have to arrest you."

Gretchen's eyes widened. "You don't understand. What I've done—what I've been doing—it's despicable. It's unforgivable. If Jenn was alive, she would never speak to me again."

"Spit it out, Gretchen." I pulled a pair of handcuffs I'd hidden in the pocket of my robe and rattled them in her face. "Or you're heading straight to your stateroom to stay there for the rest of the cruise on house arrest."

"Okay, okay!" She held up her hands. "I'm having an affair with Alan Spitz!"

I lowered the handcuffs. "Go on."

"That's why I was at Jenn's house that morning," she continued breathlessly. "Alan called to tell me she'd left early. We hadn't been able to meet in a few days. I was missing him, so I drove over there. My boyfriend *was* asleep, and he has no idea about Alan. That's why he verified my alibi with the police. Please, Detective. I didn't kill Jenn. I'm only having sex with her husband."

I studied Gretchen's flushed cheeks and trembling fingers. "Who's been calling you so often on your cell phone?"

"Alan," she answered. "He's a mess. He can't handle the kids without Jenn. I thought it would be a good idea to go on this cruise and get away from everything for a while, but Alan needs my help. I'm trying to be a good person."

"I have to corroborate your story." With great relief, I removed myself from the heated bench. "Wait here. If you move, I'll take it as an admission of guilt."

I left Gretchen in the Quiet Room and returned to the lockers to fetch my notes and my phone. I wiped the sweat from my face before dialing Alan Spitz's cell number.

"Hello?" he answered in a groggy voice.

"Hi, Alan. It's Detective Ryder. Remember me?"

He cleared his throat and attempted to sound less hungover. "Yes, hi. I'm sorry. I'm a bit confused. Wasn't my wife's case reassigned to another detective?"

"Yes and no," I replied. "I have a question for you. At the time of your wife's death, were you with Gretchen Wagner?"

A pause. "Who?"

"Gretchen Wagner," I repeated and rolled my eyes. "She's one of your neighbors. Blonde. Thirties. About five foot two?"

"Detective," he said wearily. "A lot of my neighbors are blonde, thirty, and five foot two. I'm not sure which one is Gretchen Wagner. Do you need anything else from me? I have to make the kids' dinner."

"No, Alan. That'll be all. Have a nice evening."

Gretchen emerged from the Quiet Room as I was about to exit the locker area. I stalled in the doorway and watched as she checked up and down the hallway for a glimpse of me. When she didn't find me, she walked purposely toward the spa's exit.

"Gretchen Wagner!"

She broke into a run, and I sprinted after her. We careened through the spa doors, past the startled employees at the front desk, and into the busy hallway beyond. The robe tangled around my shins and the rough skin on my thigh stung, but I refused to let Gretchen get away from me. In front of at least ten people, I tackled her to the ground.

"Gretchen Wagner," I said, pinning her arms behind her back. "You are under arrest for the murder of Jenn Spitz."

The crowd gasped and parted as I handcuffed Gretchen and pulled her to her feet. Gretchen sobbed openly.

"I didn't do it," she cried. "I was with Alan the whole time."

"Oh, yeah? Then why doesn't he know your name?"

AFTER ESCORTING Gretchen back to her stateroom, I called security. Clint arrived shortly, with Russo in tow.

"I almost forgot about you," Clint said gruffly. "What's going on?"

I jabbed my thumb at Gretchen's door. "I made an arrest. She might have had something to do with the murder I'm following back home, but it seems doubtful that she killed Christine Sherry too. Either way, I need someone stationed outside this door twenty-four-seven until we make it back to Tampa."

"I can handle it for now," Russo said, taking up an easy watch stance beside me. "Relief in an hour or so, boss? Rotating schedule?"

"I'll put some guys on it." Clint patted my shoulder with his heavy hand and glanced down at my leg. It was bleeding through the gauze. "What the hell happened?"

"Hazards of the job."

"Go to first aid and get cleaned up," he ordered. "No one wants to see that."

I DIDN'T GO to first aid, tired of being stared at in the hallways. Instead, I returned to my room and called guest services to request new bandages and ointment. While I waited for the supplies to arrive, I called Angela to let her know I'd arrested Gretchen. She didn't answer her phone. Neither did Carter. I didn't have the balls to phone the station's general line, so I decided to try again later.

One of the room services attendants delivered the first aid materials. I tipped him and got to work. Beneath the wet, dirty bandages, my road rash had gone pink around the edges, the first sign of infection. I got in the shower and washed it with complimentary soap. It stung like a bitch, but at least it was clean. Afterward, I covered the entire rash in antibiotic cream and rewrapped it with a fresh layer of gauze.

I fell asleep sometime after that, succumbing to the exhaustion that had been creeping up on me for the past several days. For once, I slept without dreams, nightmares, or terrors. When I woke up, the sky was dark and the ship had begun chugging through the black water again. Gingerly, I pulled on a fresh pair of pants to hide the bandage and left my stateroom.

As I passed through the hallway, a number caught my eye. 7031. The stateroom across the hallway from mine. I hadn't seen anyone go in or out of it in all my time aboard the ship.

"Daniella Barrar," I murmured. "Still sick, are we?"

The name had flown off my radar after Clint's young security guard had scared us off with talk of E. coli and stomach flus. Since that night, I hadn't given the nauseous woman one ounce of thought. Maybe it was time to do so.

I knocked on her door. "Miss Barrar? Are you in there? It's Detective Ryder."

Unlike last time, when we could hear Daniella heaving her dinner into the toilet, no sounds came from the other side of the door. I knocked again for good measure, but it was no use.

"That's okay," I muttered to no one. "I can wait."

I sat against the wall and stretched my legs across the hallway. One way or another, I planned on meeting Daniella Barrar.

My body, on the other hand, had different plans. My nap earlier hadn't staved off my exhaustion completely. An hour into my post outside Daniella's door, my head drooped toward my chest. I dozed off.

I WOKE WITH A START. The lights were dimmed in the hallway, a sign that everyone else on the ship had returned to their rooms for the night. Hours had passed by without me noticing. I pushed myself to my feet with a groan and rubbed the sleep from my eyes. Once again, I knocked on Daniella's door. Only silence answered.

This was ridiculous. At some point during the evening, Daniella would have seen me waiting outside her door if she'd left her room. Any sane person would have woken me up and demanded to know what I was doing there. Either Daniella had died in her stateroom, or she hadn't returned to it in quite some time.

Determined to find her, I limped into the closest foyer and called for an elevator. I rode up to the top deck, intending to get to the security office. Since all else failed, I could have Clint search for Daniella on the security footage. But when I pushed on the door to get out to the pool deck, it didn't budge. They had been locked for the night.

"Shit," I muttered.

A creeping feeling skittered across my neck. The ship was so quiet and dark. The floor was lined with small LED lights to help workers see where they were going at night, but they didn't banish the strange shadows or the eerie sound of the ship's hull cutting through the waves. The lump in my throat began to grow. Something wasn't right.

I turned to go back to the elevator and stopped dead.

A woman stood at the top of the stairs. Her beautiful blonde hair flowed around her shoulders, shining in the darkness. In one hand, she held a switch knife with a red blade, but that wasn't the most alarming thing about her. No, the most alarming thing was that she was wearing the mask I'd painted at the children's hut hours earlier, with the paint that looked like blood running down her face.

We stood in silence. For how long, I couldn't tell. We stared at each other, her at the top of the stairs, me at the bottom. My heart thudded against my ribs. The lump in my throat grew to an impossible size. I struggled to breathe.

When she moved, her blonde hair fanned out like a cape behind her. For a second, I was too enraptured by the way the flaxen strands caught the light to react. Then I realized the speed at which the woman darted toward me. She took the steps three at a time.

My brain engaged. I bent down and yanked the carpet that covered the stairs, pulling the woman's feet out from under her. She caught herself on the railing, but her stumble gave me enough time to tear down the adjacent hallway.

The corridors of the ship were long and empty. You

could see from one end to the other without issue. There were no corners to hide behind. Nowhere to lose a woman with a knife chasing after you.

Her footsteps thundered behind me. I chanced a look over my shoulder and caught sight of that mask again. She was fast, gaining a half-step on me every other second.

I darted out of the hallway, pressed the button for the elevator, than ran down a flight of stairs and pressed the button again. The elevator, already halfway up to the next floor, paused to collect me. I ran in and hammered the button for my floor. It continued up instead of down.

"Damn it!"

The elevator dinged, and the doors opened.

The foyer was empty.

Heaving for breath, I peered left and right. The woman in the mask was nowhere in sight. My heart rate slowed as I pushed the button for my floor, and the elevator chugged downward. The doors opened on Deck Seven. I stepped out.

So did she. From the elevator opposite mine. I lifted my hands.

"Please," I said. "We can talk about this."

Though she wore a mask, I sensed her smile.

I screamed as she darted toward me and jabbed with the knife. Without thinking, I grabbed hold of the blade and twisted it away from my torso. The weapon's handle twisted free of her hand and thunked to the floor. She turned her head back and forth to search for it, her vision impaired by the mask. When she rotated toward me, I swung my right fist up into her rib cage, using both her momentum and mine to make the hit count. She grunted and doubled over.

I made a run for it, fleeing from the foyer and into the hallway. When I reached my room, I barricaded the door with the desk chair. Sweating, bleeding, and hyperventilating, I curled up in a ball and sank to the floor.

17

*I*f I slept at all that night, I couldn't remember it. Until dawn, I huddled beneath the lush linen covers on the bed and clutched a pillow to my chest while I watched the door and listened for any hint of an intruder. The minutes passed like hours, but no one knocked or passed by in the hallway at all. My eyelids drooped, and my body gave in to the slow rocking of the ship as it cruised across the sea.

Then it was morning, and the sun shone through the balcony doors to lay across my face like an impatient cat whining for its breakfast. I pressed my face into the pillows, unwilling to face the day. Had last night really happened? I rolled over to get my phone and dialed the first person who could make sense of all this.

"I hope you're calling to tell me you've figured

everything out," Sandy answered. "Because if I recall correctly, I gave you homework the last time we were on the phone together."

"Someone attacked me last night."

Sandy's sigh came through the phone as whooshing static. "Alex, we've been over this. It wasn't real. It was a night terror. It's borderline hallucinatory, and if you allow these nightmares to take precedence in your waking life, you won't ever see remission."

"No, Sandy. You don't understand." I opened and closed my palm repeatedly. "A blonde woman chased me through the corridors of the ship last night. She had a knife. She wore a mask."

"You're spiraling," Sandy warned. "Letting your thoughts get the better of you. Bring it back to reality, Alex. No one on the ship wants to attack you."

"Then explain the knife wound across my hand." I unfurled my palm again. It was sticky with dried blood. The cut wasn't too deep. I'd grabbed the blade at an odd angle that had saved me from cutting through the tendons. Still, it was there. "She tried to stab me. I defended myself, but next time, I might not be so lucky."

Therapists, like everyone else, had problems of their own. I presumed that people became therapists out of necessity. They'd gone through something, possibly gotten over it, and wanted to share their ways with others who couldn't dig themselves out of the hole on their own.

Therapists, like everyone else, had a tell. I'd noticed Sandy's right away. She cleared her throat in a specific manner, with a half-cough, half-scoff kind of noise at the back of her airway. She did it when she didn't like what she was hearing, to buy time to find something appropriate to say. When she cleared her throat, she gave off the vibe of wanting to shake sense into her patients. It was never a good sign.

"Do you remember what happened when you first came to me two years ago?" she began. "You'd dumped your former therapist because you thought he was a quack. Then, during one of your episodes, you punched a mirror because you thought your reflection was a demon. You sliced up your knuckles and broke your hand in three places."

I flexed the hand in question. The scars from that incident had faded to white. If you weren't looking for them, you would never have known they were there.

"This is different."

"Last time, you were strong enough to realize that you needed help," Sandy went on. "I implore you to find that strength again, Alex. One night, you may put yourself in a situation that you can't recover from."

I opened my mouth to argue, but something stalled me. The more I thought about last night, the more the details of the event slipped away. I couldn't remember what time it was when I'd awoken from my slumber outside Daniella Barrar's door or what floor I'd ridden the elevator to where the doors were locked or the shape of the woman standing at the top of the stairs. All I recalled was her blonde hair, the knife with the red blade, and the children's mask.

"Is anything coming back to you?" Sandy asked gently.

I kicked off the covers and walked into the main room. The chair I'd used to bar the door was in its original place near the desk. Not a thing was out of place, despite my tornado of action to get inside last night. Strangest of all, the mask rested on the dresser, right where I'd left it last.

I rubbed my head and tried to make sense of it all. The cut on my palm sent a jolt of discomfort through me. I went into the bathroom to wash it and found a complimentary Emerald Cruises razor with blood on the blade.

"None of this makes sense," I murmured, more to myself than to Sandy. "I was so sure everything that happened last night was real."

"That's how these things happen," Sandy replied softly. "That's why it's so important to take care of yourself. From the beginning, I was worried about what this case would do to you. That's why I asked you to give it up so many times. Am I overstepping in doing so? Possibly. But my biggest concern is your quality of life, Alex."

I rinsed my hands beneath the cool water and watched the dried blood swirl down the drain. "Thank you, Sandy. I'm sorry I haven't been listening to you. I understand. I really do."

"And yet," Sandy said, "you still won't take my advice, will you?"

"I'm sorry," I replied. "As long as I'm on this ship, I have a job to do. As soon as I get to shore, I promise I'll take a break from all of this. A real vacation. Preferably not one where I'm stuck on a boat with a murderer."

Sandy snorted. "Somehow, I doubt that."

"So little faith in me?"

"No, Alex," she said. "I have the utmost faith in you. I hope all goes well."

THOUGH THE CONDITION of my stateroom indicated last night's terrors had been nothing more than my own imagination betraying me, I had to make sure. My first order of business was heading up to the security office to speak to Clint.

"You look like shit," he observed when I walked in. He'd raided the breakfast buffet before his shift. A plate of food rested on the desk, from which he stacked eggs, bacon, and cheese onto a miniature biscuit to feed himself. Crumbs stuck to his mustache. "What the hell have you been doing all night? Beating your face against the wall?"

I caught sight of my visage in the reflection of the monitors and quickly looked away. Intense sleep deprivation often looked like alcoholism or drug addiction or any other number of ailments that spoke poorly of me. The bags beneath my eyes were so dark, it looked like someone had punched me over and over.

"Someone watches the monitors at night, right?" I asked, wiping moisture from my eyes. "This room is never unattended?"

"Yup." Clint squinted around my torso. "What happened to your hand?"

"That's what I'm trying to figure out," I said. "Who was on duty last night? Did they happen to see anything alarming?"

Clint spun around to check a clipboard hanging on the wall. "The kid was on duty last night. Tosh. His notes say everything went well, and he didn't contact me for help either. That generally means nothing out of the ordinary happened. Why?"

"Can you bring up the footage from the aft elevator foyer on Deck Ten?"

Clint rolled his chair closer to the deck and shook the mouse to wake up the computer. "What time?"

I clicked my tongue. I had no idea what time it was, only that it was the middle of the night. "Try around two o'clock."

Clint scanned through the footage at a faster rate than normal. We quickly burned through the two o'clock hour, then past three and four as well. At five in the morning, when the cruise employees woke up, unlocked the doors to the pool, and began their duties, Clint pressed pause on the security tapes.

"Well?" he prompted. "I don't see anything. Are you going to tell me what this is all about?"

I slumped into the other chair and let it roll me halfway across the office. "I had an incident last night."

"What kind of incident?"

I lifted my bandaged hand. "A nightmare kind of incident. I wanted to make sure it wasn't real."

Clint chewed slowly on a fresh biscuit. "Are you sure you're cut out for this? You're talking about what's real and what's not. That's a bit worrisome for a homicide detective."

"I'm out of my depth," I admitted. "Can I have a piece of bacon?"

He slid the whole plate toward me. "Bacon's not gonna fix what you got going on, honey."

"When do we arrive at port tomorrow?" I copied Clint's idea and fixed myself a small breakfast sandwich. "Early, right?"

"Five AM."

"And when does everyone disembark?"

"After breakfast," he answered. "Usually around eight o'clock. No later than nine. We gotta get the ship ready for the next batch of guests."

"Can people leave earlier?"

"Sure, if they want to," Clint said. "You can request an early disembarkation at guest services, but you have to carry your own bags off the boat. No luggage service."

"That's fine. I don't need it." I mustered a wry grin. "I didn't get on with luggage, remember?"

Clint's chuckle made his belly bounce. "Was it only four days ago we met? Feels like it's been years."

"It sure has," I muttered.

He plucked a burned sausage off the plate and munched on it like a candy bar while he returned his attention to the monitors. Before he switched back to the live feed, a shadow in the right corner of the screen caught his eye.

"Wait a minute."

He rewound the tape. The picture was of the staircase between Deck Ten and Eleven. A figure was crouched on the stairs, waiting for something. Or someone. A minute later, the toe of my foot entered the frame of the elevator foyer. Then it disappeared, as did the figure on the stairs.

"This footage has been looped," Clint growled, rewinding the tapes again to get a better look. Once more, my foot stepped in and vanished, like I was no more than a ghost. "Someone's messed with our security system."

My pulse raced as I leaned over Clint's shoulder for a better look. "Can you get a better picture of the person on the stairs?"

Clint combed every angle for another glimpse, but each tape had been scrubbed and looped over to make it look like nothing had happened last night. We only had the one angle that showed the figure from the back for a brief moment. Clint paused the footage once more and zoomed in.

"Looks like a woman," Clint observed. "Relatively small. Look at the shoulders and waist. She's petite. Long hair—what's that?"

He pointed to a thin line around the back of the woman's head.

I bit my lip, hard, to make sure I was awake. "It's holding the mask on."

My phone rang, startling both me and Clint. I answered hurriedly.

"Yeah?"

"It's Angela." Her voice was terse. "I've got something for you."

"Hit me with it."

"Alan Spitz showed up at the station last night," Angela said. "He was drunk again. He admitted to having an affair with Gretchen Wagner. Apparently, she was at his house the morning Jenn was killed. He even brought in security footage to prove it."

I sagged in my chair and squeezed the bridge of my nose. "That makes sense."

"Does it?" Angela said. "I figured you'd be pissed you lost another lead."

"It resolves one of my problems."

"What problem?"

I picked at the bandage on my palm. "I was attacked by a blonde woman last night, but I put Gretchen on house arrest yesterday. She was in her room all night, so it couldn't have been her."

Vigorous tapping echoed through the phone, like Angela was jostling her foot up and down beneath her desk. "You were attacked?"

"It's fine. I got away."

"Yeah, but you know what this means, right?"

"No, what?"

Angela's voice trembled. "It's the same killer. It's one case. She murdered Jenn *and* Christine. Alex, she followed you onto the *Adventure*."

I swallowed hard. "Or she was already on it to begin with."

THE LAST DAY at sea was a melancholy one. Though the guests attempted to enjoy their final day of vacation, a dreary pall hung over the ship. The weather didn't help either. Instead of sunshine, we sailed into an overcast day of gray skies and dark clouds. The forecasted storm never emerged, but a steady drizzle kept everyone but the most determined from enjoying the various pools.

For most of the day, I followed Sandy's advice. I made sure Clint and the rest of his team were on high alert and stayed in my stateroom. I went over the evidence and notes I already had, reading and rereading until my vision blurred. At lunch time, I ordered room service and requested that the person who delivered it be a brunette. When it arrived, I checked the peephole before allowing the employee entrance to my stateroom.

I changed the gauze on my thigh. The wound had crusted over. Each time I moved, the fragile scabs cracked and oozed. The cut on my hand was no better. I couldn't hold a pen without bleeding through the bandages. My sunburn had finally begun to peel, resulting in a layer of flaky white skin across my entire body. All in all, I had never looked worse for wear, and that included the time I thrust my fist through a mirror.

As the day wore on, I listened to the recordings of my interviews with suspects and witnesses. I gleaned no new information. Everyone spoke so surely of themselves when they claimed they had nothing to do with Jenn's or Christine's deaths. Usually, I was quick to catch a liar. A hitch in someone's voice or an involuntary tic gave a lot away, but not one of my recordings made me doubt someone's story.

By that evening, I had grown weary of my self-imposed detention. I joined everyone else for dinner in the assigned dining hall. In such a crowd, the killer would never dare to show her face. I felt safe enough as the throng jostled me along. Then I remembered that Christine had been murdered among hundreds of other people, and my ribs clamped around my lungs.

I sat alone at my table. Several people had skipped dinner, preferring to order room service and make the most of their last few waking hours aboard the *Adventure*. Gretchen caught my eye as she sat across from LeeAnn, then quickly looked away. Earlier, I'd ordered Clint's guards to stand down and let Gretchen out of her room. She hadn't been confined for that long, but her contempt for me radiated across the busy dining area. In some way, I'd always known Gretchen wasn't the killer. She didn't have the stones for murder. Besides, the woman who'd chased after me last night had had a lightness of foot that Gretchen didn't.

As dinner began, I let my mind rest and focused on my food. The menus aboard the *Adventure* were exquisite, and I'd hardly taken advantage of them. I ordered a stuffed baked potato soup to start with, a wedge salad with giant chunks of gorgonzola, and the pecan-crusted trout. Halfway through my main dish, I looked up to see that Corrine Corral had never joined her two friends for dinner.

The fish turned in my stomach. Something didn't feel right. I wiped my mouth, abandoned the food, and approached Gretchen and LeeAnn's table.

"You better be here to offer me an apology," Gretchen spat, trying and failing to sound intimidating. "Otherwise, you can keep moving."

"Where's Corrine?"

LeeAnn viciously stabbed a piece of filet mignon. "You don't know when to quit, do you? Face it, Detective. You're on all the wrong paths."

I planted my palm between LeeAnn and her plate,

leaned forward, and said in a low voice, "Tell me where she is or I'll arrest you for obstruction of justice. I'm not stupid, LeeAnn. I know your secret."

It was a huge bluff, but with the way she'd been acting since I first met her, LeeAnn had to be hiding something. Her face paled, and she turned away to avoid the scent of pecans and baked potato on my breath.

"She's in the room," LeeAnn said. "She said she was too tired for dinner. Now get out of my face, Detective, or you'll find out how much you've inconvenienced that secret of mine."

Something told me LeeAnn was bluffing too, so I didn't take the bait. LeeAnn had never been a suspect in this case purely because of her complexion, but if I didn't already know my murderer was pale and blonde, I would have arrested LeeAnn on the spot.

CORRINE WAS NOT in her room despite LeeAnn's report. I knocked loudly several times without a reply. The sourness in my stomach intensified as I began to roam the ship in search for her. I checked the bars first, then the pool parties, and finally the spa and gym areas. She was nowhere to be found. As I crossed the top deck again, Derek waved at me from the other end of the crowd. I waved back, and he frantically beckoned me toward him. Acid bubbled in the back of my throat as I made my way through the dancing crowd.

When I reached him, Derek grabbed onto me and pulled me away from the party on the pool deck. It seemed fitting that the last night of the cruise mimicked the first one. All we needed was another bloody body in the pool to make the evenings match.

"What's wrong?" I asked as Derek led me inside, where the pumping music was muffled and low.

"She's gone," he reported. "Andrea. My girlfriend." He shook his hands like he was trying to get a pack of spiders off of them. "God, I knew this was going to happen. She looks exactly like the killer's type. I left her alone for one second while I went to get drinks. By the time I got back, she had disappeared!"

I seized Derek's shoulders and forced him to look at me. "Stop it. Don't go there yet. For all we know, Andrea got tired and went back to your room. Talk to me. Did you text her?"

"I paid for the cheap Wi-Fi plan," Derek moaned. "I'm out of data. I can't reach her."

"Well, did you actually check your room to see if she was there?"

"No, I was afraid she might turn up at the pool deck again and wonder where I was."

I let go of his shoulders. "First of all, download the Emerald Cruises app and see if you can get ahold of her through there. Second, go check your room to make sure she hasn't ditched the pool party. Text me through the app when you find out."

Derek took a deep, calming breath. "What are you going to do?"

"I'll wait on the pool deck in case she comes back."

"Okay." Derek bounded off to the elevators. "I'll talk to you in a minute!"

I returned to the pool deck. Anxiety rose in my core and spread to my limbs. After a few minutes, my entire body felt like it was vibrating. Sandy's assigned breathing exercises didn't help. I stuck to the edges of the makeshift dance floor and scanned each face for a glimpse of Derek's girlfriend. Each time I spotted a pretty, blonde woman, my stomach dropped. It wasn't her.

My phone rang, interrupting my process.

"Not a good time, Dominique," I answered.

"You haven't had much time for me at all lately," she replied. "Is something going on?"

"Yeah, a murder investigation," I said, more snarkily than I meant. "Sorry, I'm in a bit of a pickle. Can I call you back later?"

"Don't bother."

A moment after she hung up, I got a text from Derek on the Emerald Cruises app. *Andrea's not in her room or replying to my messages. SOS.*

I texted back: *Regroup at the security office. I'll meet you there.*

I messaged Clint to let him know Derek was coming then headed to the elevators. I wanted my notes on hand if Andrea was actually in trouble. It was our best bet of rescuing her before something disastrous happened.

I rode in the elevator with a few other people who were turning in early for the night. They all got off at other floors, nodding polite goodbyes, and left me alone to travel to Deck Seven. The hallway beyond the elevator was clear. I fumbled for my keycard in my pocket then stumbled to a halt.

The door to my stateroom was already ajar.

I inched along the hallway, keeping to the wall. I had no weapon on me. My gun had remained locked in the safe since Carter had berated me during the first day of the cruise. I reached the door and pushed it fully open.

Andrea, Derek's girlfriend, struggled on the floor. Above her stood a blonde woman wearing the children's mask from my desk again. Between them, the knife with the red blade steadily sank toward Andrea's heart. She wasn't as strong as her attacker. Her hands slipped on the other woman's forearms, and the knife pierced the skin of her chest.

"No!"

I dove for the woman and careened into her legs. She toppled over but kept hold of the knife. As she untangled herself from me, we made eye contact. A sense of familiarity washed over me. I knew those brown eyes from somewhere, but I couldn't place them.

The attacker ripped her gaze from mine, got up,

and ran out into the hallway. I almost followed her, but Andrea grabbed my hand. Other than the small wound on her chest, she was okay.

"Thank you," she gasped. "She dragged me in here. Had a key and everything. I don't understand—"

"Stay put," I ordered. "Put the lock on behind me."

As I sprinted from the room, I heard Andrea barricade the door. At the end of the hallway, a wisp of blonde hair disappeared around the corner. I flew after the attacker.

When I turned the corner, she was gone. The children's mask lay in the middle of the foyer. I picked it up and found something underneath: a gaudy bracelet made of bright orange jewels.

"We have to put the ship on lockdown again." I drove my finger into the security desk. "It's the only way to ensure everyone remains safe."

Clint shook his head. "Can't do that. It's the last night of the cruise. People will riot if they aren't allowed to enjoy their last night."

"People will riot if someone else gets killed," I said. "Emerald Cruises won't see business for years. The company may never recover from this as it is."

"What's the point of a lockdown if your killer has a key anyway?" Clint demanded.

"What are you talking about?"

"The doors on this ship lock automatically," he said. "But she got into your room while you were away from it. She has a damn key."

I tossed my hands up. "She probably waited for me

to leave and propped the door open. It doesn't mean she has a key, and it doesn't mean she has a key to anyone else's door either. Clint, come on. Are you seriously not going to protect the people on this ship?"

"I am going to protect them, but I need to do what's best for both the guests and this company," Clint bargained. "I've already spoken to the Captain, and she agrees with me. We're not putting the ship on lockdown, but we're tightening security measures."

"Tighter than before?" I questioned. "Because that didn't seem to work last time."

Clint glared at me with his beady eyes, then turned to face Russo, who'd been listening to us argue for at least twenty minutes. "Sweep the entire ship. Check the security footage for a blonde woman coming out of Detective Ryder's room. There has to be a record of her somewhere. She can't have wiped all our feeds."

Russo nodded and left to assign duties to the other guards. Clint dropped his erect posture and sank into one of the rolling chairs. He rubbed his temples, reaching both with one hand.

"Why do I have a feeling this is the end of my career?" he muttered.

"It doesn't have to be," I said. "If you help me catch this woman, it might be the most successful day of your career thus far."

He uncapped a water bottle and drained half of the contents in ten seconds. Sweat beaded near his hairline, but it wasn't too hot in the security office. He was nervous.

"Are you scared?" I asked him.

He set the bottle down harder than intended, and the water bounced up and spilled over. Clint wiped it with his sleeve. "Of course I'm scared. I've been scared since day one. My job is to keep everyone on this ship safe, and I've failed spectacularly to do so."

I took the risk of resting my hand on his broad shoulder. "Please. Help me figure this out. I don't care if it takes all night. By the time we make port, I *will* have the killer in hand. I already have a feeling I know who it is."

That caught his attention. "How do you figure?"

I dropped the orange bracelet on the table. "That was under the mask the killer left in the foyer. She must have dropped it."

Clint examined the bracelet stone by stone. "Good grief, this is ugly."

"Corrine Corral sells that jewelry," I told him. "She happens to have a ton of pieces for herself, and her favorite color is orange."

"Corrine Corral," he mused. "I thought you already spoke to her? Didn't you say she was no longer a suspect?"

"I never said that," I replied. "She made a convincing argument against Gretchen Wagner, which is why I put her on the back burner momentarily. But Corrine was my main suspect to begin with. Everything lines up.

She was friends with Jenn, no one can corroborate her alibi, and she fits the killer's look."

"A housewife." Clint held up the bracelet. "You think a woman who sells this shit for a living has it in her to torture and murder a bunch of other people?"

"I think a woman who's stuck selling that shit needs an outlet."

He knocked the gemstones together as if to test whether they were real or not. "Okay then, Detective. What's the plan?"

"I need to check on Derek and Andrea," I said, "and I need to scope my room for any more clues. The killer led Andrea there for a reason. She wants my attention, but I'm betting she didn't expect me to walk in on her while she was in the middle of the act."

"Why would Corrine Corral want your attention?" Clint asked. "Do you know each other?"

I didn't have an immediate answer for that. Before this case, I'd never seen Corrine a day in my life. Unless you counted my first day as a rookie, when I'd watched the killer slip out of mine and Carter's hands without doing anything about.

"Me and the killer go way back," I said. "Keep an eye on your guys. Make sure they're on the lookout for any blonde, attractive women between the ages of twenty-five and thirty-five. At this point, we need to be watching for both the killer and her potential victims."

. . .

DEREK AND ANDREA had locked themselves in their room based on my advice. I knocked on their door lightly and called, "It's Detective Ryder!"

Derek answered. His eyes were puffy and red. "Come on in, Alex."

Andrea sat on the bed, wiping her tears with a saturated tissue. When she saw me, she straightened up and tried to maintain her composure. Derek put the lock on the door and immediately went back to Andrea. He wrapped his arm around her, and she nuzzled against his neck.

"I know this is hard for you," I said to Andrea, "but you're the first person who's ever survived this woman. I need you to tell me everything that happened."

Andrea sniffled and drew a fresh tissue from the box. "The details are fuzzy. I was a little tipsy."

"That's okay," I said. "Do your best. Let's start with the woman. When did she approach you?"

"Right after Derek went to get more drinks," Andrea reported. "As soon as he left, she came up to me and asked about my dress."

"What did she look like?"

"Blonde," she replied. No surprises there. "Brown eyes. High cheekbones. Maybe about thirty years old? She was really pretty."

"She looked like you," I commented.

"I suppose so," Andrea said. "Why?"

"It's her thing," Derek answered. "She picks victims

that resemble herself. A good a way as any to keep detectives guessing."

I patted Andrea's hand to get her attention back. "Would you recognize the woman if I showed you a picture of her?"

Andrea wiped her nose. "Maybe. Like I said, I was a little tipsy."

"How did she get you away from the pool deck and down to Deck Seven?"

"She asked me to hold her purse while she went to the restroom," she replied. "I figured it was no big deal. Just helping another woman out. But we didn't go the restroom nearest the pool deck. She said it was too dirty, so we got in the elevator."

"Didn't you suspect something was wrong when she didn't lead you to the bathroom?" I asked.

"Not really," Andrea said. "She wasn't weird or suspicious or anything. She said she'd forgotten something in her room, and asked if I'd mind coming with her. I didn't think much of it. Not until we got to her room—your room—and she put the mask on."

"The mask from my desk?"

"Yes." She added the used tissue to a pile on the floor. "She put it on and pulled out the knife from inside her sleeve before I realized what was happening."

Derek leaned his forehead against Andrea's. "You fought back though. I'm so proud of you."

"How did you manage that?" I added. "She attacked me too, and I barely got away."

"She attacked *you?*" Derek gasped. I nodded.

"She seemed distracted," Andrea said. "She didn't go after me right away. She made a phone call before she put on the mask. Afterward, she started going through your things. I didn't know it was your room, Detective Ryder. I'm sorry."

"Did she find anything she liked of mine?" I asked.

Andrea's brow furrowed as she thought back on it. "She tried on a bracelet. It had a small charm on it."

"Gold?"

"Yes. Does it mean anything?"

My teeth grated against each other. "Just that she remembers her other victims. So when she pulled the knife on you, you'd already suspected she was going to attack?"

"Yes," Andrea said. "Derek told me about your case. He said to be extra careful around other women on the ship. I'm so stupid to have forgotten."

Derek smoothed Andrea's hair. "You're not stupid."

"How did she attack you?" I asked Andrea.

"She charged," she replied. "Knocked me to the ground and straddled me. I punched her in the—um" —she gestured to her breasts— "which looked like it hurt. It gave me time to grab her arms, so she couldn't stab me. She was stronger than me though. If you hadn't walked in, she would have killed me for sure."

I almost chuckled at the thought of Andrea

punching the killer in the boob but contained myself at the last second. "I'm proud of you, Andrea. You put up a good fight." I scrolled through my phone and found a picture of Corrine that Angela had sent me a few days ago. "Is this the woman that attacked you?"

She squinted at the picture. It showed off Corrine's profile, her high cheekbones and pointed chin. "It looks like her, but I'm not sure. Same build though, and she was wearing that bracelet." She pointed to the unpleasant orange gemstones. "I remember wondering why anyone would buy something like that. It's tasteless."

"You're telling me," I muttered.

FOR THE REST of the night, I stayed with Clint. We patrolled the ship together, checked in with the other guards, attempted to track down Corrine, and reviewed the security footage from the attack against Andrea. Nothing seemed to go our way.

"No sign of her," Russo reported over the radio. "We've swept the whole ship twice. No idea where she's hiding."

Clint clutched the radio so tightly that I thought it might crack under the pressure. "Sweep it again. In fact, keep sweeping it until you find something."

"Yes, sir," came the crackly reply.

Clint clipped the radio on his belt. "I can't believe this."

"They searched everywhere?" I asked. "Every room?"

"We can't search the rooms without the guests' consent."

We had already checked for Corrine in her own room. It had been LeeAnn who answered the door and haughtily informed us that Corrine hadn't returned yet. She reluctantly let us inside to make sure she wasn't lying. Corrine was nowhere to be found.

To make matters worse, the security footage was inconclusive. Though we managed to locate the exact moment the attacker lured Andrea away from the pool deck, there was no clear angle of her face. The killer made sure to keep her visage away from the cameras, turning away from them or keeping her head down to stay under the radar. She was a smart pain in the ass. She knew exactly where each camera was, despite that they were all hidden within the ship's architecture.

Clint and I kept up our circuit. We watched the security monitors for an hour until Russo came to relieve us. Then we walked the ship for an hour. Then we checked Corrine's room again. After that, we started the whole process over again. It was no use. Corrine never appeared on the monitors or in the hallways. When I fell asleep at the security desk, Clint kicked my chair and ordered me to return to my own room. Russo escorted me there, just in case.

. . .

I AWOKE to the sound of my phone ringing and scrambled around in the bedsheets to find it. I'd gone to sleep fully-dressed, and my phone was still in my pocket. I fished it out and answered the call.

"Hello?" I said groggily.

"You'll never believe this." It was Angela.

I sat straight up and rubbed the exhaustion from my eyes. "You got something?"

"More than something," Angela said. "We found Jenn Spitz's car. Guess where it was?"

"An impound lot?"

"In Corrine Corral's garage."

I choked on my own spit. "You're shitting me."

"I am not," Angela replied. "Her husband called this morning and asked if we could get rid of it. He had no idea it was there. I guess he keeps his car in the driveway."

I ran my fingers through my messy hair. "Do you know what this means?"

"That Carter granted you a warrant to search Corrine's stateroom?"

"No shit."

"Get in there, Detective." I could practically hear Angela's grin through the phone. "You're officially unsuspended. By the way, we're on our way to the port now. Meet you there."

I hung up and glanced out the verandah window. Sometime in the wee hours of the morning, the *Adventure* had returned to Tampa. The ship was docked, and

I had a clear view of a familiar bit of land. I could even see my car in the parking lot from here.

Guests had already begun to disembark. I checked my watch. It was a few minutes after seven o'clock. These were the early-risers, the guests who preferred to beat the rush off the ship rather than stick around for one last resort-style breakfasts. I quickly dialed the number for the security office.

"Security," a deep voice answered.

"Hey, Russo. It's Detective Ryder."

"Morning, Detective. What can I do for you?"

"Can you check if Corrine Corral put her name down to disembark early?" I asked. "If so, I need someone to check if she's already left the ship. If not, I need someone to detain her before she leaves."

Russo's keyboard clacked. "Let's see here. Corrine Corral. Nope, she didn't sign up for early disembarkation. She's probably at breakfast."

"Perfect. That gives me time to search her room."

CORRINE, it turned out, was not at breakfast. She answered her door when I arrived at her stateroom. For someone who had been missing for the entire night, she appeared well-rested. She wore yet another floral summer dress, this one printed with sunflowers, and the matching yellow necklace that she'd sported on her first day of the cruise.

"Detective Ryder," she said, her perfectly plucked

eyebrows arching in surprise. "What can I do for you this morning?"

I turned the screen of my phone to face her. "This is a warrant to search your room. You can read it in detail when my team gets here. For now, take a seat."

Corrine stumbled backward as I forced my way into her stateroom. She sat on the edge of the unmade bed. "What the hell do you need a warrant for? I thought we were past this."

"Did you know we've been looking for you all night?" I asked. "Where have you been if not in this room?"

"I was next door with Gretchen," Corrine replied. "She was upset after you quarantined her to her room all day. She needed someone to comfort her."

"LeeAnn said you didn't come back to your room."

"I didn't. I was next door."

"Where is LeeAnn anyway?"

Corrine patted the gems around her neck. "She got off the ship early. Apparently, she had to go back to work today."

I started sweeping Corrine's room from top to bottom. I began with the high shelves and moved downward, leaving no stone unturned. Corrine watched from her spot on the bed.

"I don't know what you expect to find," she said. "I've packed everything already."

"Unpack it."

"You're joking."

I slid her suitcase across the floor to her. "I'm not. Get moving."

As Corrine unzipped her suitcase and laid her clothes neatly on the bed, I continued my search. I rifled through the bathroom, checked the side drawers of the bedside table, and looked under the bed. Finally, I reached the closet.

"What's the code for the safe?" I asked.

"I don't know," Corrine replied grumpily. "I didn't use it."

"It's flashing. Someone used it."

"It wasn't me."

For the hell of it, I tried the default code. Four straight ones. The safe beeped, the light turned green, and the door popped open. I shined the light of my phone inside. It reflected off something shiny and red.

I pulled my sleeve down and used the fabric to take the object out. "Explain this to me, Corrine. If you're innocent, what is the murder weapon doing in your room?"

The red-bladed switch knife glinted in the sun streaming in from the window. Corrine stared open-mouthed at it.

"I've never seen that before in my life," she said.

I dropped the knife into a plastic bag I'd had Clint steal from the kitchen for me and set it aside. I took my handcuffs from my belt. For the first time in five days, I had all of my effects, including my weapon, with me.

My badge shone brightly. I had proof of Corrine's guilt. All was right with the world.

"Get up," I ordered Corrine. "Turn around and put your hands behind your back. You're under arrest for the murders of Jenn Spitz and Christine Sherry, along with several others I'm sure."

"No!" Corrine yelled.

I grabbed her as she tried to run from the room and forced her arms behind her back. She let the waterworks go, sobbing as I cuffed her and made her sit on the bed again.

"Eight years," I said as adrenaline pumped through my chest. "I've been chasing you for eight years. I can't believe you thought you could get away with this."

Corrine was beyond words. She slumped across the bedspread, overcome with tears. I dialed a familiar number on my phone.

"Lieutenant Carter."

"It's Ryder," I said. "I got the perp."

"Nice job, Detective. We're waiting for you outside."

CORRINE DIDN'T GET her last breakfast. I led her off the ship, down the gangplank, and over to the pickup loop, where Carter and Angela were waiting for us. Carter wore her usual look of disapproval, but she didn't direct it at me this time. Instead, she let Corrine take the full brunt of it.

"I don't like you," Carter announced to Corrine.

"Get in the car. Watch your head. Or don't. I don't care."

"P-please," Corrine sobbed. "It wasn't me. I swear!"

Angela took over, placing her hand on top of Corrine's head as she loaded the culprit into the back seat of the squad car. I handed over the baggie with the red switchblade and another one with Corrine's orange gemstone bracelet. Carter took both and patted me on the back.

"Don't get me wrong," she growled. "I'm still pissed at you for how you handled this case, and there *will* be repercussions. First of all, you're taking a leave of absence for at least a month to think over this."

"What?" I exclaimed. "You said I was un-suspended!"

"That doesn't mean I trust you in the field," Carter said. "You need to clear your mind, Ryder. Take a damn break. You deserve it anyway. I put a whole team of detectives on this case, and no one made any progress except for you. I know you're good, but I also know you need to rest. Get out of my hair."

Carter rounded the car and got in on the driver's side without saying goodbye. Angela smirked and cuffed my shoulder.

"You look tan," she said.

"You look the same."

She rolled her eyes. "Don't worry. Carter will come around. In the meantime, we should celebrate. Wanna meet up for drinks later?"

"Sure."

Angela looked taken aback. "Really?"

"Yeah, why not?"

"You usually don't—I mean—you don't make plans —" she stammered.

I nudged her with my elbow. "I'm turning over a new leaf. Why don't you invite Jess as well?"

"I'm officially stunned."

As I laughed, Carter rolled down the window. "Pennacchi, let's go! I haven't got all day!"

Angela grimaced, waved goodbye, and got in the passenger seat. Carter's squad car peeled off with Corrine's teary face pressed against the back window. I watched until it had disappeared from the parking lot, then headed to my own car.

I fit the key into the ignition, turned the AC on full blast, and joined the line of cars to get on the main road, braking to let a cute travel van go in front of me. A smiling sun sticker was stuck to the back windshield. The driver's hand went up in between the seats to thank me. I smiled and nodded back.

"Then I cuffed her and led her off the ship right into Carter's hands," I said. "I don't think I've ever felt that kind of relief after a case."

Dominique's voice echoed through my car's bluetooth system. "That's great, Alex. I'm so glad for you."

The sentiment sounded flat. A light turned yellow in front of me, and I couldn't decide whether to go or stop. I hit the brake then changed my mind and floored it through the intersection right as the light changed to red. Another car went behind me, and the traffic camera flashed, catching them in the act.

"Listen, Dom," I said. "I know I haven't been the best friend this past week, and I don't want to make excuses for myself. But this case has been haunting me every day since my first day on the job. Do you know I slept last night? Soundly? I haven't felt this rested in a long time."

"It's not that," Dominique sighed. "I'm happy for you. I really am. It's that—never mind. Don't worry about it."

I turned into the parking lot of the station and pulled in next to Carter's spot. I pinned my badge onto my belt. "You can tell me anything. I won't be offended."

"I guess I'm not used to you not paying attention to me," Dominique said. "I know that sounds weird, but I'm jealous. I'm jealous that Corrine Corral is getting all of your brain power."

I let out half of a laugh, unsure where Dominique was going with this. "Dom, Corrine Corral is a criminal. You're my best friend. The kind of attention I'm giving to her is completely different than the kind I devote to you. Are you coming home or not, by the way? I'd love to celebrate my win with you. In the flesh."

"I'm already here."

"What?" I said excitedly. "You are? Where? When can I see you?"

The phone disconnected with an annoying beep. I checked the screen. Call Failed. I dialed Dominique back, but she didn't answer. Oh, well. I'd speak to her after work.

I expected one hell of a cheer when I walked into the station, but the thing about expectations was that, most times, you ended up disappointed. I crossed the threshold, grinning from ear to ear, but the first cop I made eye contact with quickly looked away from me. No one cheered or patted me on the back. No one came up to ask how I'd cracked a case that had been open for years. No one congratulated me. No one even smiled.

Instead, I got shaking heads, stolen glances, and sympathetic grimaces. I walked up to the front desk. The rookie manning the phones gasped when he saw me and answered a phone that wasn't ringing.

I reached over to take the receiver from him and put it back on the hook. "Nice try, Hunter. Are you going to tell me what's going on or do I have to find out for myself? Who fucked up?"

Hunter's throat bobbed as he swallowed his nerves. "Uh, sorry, ma'am. I don't know what's going on."

"You better not be lying."

"Lieutenant Carter asked to see you in her office as soon as you got in," Hunter reported. "That's all I know."

My heart splashed into my stomach, dousing my other organs in bile. Every part of me felt sick and sour. Carter shouldn't be holed up in her office right after we put away a murderer. She was the first one to buy cake and champagne whenever one of her detectives made a huge save. Had Corrine Corral somehow escaped custody?

"Good luck," Hunter muttered as I slogged around the front desk.

I passed through the bullpen. Heads turned to

watch me take the walk of shame to Carter's office. I didn't have the strength to square my shoulders or lift my chin. Every pair of eyes followed me across the room, all the way to Carter's door. Angry voices emanated from the other side. I knocked.

"Who the hell is it?" Carter yelled.

"It's Ryder."

A slight pause. "Get in here, Ryder."

I opened the door. Carter stood behind her desk, palms planted in front of her. "Carter, what's going on? Everyone's acting like someone died. Did someone die?"

Carter pointed behind me. I turned around. My mouth dropped open.

LeeAnn Rhodes stood in the corner of Carter's office, dressed in full Tampa Police regalia. Her lip curled upward in a sneer as she looked me up and down. "Allow me to introduce myself," she said, stepping forward. "Officer Liz Hutton from Narcotics."

"O-officer?" I stuttered. "What the hell is going on?"

"Liz is from the next division over," Carter said. "It turns out the only thing Corral's guilty of is using her jewelry business as a front to sell pharmaceuticals on a wide scale to her neighbors."

My mouth dropped open. "She's a drug dealer?"

"She sure is," LeeAnn—Liz—said. "But since your stupid ass ruined my cover, we couldn't apprehend her for the *actual* crimes she committed."

"You were undercover?" I stammered.

"I told you to let it go," Liz reminded me. "I told you more than once, but you were so damn determined to be the hero."

"I thought you were a suspect," I said hotly. "Why didn't you tell me you were a cop?"

"It would have risked my operation," Liz replied. "I've been tracking Corrine Corral for months, since before she moved to Pelican Point. She didn't kill Jenn Spitz. She had an alibi."

"But Jenn's car!" I argued. "It was in Corrine's garage."

"Because she had recruited Jenn to join her business," Liz countered. "Corrine made a run that morning to her supplier, but she was scared someone was catching on, so she borrowed Jenn's car instead. We have footage from traffic cameras of her on the road during the time Jenn was murdered."

I sank into the chair across from Carter's desk and let all of it catch up to me. It didn't work. My brain wouldn't absorb the information. "There has to be a mistake. I found the murder weapon in Corrine's stateroom safe."

"The killer on the cruise ship got into multiple staterooms," Carter said. "We think she might have had a master key."

"Weren't *you* there?" I accused Liz. "Wouldn't you have seen the perp come in and plant the knife?"

"After you showed up, I needed a damn drink," Liz

spat. "I was out of the room for most of the night. When I got back, I went straight to sleep."

"This is impossible." I pressed my palms against my eyes and focused on the floating colors in the darkness. "This can't be happening, because if this is happening—"

"It means the perp is still on the loose," Carter finished for me.

"No," I said firmly. "No way. All the clues pointed to Corrine. Everything fit!"

"This isn't an episode of Blue's Clues," Liz snapped. "Wake up, Ryder. Someone framed Corrine. They set you up. You got pranked."

Carter stepped out from behind her desk and cupped Liz's elbow. "Thank you, Officer. That's enough for right now. I'll call you if I have any updates."

Liz left the room, fixing her glare on me on her way out. Once she was gone, Carter dropped her shoulders and sagged into her desk chair. At least we were on the same level now.

"Tell me," Carter said softly, "how this could have happened."

I didn't have an answer for her. "Did you arrest Corrine for the drug counts?"

"We couldn't," she answered, "because she had already been charged for murder. She had an attorney on standby who got her out of here in record time."

"But—"

"You screwed up," Carter interrupted. "That's the

only way to see this, Alex. I should have known better than to put you on this case. I knew you were too close to it to see things clearly. I should have stuck to my guns when I suspended you, not that it would have meant much. I know you were operating aboard that ship after I told you not to."

"People were in danger."

Carter slammed her fist on the desk, making me jump. "You did nothing to prevent further danger from occurring! Worse, you interfered with a legitimate investigation! Don't act like the hero, Ryder. You are not a hero."

"Carter, I seriously thought—"

"Get out of my office," she ordered. "Do some fucking paperwork, and don't go near anyone else's cases until I've decided what to do with you."

"Lieutenant, please."

Carter gave me a long look. "I thought you were going to be one of the best, Alex. I really did."

BEING FORCED to sit at my desk was a worse punishment than probation, and Carter knew it. She knew everyone would stare at me as they passed by. She knew they would whisper behind their hands about how badly I'd blown it. She knew the weight of my embarrassment would force me to melt into the chair and color my cheeks bright red.

Angela set a cup of colorful liquid on my desk and

patted my shoulder. "It's beet and carrot. Sounds gross, but it's actually pretty good. I thought you could use a healthy pick-me-up. Coffee's not the best thing for the nerves."

"Didn't you hear?" I grumbled. "I'm the office's court jester."

"I heard," Angela said, "and I'm sorry. What did Carter say?"

"That I was the worst detective in the history of Tampa."

"She did not."

I groaned and leaned back in my chair. "She might as well have."

Angela sat on the corner of my desk and sipped her own bright-green juice. "What are you going to do about it?"

"What am I supposed to do?" I asked. "I got played. I found the wrong person."

"You can't give up," Angela insisted. "You know this case better than anyone. If you can't figure out who killed Jenn, no one else is going to either."

"You keep saying that," I muttered.

She forced the cup of juice into my hand. "Because it's true."

Once Angela was gone, I went back to slumping behind my desktop and hoping no one would notice me. When my phone rang, I hastily picked it up so the ringtone wouldn't attract attention.

"Hello?"

"Hey, it's me," Dominique answered. "We got disconnected earlier. Did you get to work okay?"

"Uh-huh."

"Uh-oh," she said. "What happened?"

"Oh, you know," I replied casually. "Apparently, I caught the wrong person."

There was a moment of silence. Then Dominique laughed. It wasn't her usual subdued giggle. It was a deep, from-the-belly kind of laugh, one I hadn't heard her use before.

"I'm glad you find that so amusing," I barked. "I'm in deep shit."

Dominique's laugh died down to a chuckle. "Oh, gosh. I really needed that."

"What exactly is so funny?"

"You have no idea, do you?"

Again, the line went dead, but this time, it was because Dominique had hung up on me. I stared at the home screen of my phone, flabbergasted. What the hell was she talking about?

My computer chimed. I had a new email. I clicked on the link to open it. It was a survey from Emerald Cruises, thanking me for my time aboard the *Adventure* and asking how likely I would be to recommend the cruise line to someone else. As I exited the window, a memory from yesterday flashed in my mind: the travel van I'd let in front of me in the line to get out of the terminal's parking lot.

I dialed the number for the Port of Tampa.

"Hello, this is Charlene with customer service. How may I help you today?"

"Hi, Charlene," I said hastily. "This is Detective Alex Ryder with the Tampa Police Department. I'm working on a homicide case, and I need the security footage of your parking lot from yesterday morning between the hours of seven and ten o'clock."

"I'll transfer you to someone who can help you out, Detective."

A few minutes later, I spoke to the head of the security at the port, who emailed me the footage I needed. I scanned through it and located the travel van parked in the far corner of the parking lot, away from most of the other cars.

I chewed my fingernails as I watched everyone disembark from the *Adventure*. There was Derek and his girlfriend. Owen, Max, and the others from the support group. Me and Corrine. Liz Hutton chasing after us a few minutes too late. And a blonde woman with wide sunglasses that obscured half of her face. She made a beeline for the travel van, tossed her small duffel bag in the back, and got into the driver's seat. The van backed out of the space, drove down the aisle, and reached the trafficky center lane. There was my car, pausing to let the van in.

I rewound the footage and zoomed in to get a better look at the woman's face. The sunglasses hid almost every defining feature, and the grainy black-and-white security video didn't help either. There was no way facial recognition software was going to help me here. The van, on the other hand, might serve a purpose. I looked up the license plate number in the database. Nothing turned up. The stupid smiling sun sticker on the back window mocked me.

I reclined in my chair and huffed through my nose. If the van wasn't registered, it was another dead end. No lead to follow. Unless...

I scooted closer to my desk and went through my old saved files from before I'd left on the cruise. Everything for this case was saved to one folder. I'd been too stupid to organize or label them, so instead of being able to search for what I needed, I had to go through each unlabeled file one by one to find what I was looking for. At long last, the security footage from Day Moon Yoga Studio on the morning Jenn died popped up. I played it from the beginning.

At half-past five in the morning, the white maintenance van pulled into the back lot and parked in front of the camera, obscuring the footage. A few minutes later, it pulled out again. In between those times, someone had murdered Jenn Spitz at Day Moon. I rewound the footage and played it again, this time in slow motion. The van backed in, blocked the camera—I rewound it again.

On the tenth viewing, I saw it. Right before the van parked, there was a half-second where the camera was able to see the corner of the back windshield. In that corner was a sticker of a smiling sun.

I let out a deep breath. I fiddled with my bracelet, the one Andrea had told me the killer tried on in my room. The silver charm featured a smiling sun.

Angela passed behind me and paused when she saw the frozen footage on my screen. "Going over everything to see what you missed, huh? Any luck?"

"Maybe." I tucked the bracelet under my sleeve. "Hey, can you do me a favor?"

"Sure. What's up?"

"I need a phone number," I said. "For the parents of Dominique Benson."

She toasted me with her half-empty juice cup. "I'll see what I can do."

A FEW MINUTES LATER, Angela sent an instant message my way with the number. I wrote it on a sticky note, went outside, and dialed my phone with shaking fingers. The sun beat on my forehead, reminding me that my burn had not yet healed.

"Hello?" answered a soft voice.

"Hi, this is Detective Ryder with the Tampa Police Department," I said. "Is this Frances Benson?"

"Yes, this is she. Is everything okay?"

"I'm a friend of your daughter's," I said.

Frances sucked in a deep breath. "Dominique? Is everything okay?"

"That's what I'm trying to figure out, Miss Benson." I leaned against the building, feeling the rough brick snag against my shirt. "Can I ask you a personal question? How's your pottery class going?"

"Pottery class?" Frances sounded confused. "I've never tried pottery before. What does this have to do with Dominique?"

I squeezed my eyes shut. "What about your husband? Would he happen to have a senior league softball tournament coming up?"

"I'm afraid I wouldn't know," Frances replied. "We divorced almost eight years ago."

"Can I ask why?"

She sighed heavily. "After what happened to Dominique, we had trouble seeing eye to eye. My husband thought we should go after her. I told him she needed time to process everything. I was wrong. She never came home, and her absence drove a wedge in our marriage."

"Miss Benson, when was the last time you spoke to Dominique?"

"Right after she was rescued from that awful house," Frances answered. "She texted me to say she couldn't come home. She couldn't go back to her regular life because it felt wrong. She said she was going to travel the world by herself to find what she really wanted."

"When was the last time you saw her?"

"A few months before that," Frances replied. "She and her husband had visited us for Easter. I'm sorry, Detective. Has something happened to Dominique? I

337

know we aren't in contact anymore, but she's still my daughter. I would be devastated."

"I'll let you know as soon as I figure it out myself," I told Frances. "For now, try not to worry. Can I keep your number on file, Miss Benson?"

"Of course."

"Thank you. Buh-bye now."

I hung up and tipped my head against the brick. A dark cloud crossed the sky and blocked out the sun. One fat raindrop landed on the center of my forehead.

Angela emerged from the station. "There you are. Are you okay? What's going on?"

I looked her in the eye. "I think Dominique Benson is dead."

2 0

J wore the smiling sun charm bracelet, as well as a pair of comfortable jeans and a light T-shirt. Angela recommended I add body armor underneath, but I knew I had to go into this looking as ignorant as possible.

"*Hi, Dominique! It's me. I don't know why our conversations keep getting cut short, but I'm tired of always missing each other. We should meet up! I know a great place for coffee. I'll send you the address. Eleven o'clock?*"

I recorded the message ten times before I was finally satisfied with it. Thankfully, Dominique hadn't answered her phone, so I didn't have to speak to her live. The pressure might have eaten me alive. Then again, the hardest part was yet to come.

Ten minutes later, Dominique texted me back. *Hey! Guess I don't have the greatest service in the 'burbs. I'm down to meet, but my van broke down! Wanna come to me?*

Angela read the message over my shoulder. "Where is she?"

Dominique dropped a pin to share her location with me. I let out a laugh of disbelief.

"In the Day Moon parking lot."

Angela squeezed my shoulders. "You can do this, Alex."

AT ELEVEN O'CLOCK on the dot, I drove to the quaint little strip plaza and parked in front of Crescent Cakes Bakery. Day Moon was not open for business yet, but at least all the crime scene tape had been cleaned up. I put my car in park and glanced in the mirror. At the far end of the lot was the cute white travel van, complete with the smiling sun sticker. The license plate was different than the one she'd had at the Port of Tampa. I wondered where she'd stolen it.

The summer afternoon shower came early that day, but it wasn't the torrential downpour that I was used to. I slipped into the arms of my rain jacket, pulled the hood up, and jogged into the bakery. It was a slow morning. Only two customers sat inside. The glass case of pastries was almost full. Few people had bought breakfast today. Becca Bailey leaned on the counter, tapping her fingers against her cheek in impatience. On a normal day, she'd be in the back whipping up new treats to satisfy her ever-hungry customers. She straightened up as the bell over the door rang, but her face fell when I swept my hood back.

"No, no," she said. "I don't want you in here. I've seen the news. You haven't caught the person responsible for what happened next door yet, and I'm not going to get caught up in the drama. I've lost business already as it is. Look at this place! It's dead."

The two remaining customers exchanged nervous glances with each other. One poured her coffee into a to-go cup and fled the scene. The other smiled anxiously at me then returned her gaze to her computer.

"I'm not here to cause trouble," I told Becca. "I'm sorry that your business is suffering, but it's only been a week since the incident. Cases like this aren't resolved overnight."

"So you're not going to question me again?"

"Nope." I pulled out my debit card. "Actually, I was hoping for coffee and croissants."

A FEW MINUTES LATER, I jogged across the parking lot and knocked on the door of the travel van with the hand that wasn't carrying the coffee and treats. My whole body felt like it was vibrating. Adrenaline rushed through me like a hurricane as I waited for someone to answer. I took a deep breath, taking in the misty mid-morning air. The van door slid open.

"Hi!"

With a huge smile, Dominique yanked me into the van and pulled me into a tight hug. My body stiffened, but I had the perfect excuse to draw away. "Watch out! The coffee's going to spill."

She released me and stepped back, giving me the first real view of her I'd had since she'd left town eight years ago. She looked different. Most noticeably, her hair was brown instead of blonde, and it had been cut up to her chin. She'd also gained some muscle mass in her arms and legs, as if she was spending more time in the gym these days. She wore denim shorts and a cute tank top, showing off all of her tan skin. The scars from the torture she'd supposedly endured had faded to white. Unless you knew they were there, you wouldn't notice them.

"Well?" She beamed, and her smile was radiant. "Aren't you going to say anything? Haven't we been waiting on this reunion for almost a decade?"

"Uh—"

"Get in character, Ryder," a curt voice whispered in my ear. It was Angela, and the fact that she was within range to be heard through my hidden earpiece helped relax me. If this went south, backup was nearby.

I stifled my nerves and mimicked Dominique's grin. I set the coffee and croissants aside and threw my arms wide. "Get in here!"

She folded herself into my embrace, and I forced myself to wrap my arms around her. We hugged like two friends who hadn't seen each other in years, but was that what we were? I hoped so, but the sinking feeling in my stomach told me something different.

"I can't believe this," Dominique said, pulling away first. She inspected me from head to toe with a satisfied smile. "Detective Alex Ryder in the flesh!"

"Hey, I've always been here," I reminded her. "You could have come to see me whenever you wanted, but you didn't."

"I was busy conquering the nation," she said. "Besides, you know why I haven't come back here before."

"Because of what happened to you," I said. "I know. I understand. Is it hard for you to be here? I don't want you to force you to stay if you're uncomfortable."

"It's fine," she said. "It's all in the past." She spread her arms. "So what do you think? It's cute, right?"

I looked around the van. It *was* cute. Every square inch of it had a purpose. The breakfast table doubled as a desk. The small bed could be folded up and put away to make more room for guests. Each spare corner served as some kind of storage area. The whole vehicle had a distinctly bohemian vibe. All in all, it was very Instagrammable.

"This is awesome," I told her. "Where do you shower?"

"At RV parks usually." She unfolded two seats from a cabinet and gestured for me to sit down. "Or at the beach if they have public showers. Technically, I'm not supposed to do that, but I don't often get caught."

"And, uh, where do you go to the bathroom?"

She got up and pulled on a handle beneath the bed. An enormous drawer came out, in which sat a weird-looking toilet. "It's a composting toilet."

"That's gross."

"It's resourceful," she countered, then grimaced. "Well, emptying it out is gross, but you gotta do what you gotta do, right?"

I pulled the croissants out of the bag and offered one to Dominique. "So what made you decide to finally come home? Desperate to catch up with me, right?"

Her lips twitched, almost like she had to fight to smile. "You're the one who kept begging me to come back. What am I, your only friend?"

I lifted my coffee cup in a toast. "Pretty much."

"Thanks a lot," Angela grumbled in my ear. *"Get to talking, Ryder. I haven't got all day."*

I scratched my ear, subtly checking to make sure the earpiece wasn't visible from where Dominique sat. "Didn't you say your dad had a softball tournament coming up? We should go together. That would be so much fun."

"It got cancelled," she said, shrugging. "Something to do with a scheduling mix-up. Lame, right? He was really looking forward to it."

"Aw, that's a shame," I replied. "Where does he play? Maybe I can pull rank and help out."

"Oh—uh, I'm not sure." She picked a piece of burnt

chocolate off her croissant. "Somewhere on Dale Mabry, I think?"

"There's a softball field over there?"

"A few actually." She swirled her coffee. "Not sure which one he's at."

"He didn't give you the address?"

"He's in his sixties," she reminded me. "He's getting a little senile."

"Hmm."

She went to the small fridge, brought out a small carton of coconut coffee creamer, and poured a dollop in her to-go cup. "Want some?" I shook my head, and she put it away. "Enough about me! What about you? You look—uh…"

"You can say I look like crap," I told her.

"It's the sunburn and the bags under your eyes," she said with an apologetic look. "You kinda look like Tom Hanks after he got back from that deserted island. Aren't cruises supposed to be relaxing?"

"Sure, if you're not hunting down a killer the entire time."

She laughed. "I guess you have a point there. At least you closed the case." She shook her head. "Corrine Corral. Who would've guessed a suburban housewife had it in her?"

I rested my hand on top of hers. "Hey," I said softly. "You don't have to act like you aren't affected by this. Corrine Corral tortured you. She killed your husband.

Don't pretend to be strong for my sake. This is your win as much as it is mine."

She stared at our hands, stacked on top of each other. Gently, she pulled hers out of my grasp. "How many cops are outside?"

I sat back and crossed my legs. Comfortable. Confident. "None."

"Liar."

"So that's what gets you, huh?" I asked. "Genuine affection. Pity. You can't stand someone pitying you when all you really want to do is brag about what you've done. It's true, isn't it?"

She set her coffee aside. She hadn't taken one sip, scared I'd drugged it. She crossed her arms and stared at me.

"I want to hear you say it," I told her.

"Say what?"

I leaned across the small fold-out table. "Tell me what happened to the real Dominique Benson."

A terrifying smile spread across her pretty face. She said nothing.

"Tell me," I insisted. "This is what you wanted, right? Credit for your work? *What happened to Dominique Benson?*"

"I killed her."

She said it so simply, as if the statement didn't affect her at all. As if taking someone's life was as routine to her as brushing her teeth in the morning. Blood rushed through my body and made my fingers and toes tingle.

"Keep it together, Ryder," Angela said in my ear. *"Keep her talking. We want a full confession."*

"What's your real name?" I asked.

"I don't really have one," she said casually. "But for most of my life, people called me Sydney. Sydney Mallone."

"Sydney."

She smiled when I said it, like she'd been waiting to hear it from me for years.

"How did you do it?" I asked. "*Why* did you do it? How many people have you killed?"

"Fourteen," she replied. Again, casual. Nonchalant. "All across the country. I have to say though. None of them are going to be as special as you."

My heart jumped into my throat. "You're going to kill me?"

A soft smile touched her lips. "Not right away. Don't you think I deserve a little time to play with you first? After all, this is my longest game yet. Eight years, Alex. For eight years, you've been tracking a killer, and you never suspected your best friend. *This*, Alex, is my finest work."

"Do you want a sticker or something?" I said sarcastically.

Her smile dropped. "Don't speak to me like that."

"What do you want from me?"

"This moment." She pushed the coffee cup aside and took a bite of the croissant. "I wanted to see the look in your eyes when you realized you had completely and utterly failed. You didn't save Dominique Benson all those years ago. In fact, it's your fault that she's dead." She brushed crumbs from her hands. "If you and your lieutenant hadn't broken in, she wouldn't have made a break for it. I had to go track her down and kill her in the freaking swamp land behind that neighborhood. It was messy. I don't like messy."

"But you had torture wounds," I argued. "You had wire marks around your fingers."

"I was a big fan of self-harm back in the day," Dominique—Sydney—said. "You see, Alex, I have a hard time feeling anything. I'm bored all the time, so I do whatever I can to feel something. Back then, I tortured myself like I tortured my victims. It made me feel connected to them. Of course, I never did enough to put myself in danger. Dying's not really my thing."

"Just killing."

"Right-o," she said. "Besides, having torture wounds was a great defense mechanism. Take yourself for example. You took one look at me, bleeding and wounded, and decided that I was a victim. You saved me from years of incarceration."

"Why?" I growled. "Why did you orchestrate this whole thing? Was it all your idea? Did you murder Jenn to get my attention? Did you send me on the damned cruise ship so you could play cat and mouse with me the entire time, *Daniella Barrar?*"

She snorted with laughter. "I can't believe you didn't follow up on that lead. The stomach flu? Really?

Come on, Alex. Both my alibis have the same initials. I thought you'd at least catch on to that."

"So the cruise *was* planned."

"Actually, no," Sydney said, taking another bite of her croissant. "I had no idea you were going to go apeshit and follow a suspect onto a cruise ship. You almost ruined everything. Do you know how hard it is to get a fake identity and passport in less than twenty-four hours? I had to pay four times what I usually do for those services."

"How did you do it?" I asked. "How did you go unnoticed all that time? No one saw you murder Jenn or Christine."

"A lot of planning went into Jenn's murder," she replied. "I staked out a lot. Studied the area. Wondered where the best place was to draw you out. Jenn, it turned out, had been arguing with her husband a lot lately. She started getting to Day Moon earlier and earlier, sitting in her car in the parking lot while no one else was around. It was easy to pretend to be a new member of the studio. We became quick friends. Once I convinced her to get out of the car, all I had to do was break into the studio and get her inside. I'll admit the set-up was a bit much—the chakras and all that—but I wanted you to know it was me."

I swallowed the bile rising in my throat. "And Christine?"

"I had to keep you on your toes, didn't I?" Another disarming smile crossed her face. "It was so easy.

349

Everyone was so drunk that night. No one noticed when I jammed that knife into her leg. Not even Christine."

I couldn't catch my breath, too stunned by Sydney's stories to say anything. She was so unassuming. It seemed impossible that she was guilty of the things she boasted of. Out of the corner of my eye, I saw a box of brown hair dye and a pair of scissors. She noticed my gaze.

"Stupid, huh?" she said, tugging on her newly shorn and dyed hair. "I thought it might help throw you off the trail, but you're too smart to fall for that. Aren't you, Alex? I have to say, I like being blonde so much better."

"You picked victims that looked like you," I realized. "So that if you were ever caught, you'd blend in."

"You're finally catching on."

I ran my fingers through my own blonde hair. "All this time. This was all for me?"

"You were the most interesting person I'd ever met," Sydney said. "You were so *determined* to catch the killer, to avenge Dominique's torture and the death of her husband. Not to mention, all the girls who came before. God, I loved watching you solve a case. You get this look on your face—your nose scrunches up—it's cute."

"Shut up. Have you been watching me? Lying about traveling in your stupid van?"

She shrugged and leaned back. "Whenever I got

bored with you, I'd drive somewhere else to deal with my restlessness."

"You mean you'd go kill someone else?"

"It's just a hobby." She picked croissant crumbs from beneath her nails. "Don't be jealous of those other girls. You're my favorite."

"Lucky me."

She closed the distance between us and planted her hands on either side of my chair. Her breath tickled my neck. "We're going to have so much fun together. But first" —she yanked the earpiece out of my ear, tossed it to the floor, and stomped on it— "you're going to have to learn to trust me."

I curled my knees up, planted my feet on her chest, and kicked her as hard as possible. She flew across the van and crashed into the cabinets, sending reusable cups and plates flying. The scabs on my thigh ripped open, staining my jeans with fresh blood, but I ignored the pain. I aimed another kick at Sydney's midsection, but she rolled out of reach. The missed kick sent me off-balance, and she took advantage of my wobble. She yanked my other foot out from under me, and I went down face first. My chin clipped the counter and knocked my head back at a dangerous angle. I groaned and cupped the back of my neck as it throbbed.

Sydney rolled on top of me and pressed me to the floor with her weight. She whispered in my ear, "This is practically foreplay for me. You know that, right?"

I grabbed a plastic fork that had fallen from the

shelves and blindly jabbed it behind me. It connected with some part of her face because she howled with pain. As she lifted away from me, I flipped over and pulled my legs out from under her. She had four bleeding fork marks down her left cheek. Still on my back, I lashed out like a threatened cat and aimed another kick at Sydney's nose. She dodged it just in time. My foot hit her shoulder instead. She trapped it against her body with one arm and hammered down on my shin with the other. I let out a strangled scream as my knee hyperextended and the ligaments popped.

She straddled me and pinned my arms to my chest. "I could do this all day," she announced with a roguish grin. Her eyelids, on the other hand, had begun to droop. "Can you?"

"No," I grunted, trying to breathe through the pain in my knee. "But that's why I put a sedative in your fucking croissant. It just takes a few minutes to kick in."

If she killed me, the panic in her eyes at that exact moment would have made it worth it.

"You're bluffing," she growled, pressing her forearm against my throat.

"Don't you feel it?" I gasped. "You're getting sluggish, aren't you?"

She blinked rapidly and shook her head, trying to clear the fog that was taking over her brain. "You stupid—I hate you—Alex—"

With her fading strength, she pulled a switch knife

from the back pocket of her denim shorts, flicked the blade out, and buried it in my stomach. I felt it slide in all the way up to the hilt, and an ear-splitting scream tore its way out of my throat. Sydney wrapped her fingers around the handle.

"Don't," I pleaded. "Don't pull it out."

With her teeth bared, she yanked the blade free. Blood spurted across my shirt, spilling from my abdomen at a rapid pace. Sydney rolled off of me and stumbled across the messy van and through the door. In a few minutes, she would be unconscious, but if she was smart, she'd have enough time to disappear. I couldn't let that happen.

I grabbed a nearby dish towel and pressed it against the knife wound with as much pressure as I could muster. Then I rolled up from the floor, yelling from both pain and determination. I dragged myself across the van and fell out of the door and into the parking lot.

Sydney was on her knees, her hands in the air.

Fifty cops circled her, each with a gun pointed to her head. Angela and Carter stood front and center.

"Oh, good," I gasped, collapsing to the pavement. "You got her."

Then I passed out.

"—AND the blade missed her vital organs. She'll make a full recovery. She's a lucky girl."

"And a hero."

"Thanks, Doc."

"Sure thing, Lieutenant. I'll have an intern keep you posted on her stats."

Groggy and disoriented, I opened my eyes. Everything around me was a calming shade of mint-green. The walls, the bed sheets, the plastic cup of water by my bedside. That color was supposed to be calming—that's why they painted hospitals in all mint-green—but all I could think about was how much I wanted some mint chocolate chip ice cream. I groaned and tried to sit up.

"Whoa!" Angela sat on the edge of my bed and helped prop me up against the pillows. "Easy, Ryder. You're not in the best shape."

Everything hurt. My busted knee throbbed. The scabs on my thigh burned. Inhaling was the worst. Every time I did it, the stab wound in my stomach sent a wave of pain across my body.

"Did you get her?" I asked breathlessly. "Sydney?"

"We got her." It was Carter that answered. She stood by the door as if on guard duty, arms crossed firmly over her chest. "Thanks to you, Ryder."

"I wasn't sure you'd come," I admitted.

"Angela explained the situation to me," Carter said. "I asked her if she trusted you. She said without a doubt. That's when I knew I had to let you do your thing."

"Where is she? Sydney?"

"In custody," Angela said. "Right where she belongs."

I looked over at Carter. She wore a strange expression I'd never seen before. "Everything okay, Lieutenant? That doesn't look like the face of a woman who just put a serial killer behind bars."

Carter wandered away from the door to stand at the foot of my bed. Her bottom lip trembled as she leaned over me and drew out her index finger. "Don't you *ever* scare me like that again, Ryder. Do you understand me?"

I suddenly understood the weird look on her face. It was relief. Lieutenant Carter was *relieved* that I hadn't died under Sydney's knife.

"I won't," I told her. "I promise. Does this mean I don't have to do paperwork anymore?"

Angela laughed. Carter tried to hold it in, but the joke eventually got the better of her and she let out an amused chuckle.

"You'll live to see plenty of new homicide cases," Carter said. "But I'm not assigning you a damn thing until you're all healed up."

"Fine," I grumbled.

Angela patted my arm. "Look on the bright side. You'll finally have time to hang out with me and Jess."

"Oh, what joy."

A knock sounded on the door. It was Officer Peck, one of the guys from our division. "Uh, Detective?" he said tentatively, peeking his head around the frame. "A couple of the guys are here to say hello. Are you well enough for visitors?"

I beckoned him into the room. "Sure, Peck. Bring 'em on in."

A line of officers filed into the room, each one stopping by my bed to congratulate me on my catch. Most of them had been in the Day Moon parking lot. They had all seen what I'd looked like coming out of that van. They had all, in a way, saved my life.

"That was a hell of a save, Detective."

"You're a badass, Ryder."

"You're making the rest of us look bad. You know that, right?"

I grinned from ear to ear and kept shaking hands even though it hurt. I was wrong to think I didn't have any family. The people in this room cared for me more than I could have ever imagined. They supported me in spite of my mistakes. They respected my choices. They loved me.

I couldn't wait to tell Sandy.

Made in the USA
Las Vegas, NV
28 December 2021